THE VICTIM'S DAUGHTER

a novel

ROBLEY WILSON

SIMON & SCHUSTER
NEW YORK LONDON TORONTO SYDNEY TOKYO SINGAPORE

Simon & Schuster
Simon & Schuster Building
Rockefeller Center
1230 Avenue of the Americas
New York, New York 10020

SIMON & SCHUSTER and colophon are registered trademarks
of Simon & Schuster Inc.

Designed by Deirdre C. Amthor

Manufactured in the United States of America

Library of Congress Cataloging-in-Publication Data
Wilson, Robley.
    The victim's daughter : a novel / Robley Wilson.
      p. cm.
    I. Title.
  PS3573.I4665V5 1991
  813'.54—dc20   91–15655
                                                          CIP

ISBN 0-671-72618-8

Completion of this novel was made possible in part by a grant from
the John Simon Guggenheim Foundation.

Portions of Chapter Three appeared originally in a short story,
"Nam," in *The Georgia Review*, later collected in *Terrible Kisses*,
published in 1989 by Simon & Schuster.

Remembering Norman "Red" McCann
and Carl R. Miller,
toughest editors and best teachers

Prologue

FOR A LONG TIME *after his lover had dressed and gone, Raymond Cooper lay in the disordered bed under the windows that opened onto Ridgeway Avenue and smoked one cigarette after another. He smoked absent-mindedly, as if the act were nothing he cared for—something habitual rather than pleasurable. When he caught himself tapping the next-to-last Pall Mall from a pack which only this morning had been full, the discovery startled him and he stopped. He knew he smoked too much, especially when he was alone in the house. Sometimes he wondered if he would go of lung cancer after all—if he might not already have it in some secret fold or cranny no doctor was shrewd enough to probe or brave enough to announce.*

Morbid.

His mother had died that way, slowly, painfully, finally eaten up and vanished. But if it was true that mothers poisoned daughters, he would of course take after Father—a solid inheritance, the old man still alive at ninety-one in a Portland nursing home. It was only six—no, seven years ago that time had begun to outdistance Father—the old boy suddenly not competent, enduring the degradation and humiliation of incontinence. There was no choice then: you called on the professionals to deal with such things—family loyalty was beside the point. Raymond felt no special guilt about his father, but visits depressed him; he had made them into an event more and more rare. That old man, half-blind, toothless, sitting in the home's solarium like a lizard on a rock, nodding, smiling endlessly. Skinny, shriveled creature—he probably didn't weigh more than seventy, eighty pounds. Was death better? Skin mottled as parchment, Dad's every bone with its knobby ends showing—like the nightmare pictures from the old-war concentration camps, the death camps.

The ultimate nursing homes.

·   ·   ·

When Raymond remembered his daughter, he tossed the bedsheet aside, stretched, began mustering the will to get up, shower, think about supper. Lissa would be in town tonight, late, coming from Chicago with the granddaughter. Fifteenth high school reunion. Time to clean this place up. He could hear his daughter: "Ever since Mother dumped you, you've lived like a gentleman slob." But this was no unpleasant way to deal with the fact of a life: a decent law practice, nice house, plenty of money above and beyond alimony. Beyond acrimony. A handsome daughter, educated and on her own. Good position in personnel management. Not that her own life hadn't been a tangle. A wild kid when she was in school. A husband the war made crazy. Widowed—that was the one blessing, thank heaven. "God, how can you function in this chaos? Papers everywhere." Paper came in faster than he could get it out—wills, deeds, contracts, briefs, letters. "I gain on it," he would say. "I'm always gaining on it."

And that was their intimacy—Lissa offended by disorder as if her own life were irreproachable; he amused, defensive. When she visited—seldom now—sometimes, watching her move about the house, careless, easy, unselfconscious, he drifted into reveries about youth: the freshness, the innocence around him in this straitlaced town. Young bodies, slender; how firm the flesh, how smooth—silken—the skin; the warmth of them. Naïve, wanting to learn. Tell me what you like, they said. Tell me what to do. He was an old bachelor now, true, and told Lissa so, but he was no fogey, either. "Oh, Dad," she'd teased when he visited her a couple of years back, when he'd wanted to paint the town—Rush Street, the Near North Side, a bit of nightclubbing—"I think you're one of those swingers people talk about."

Oh. If she had been here earlier, a fly on the wall, she'd have seen. He still had a good body, no potbelly like so many men his age—noticing them at Rotary and the City Club—no flab, not even aching joints to make him feel his age. Maybe a touch of the arthritis in his hands, a twinge now and again from an old ankle fracture, the tennis elbow—

not anything real. He flexed his legs; the veins were getting prominent—
a more vivid blue under the pale skin, hairline maps of purple, the blood
fighting a little through its channels. . . . The wasting image of his father
glowed in his mind and he felt himself flinch. We became our fathers—
looked like them, acted like them, said the things they said to us that
we swore we'd never repeat to our own children. Such contradictions
men were, loving and punishing.

He took a long, hot shower, toweled dry under the heat lamp in the
ceiling, wiped the steam off the medicine-cabinet mirror with one of the
guest towels, and shaved meticulously. He rubbed his fingertips against
the bags under his eyes; unavoidable, he supposed. He vowed to get
more sleep. He slapped his cheeks with aftershave, stroked it under his
chin, wincing as the alcohol stung him. Tired eyes—he peered into the
mirror; the image blurred. Farsighted. He remembered his father a few
years ago, when he could still read magazines and newspapers, holding
the reading matter close to his face, glasses (such thick lenses!) pushed
up on his forehead. Nearsighted; damned mole. Am I being smug?

He gathered up the pile of soiled clothes under the bathroom sink and
stuffed them into the laundry hamper. It was early—barely dusk. He felt
vaguely hungry, but not hungry enough to hurry into his clothes and go
out to Walden Pound for a lobster dinner. Drowsiness was what he felt:
a kind of pleasant lethargy he wished not to see dissipate. It was a good
life, he thought. It was a life better than he deserved. Good profession.
Love where he could find it. Once in a while—not often; no, not at all
often—he missed Jillie. A good young life, twenty-odd years together,
no hassles until near the end. How he had betrayed her, shocked her.
"I never thought that of you, Raymond. I never did." Dear Lord, what
can we do about the way we're bent? See my side of it, Jillie. And she
tried, yes. Poor Jillie. She said, I never thought that of you. He had
wanted to say, For a long time, I never thought that of myself.

He sat on the bed, lay back against the pillows, the last light flowing
into the room above his head and swimming high on the opposite wall
like slow currents on a pond. He stretched, sighed, rested both his opened
hands like a cup over his genitals. I'm for the long life, he thought.
Then he said it out loud, if softly: "I'm for the long life." He closed his
eyes and conjured up the young face of the recent lover—that boy with
skin smoother than porcelain; gray eyes of such maddening innocence!—
and felt himself slipping off into a satisfied sleep.

·   ·   ·

He woke up sweating, his heart hammering. Sometimes at the end of making love he felt his heart beating this hard, felt his breathlessness tighten the muscles of his chest, felt sweat turning cool all over his face and body. A circumstance not to die in, not to dare be found in. He turned onto his side, dropped his legs over the edge of the mattress, sat up, and collected himself. Damp bed linens. He'd ought to trundle them down to the cellar, run them through the wash while he thought of it. Take the hamper down, too. What in the world was that dream?

He felt an extraordinary self-consciousness—an awareness of himself as a physical object—as if the dream had sensitized him. A death dream, was it? Dreamland. Anywhere else we were delicate as crystal, soft as flowers. No wonder his mother had been sentimental, amazed to die. She wept for her fragility and his. What a universe. What a remarkable coming together of billions of chance instances. That was God, after all. Chance. Pure chance.

He stripped the bed, gathered up the damp sheets and pillowcases and heaped them on top of the hamper. The sheets, a fashionable shade of pale gold, smelled sharply sexual; they carried the moist stains of his seed, of the perfumes and unguents of love. Ray-Ray, what have you done? his angel mother would have said. Mummy isn't going to wash this kind of dirt. As if a child was any better able to control his dreams. How long had he not even known what was happening to him? Why had his father never sat him down and said not what he had in fact said about the sexual process—the mechanics of it, the tired analogies in Nature—but something that would better have explained the accidence of life? Somewhere below our consciousness of it lies a thing called passion, which waits to be tapped. Which desires to be tapped, which is worthless unless it's used, which seethes and boils, which once in a great while—but especially when we are young—breaks through the restraint and timidity of the body and messes the sheets. It is one kind of love, if we're lucky. This afternoon, a brief hour, he could not have been made to believe that he was not still young. He had again been a vessel overflowing, an object insufficiently used.

Now what? He considered the discovery that he was aroused. The mind did that; what, exactly, had he been thinking about? Perhaps he would go out this evening after all. My gosh, he thought. The heat and humidity of the season; the attractions of youth and of pale, willing flesh. I'm sixty years old, he reminded himself. When shall a man be old enough to have grown beyond lust?

·   ·   ·

He put on the dressing gown, light gray with scarlet piping, that Lissa had sent him last Christmas; heard himself whistling some nameless tune he'd found on the car radio early in the afternoon. He stuffed the soiled bedclothes into the hamper and carried it ahead of him like a battering ram, edging his way gingerly down the narrow back stairs, his left hip keeping contact with the railing. Even in the safety of the nursing home his father had fallen twice—once a fractured pelvis, once a broken wrist. One indignity after another as we get along in years. Wheelchair. Walker. Jungle gym for geriatrics. Ten erotic things to do with crutches.

He paused at the cellar door, contrived to trip the wall switch with his elbow. Light streamed up the stairs to meet him as he felt his way downward, barefoot. He flipped up the top of the washing machine and fed the laundry into it. Light things first, he thought; he needed the bedclothes. Darks he set aside on the ping-pong table—there was an item that got precious little use nowadays. There had been a time when "Cooper's place" was a center for the young, friends of Lissa's. His very popular daughter: knocked up at fifteen, secret abortion. Jillie beside herself. A houseful of weeping women, shouts, blame for anyone and everyone. Raymond had had his suspicions—who could afford to pay? Not some millhand's kid, you could bet your bottom dollar. Lissa never told who. Bless her for that. Whoever he was, she swore love for him— wanted the baby, had to be reasoned with and argued at and forced away from young motherhood. This was the other kind of love, the kind that concerns itself not with pleasure, but with fulfillment, responsibility. Was she fulfilled now, his daughter?

Anyway, God knew all the rest of the wildness that had gone on in this cellar with its jukebox, its wet bar, its secondhand sofas. A lot of sweaty dancing, a lot of petting in the dimmed light. Godawful music— but those young bodies, those smooth limbs. Did they think he was a neat father when he brought down popcorn, not knowing that it was just so he could let the vitality of the young rub off on him? Even those *pimply faces—lord, how painful to be adolescent. What was this? he wondered. Normal load? Large?*

He dumped in a quantity of blue detergent without measuring it, then added what he guessed to be a half-cup of dry bleach. Oxygen bleach— light as air. He set the dials. He punched the control knob and the washer sang with incoming water. My gosh, he thought, there's no such thing anymore as "woman's work."

.   .   .

In the kitchen he bowed before the refrigerator, the light and the cold spilling out against his bare legs, looking for something to fend off appetite. He pushed aside a milk carton to see what might be hidden in the back. Yogurt, which he would save for breakfast. Perrier, a half-bottle. Opened can of tomato juice. On the bottom shelf: the box of KitKat bars, cans of Coke and orangeade. Kid stuff. Way back, a box of baking soda. Arm & Hammer.

He found a plastic freezer container of fruit cocktail and sat at the kitchen table to eat it. When he had cleaned out the container he took it to the sink to soak in warm water. Here was stuff on the counter to put away, clean up, and he ought to do something about the floor—a spot in front of the stove that stuck to the soles of his slippers. He rehearsed: I'll get to that, Melissa; I've been thinking about it. Out the kitchen window before him was not much to see—a narrow side yard, a paved driveway, the bulk of the house next door. Blakes now. Ferrises used to live there; Tom Ferris his very first client after law school, after passing the bar. That was—what? 'Forty-seven; year of the big forest fires. After the war, "the good war." Just starting his family, Tom wanted a will drawn up. Big stuff: first client, first dollar earned. Actually, ten dollars. He and Jill bought a champagne split, drank it out of beer glasses. In the darkness he could make out the bulk of the Ferris house—though the Ferrises had moved away years ago, not long after the mills shut down—its windows blank, one stark streetlight reflected off new copper flashing around the fireplace chimney. The Ferris girl—what was her name? Contemporary of Melissa's, pretty brunette with big eyes, willowy, boyish build. Anorexic? Probably, but society didn't know the word then. More than one night he'd sat in the dark of his study, peering across the drive, watching her and her boyfriend on the living-room couch. Hot and heavy. A lot of kissing and feeling, plenty of white thigh. Only once had he seen her go the limit—Patricia, that was the name—her boyfriend giving it to her dog-style in front of the couch, his buttocks pale as cream. Everything through the lace curtains was softened, like an Impressionist version of reality. Sordid, lovely reality—and why leave the shades up if not wanting an audience? Jill had come into the dark room while he was watching. "What are you up to, Raymond?" Sorry, he'd said: must have nodded off, bulb in the lamp must have burned out. Great show of changing it, throwing the old bulb away. We never know who's watching us.

·   ·   ·

When the doorbell rang, he was in the front hall, about to climb the stairs to his room to dress—he thought he would go out after all, leave a note for Lissa, have a late supper at the City Club, perhaps have a nightcap somewhere, see who or what was stirring—and his first reaction was: she's early.

That would change his plans, of course. Father-daughter things—hug and kiss, put the sweet-breathed granddaughter to bed, then sit in the parlor and chat, offer Lissa a brandy to unwind after the long day's flying and driving. My gosh, he told himself, he certainly didn't feel like a grandfather, even after eight years of practice. Grandfathers were senile old farts, buying stupid signs to stick on their bumpers, dangle from their rear windows.

He opened the front door. Not Lissa. By the time he switched on the porch light, he'd already realized something was up. He put out his hand, gesturing No, then turned to make a run for the study, to lock the door, call the police—but he wasn't quick enough. So this is how we go, he thought. We answer a bell after dark and there it is, like a late delivery. He was stumbling, losing a slipper as he fell into the study, the one bared foot tripped up by a leg of the leather desk-chair, when the first blow struck the side of his head and exploded a brilliant pink light across his field of vision. The pain was so swift, so deep, that he was astounded to feel nothing more than extraordinary paralyzing cold.

1

THE DAY BEFORE she left Chicago, Lissa's period began, so that the following evening—after the crowds at Logan, the car-rental business, the cold drink for Suzanne and the wait for luggage—the usual sense of the exotic she felt when she drove into Scoggin after dark was complicated by ordinary, mundane annoyance. It was as if her anticipation, a sensation elevated and shaken out for the decision to come to her class reunion for the first time ever, had set her too high an expectation; as if Nature, with a will of its own and reading her mood as a kind of pride, had decided to punish her. In any case, she should always have known better than to expect to find the town a welcome and reassuring place, even if she brought with her all the sentimental freight of a simplified and distant past. She had visited her hometown only three or four times in these fifteen years since high school graduation, and though she expected changes, even the most familiar places seemed radically altered. The town's streets, deserted at this late hour, were like streets in an after-Armageddon movie; she half-supposed she would see automobiles parked randomly across the curbs, the drivers frozen at the wheel, done in by invisible radiation. The leaves of the trees were colorless in the glow of the streetlamps; where there were rare lights in windows she passed, Lissa had no confidence that live human beings occupied the rooms behind the pale curtains. Only in the park in the center of town was there activity: a cluster of young people, long-haired boys and girls distributed over the benches, drinking beer, smoking. Were we like them once? she wondered, but when she had driven on and forgotten them, and when she had gone by the bronze statue of the town's founding industrialist, she was again in an empty world, hardly another car to be seen, not even a citizen walking his dog, nothing but the landscape of the science-fiction film she had fantasized. Somewhere there was a moon—ducking her head to look at the sky, she located it as a three-quarters disc with the wispy dark shadow of a cloud smudging it—and away from the center of the town it provided a soft dust of light that made the town more foreign than ever. When she turned off Main Street, then turned again onto Ridgeway Avenue, the only sounds in the world were the ticking of the car's engine and the creaking of the tires against pavement.

Stopping in front of her father's house, it occurred to Lissa that he might very well have gone to bed. She cracked the driver's door open to read the hands of her wristwatch and saw that it was now well past ten o'clock. Even if he was up, she knew how wiped out she felt, and that she couldn't possibly be at her best and liveliest—something he would be disappointed by, for he reveled in her energy. "Oh, if I had your vitality, your youth," he was forever saying to her. Thirty-three, going on thirty-four. She no longer called that "youth." Relatively, of course—although Daddy certainly seemed young for a man of his age. Pixie: even as a child she'd decided that his eyebrows, arching up and outward, made him look elfin, devilish—"mischievous" was a better word. *Sly,* Mother said once. He's a sly one.

Well—she was here, the car was at the curb. It was foolish to spend money on a motel, and there was no place else to go unless she drove to the old neighborhood and woke up Nana Simpson. They could be perfunctory tonight and let the visit begin officially tomorrow morning at breakfast—she would catch up on the local gossip, the deaths of people she remembered from her school days, then cruise the town looking for other early arrivals or visiting one of those few classmates who had stayed to make a life in Scoggin. Besides, the porch light was on, and other lights were visible throughout the house: in the cellar window behind the lilac bush, in the front hallway, in the front bedroom upstairs. Obviously she was expected.

She pushed the car door wide open and leaned to wake Susie, sound asleep on the back seat. First she touched the child's shoulder, then prodded it gently.

"Suzanne, honey, we're here."

She got no response except a small, whimpering sigh.

"Suze, come on. Grampa waited up for us." Lissa knelt on the front seat and reached back to try and lift Suzanne to a sitting posture. "Please, sweetie. The sooner we're in the house, the sooner you can go back to sleep in a real bed."

The girl's thumb was in her mouth. She shook her head.

"Suzanne. No nonsense. It's late."

The girl squirmed and pushed herself up. She looked around the inside of the car, sat up, blinked at her mother.

"That's more like it." Lissa got out of the car and folded the driver's seat forward. "Come, sweetie. Grab your little vanity case and let's say hello to Grampa."

Suzanne hauled the small blue case up from the floor and dragged it behind her, worming her way out of the back seat.

"Carry me," she said.

"Suze, no. Come on. It's just a few feet."

"I'm too tired to walk." She sat on the edge of the driver's seat with the vanity case in her lap. "I have jet lag."

"Suzanne, you know I can't carry you. You're eight, going on nine, and I can't even lift you anymore." She held out her hand. "Come on; I'll be leader, you be follower."

.   .   .

No one answered the bell. Lissa put her face to the beveled glass of the door and peered inside, Suzanne leaning against her hip, as if the child were about to fall asleep on her feet. Through the thin screen of the curtain Lissa could see that the hall was empty. A light was on in the kitchen; at the head of the stairs she saw a glow from the bedroom.

"I wonder if Grampa has gone to bed, and he just left the lights on so we could find our way."

Or perhaps he was down cellar or in the bathroom—someplace where the sound of the bell couldn't penetrate. She tried the latch. The door was locked. Sighing, beginning to have small misgivings about her timing—maybe he had a friend with him; after all, divorce didn't mean celibacy, and he wasn't answerable to anyone but himself—she fumbled through her purse for the old house key she always carried when she came to Scoggin. It was in a thin, leather key case embossed with the figure of a sea horse; she snapped open the worn case and swung out the key. Unlocked, the door stuck—it always stuck shut in the summertime—and she kicked at it with the toe of her shoe. It resisted her.

"Mother," Suzanne whined.

She kicked again and added the emphasis of her left shoulder. This time the door creaked and trembled open.

Inside the hall she hesitated, listened. Not silence, but only the hall clock ponderously ticking. No sound from upstairs—no running water, no movement. Daddy's study door was shut, but no sliver of light showed over the sill.

"Dad?" She stood at the foot of the stairs and called upward.

Susie in tow, she walked the length of the hall and looked into the lighted kitchen. A glare of white off the appliances dazzled her. Reflections in the linoleum were like the moon on water.

"Grampa's hiding," Suzanne said.

"Maybe."

"I want to go to bed."

Lissa went to the head of the cellar stairs and cracked the door open. The washer was running—in a spin cycle.

"Dad?"

"Grampa's washing his clothes in the middle of the night," Suzanne said.

That had to be where he was, poised—just like a man accustomed to living alone—to shift the clothes from washer to dryer as soon as the last spin cycle ended, no time wasted. She steered Suzanne off the hall into the parlor and plopped her into an easy chair—a blue recliner, her father's favorite.

"Just sit here for a second, sweetie. I'll get Grampa."

"Why doesn't he hear us?" The thumb went back into her mouth.

"The washer's too loud." Lissa pulled gently at Suzanne's wrist. "You'll wreck those front teeth," she said. "They're permanent, remember. You'll spend your whole adolescent career at the orthodontist's. Wires. Rubber bands. You'll forget how to smile, and people will point at you."

"I'm sleepy," the child said.

"So am I. You can lie back and doze."

She descended the narrow stairs. Surprise: he wasn't here, either, in this place of familiar objects—the oil furnace converted from coal, insulated pipes like bandaged limbs, the ping-pong table. . . . Lord, the old jukebox was still here; she wondered if it was plugged in. Old times.

Wistful times. Frightening times. Friends she was about to see for the first time in fifteen years.

The washer stopped with a heavy mechanical thump. Its orange light blinked out: last cycle. Either he had to be in the bathroom, the door shut so voices and doorbells couldn't reach him, or he'd gone out. She opened the lid of the washing machine: light colors—white, yellow, pale blue. The darks were piled on the end of the game table. That was such odd efficiency for Daddy, who never organized or bothered to pick up after himself while he was married.

She thought she might help him out—move the clean clothes into the dryer, start the dark colors through the washer—when a small sound caught her attention. Water, was it? A pipe leaking somewhere? Then, looking up to find the pipes, she saw something liquid, something dark red, the color of blood—but surely not blood; she just had monthly blood on her mind—oozing through the cobwebbed wood of the subflooring above her head and off to the right of the washing machine. It stained the boards where they joined and it had gathered along the seams in heavy droplets, like ruby chains that glowed in the bare-bulb light of the cellar. Whatever the stuff was, it fell like slow drops of wine—one drop, a long running and gathering, and then another drop—to the cellar floor, where the shapeless puddle of it shone on the bare cement. Jesus, she thought, what can this be? She felt panic begin to swell in her throat, and the simple novelty of coming home growing into a crazy premonition of— Of what? What could be happening?

She threw down the clothes she was holding and ran up to the front hall. Some horror, her mind answered her. Some unexpected, terrible thing. At the foot of the stairs she hesitated, closing her eyes, matching the layout of the cellar to the arrangement of the rooms around her. The dripping red *stuff* was under the front of the house, and her father's study, where the briefs and petitions and legal forms always grew like a cartoon office scene. *A neat desk is a sign of a sick mind.* And hadn't she known from the beginning that whatever was happening was in this place? Wasn't that why she had looked everywhere else—to avoid the one room that would answer her fears? Wasn't that what she had done five years ago, on the day she discovered her husband—looked all over the house in Oak Park before, the last thing, she opened the door to the bathroom?

For a long moment, standing before it, her stomach churning and crazy ideas filling her head, she thought she would leave this door closed. She would call someone—the police, a neighbor, anyone. *Take my sleeping daughter to a safe place. Come help me unriddle this night.* But don't be ridiculous, she told herself. This is reality; this is not some stupid horror movie.

The moment she touched the wall switch, the overhead light of the study showed her how wrong she was. Her father was dead; she knew it instantly—knew it by the way he was sprawled on the floor in front of his desk, nothing comfortable about the positioning of his arms and legs, the angle of his head. . . . His head—it was hardly his, it was hardly anyone's. He lay in a great dark stain, like an aura around his upper body, that obliterated the pattern of the Oriental carpet. The room felt humid, the air heavy. It reeked of something she could not give a name to—an ominous presence, a weightiness.

She sank to her knees beside the body—beside *it*—and opened her mouth to speak. Nothing came out but a moaning. Well, why should there be words? said a shockingly level part of her mind. Who talks to the dead? Call someone who's alive; talk to *them*.

She reached up and lifted the telephone receiver from the corner of the desk—Daddy's cluttered desk—and held it to her face. It was a beige phone, new, with squarish, sculpted lines, and it was spattered with blood. Everything in the room must be spattered with blood, she thought, and her mind began to race with the idea of blood. Blood was bonding the phone to her hand, blood like brown glue, she would never be able to let go. Meanwhile the telephone sang in her ear like the sanguine currents that had once kept her father alive. *My father is dead,* she wanted to say into the mouthpiece. My father is dead and all his blood is gone. It was everywhere, his blood. When she put the phone down her palm would be speckled with it, like odd birthmarks, death marks; stigmata— she would look like a saint, like a martyr in the missals carried by girls she'd known who went to Ste. Anne's. It would never wash off. Bring blood, she wanted to say into the phone, bottles and bags of blood. Bring something to fill him with. Or bring something to cover him with. Hide him. Hide this thing.

She punched the button for the operator. Not once since she came into her father's study had she tried to wake him with words. Witness. She was only a witness. They would have to take out her voicebox and play it like a recording; they would have to put her eyes into a projector and shine light through them and cast on a screen the three-dimensional ugliness of this room. They would have to open her heart like a book, and no one would believe what was written on its pages.

She heard the toneless ringing at the other end of the line. Her knees were ice-cold, her thighs felt chilled, but she could not make herself stand.

When I wake up from this, she thought. When this nightmare is over, and the daylight comes, and I open my eyes in a room that is pure, scrubbed white—white linens on the bed, white drapes at the windows, white walls and ceiling, white light pouring into the room from a high white sky—I will remember the deep red blood and try to make sense of it. It must mean something: an anxiety dream, a wish dream. This will make good telling, but if I went back to the analyst with it, he would sneer at me. So you dreamed your father was dead, he'd say. Doesn't that seem familiar? Same old tripe, he'd mean. Can't you be inventive for once? Can't you have a dream that will challenge me?

The operator was asking if she needed help.

Yes. Yes. But the operator kept asking—"Is anyone there? Is something wrong?"—and Lissa remembered that from the moment of finding her father she had not found words. *You are still not making words,* her mind told her. She blamed the blood. The blood was in her throat, caught there, drowning speech. She was all blood at both ends of her. Everything was amazingly difficult: the phone so heavy she could hardly hold it to her mouth; the air in the room so thin her lungs ached and she felt giddy; she thought she might faint from the very effort of finding strength to speak. And then she managed at last to do it—like a release, like breaking through a barrier.

"My husband," she said. "My husband is dead."

Once having said it, she could not stop saying it, and when the first police arrived nearly fifteen minutes later she was still saying it, hysterical, loud—"My husband is dead"—over and over and over. Though they were the wrong words, they were the only words she knew.

·   ·   ·

She woke up in her imagined white room. The room was so stunningly bright that when she opened her eyes she was obliged to close them again. She had no idea where she was. She couldn't imagine why she should be in a strange place filled with light so brilliant it blinded her. Even with her eyes shut, she could see this light; it was deep red on the screen of her lids, and all at once—of course, of course—it was nothing except the color of her father's blood. She heard a woman's soft voice saying, "Would you help? We want to remove your tampon so we can put on a clean pad." She was aware of a firm pressure on her knees, her legs raised and parted, a raw coolness. She heard herself trying to speak, and the language come out as a kind of whimper. Why is this happening to me again? she wanted to ask. She felt on her left forearm something icy, then something sharp, and her hand was fisted and bent against her shoulder. The dark red before her closed eyes faded to black. To gray. To nothing.

·   ·   ·

When she woke the second time, she was surrounded by faces, none of them—at first—familiar. She felt woozy; it was a feeling you saw made visual in the movies, she thought, translated into a wavery fuzziness on the screen—the pale shapes at the foot of the heroine's bed a blur as of something observed through an etched window, then gradually resolving into the sharp lines of concerned faces—and for several moments the reality of her waking came to nothing. Then her head hurt, and she could feel the tiny throbbing point of the needle she had been stuck with. The smell of hospital came to her, disinfectant and floor polish and the thin odor she had always imagined to be ether—they filled her nostrils; the corridor sounds grew louder; the clink of small bottles, the hiss of gurney wheels and the conversations of people who were much more than barely conscious.

She raised her right hand to her face. The hand felt contorted—no, worse, it felt as if it were still holding a telephone and could not let go. She held the hand before her eyes. The hand was empty.

At the bedside was a single familiar face and, beyond it, a host of strangers whose faces were like white balloons.

"Donnie?" she said. "Donnie Savage?"

The man smiled. "Hi, Melissa."

A classmate. One of the classmates she knew best. What was he doing here? He wore some sort of uniform, pale blue shirt and navy blue necktie, a leather strap laid diagonally across his chest, a silver badge on his breast pocket, in his hands a cap with a polished black visor.

"You've come back for the reunion too," she said.

He laughed. "I never left," he said.

"Jesus," Lissa said, "I feel dizzy."

"They gave you something to settle you down."

"Was I trouble?"

"You were raving," Savage said. "When they first got you in here you were stiff, you were a real zombie; they couldn't get a word out of you. Then all at once you just let go. Screaming, pounding on people. They zapped you with a tranquilizer."

Lissa turned her head away and looked out the window. The sky was a pale, brilliant blue with a suggestion of cloud; it must be morning, she thought.

"I *feel* zapped," she said. "Suzanne— Where's Susie? Is she all right?"

"She's fine. I took her to the Simpson place."

"Does she know I'm here?"

"She thinks you got up early and went to the store with your father," Savage said. "I checked on her, just before I came on duty."

"You're a policeman."

"Afraid so."

"Susie adores uniforms," Lissa said. She thought of Suzanne carrying around the apartment the framed picture of her father, Edwin in his infantry uniform, taken before he was shipped out; a shudder danced through her, a sensation she seemed to have no control over. "I hope you didn't scare her."

"She's totally fine. What a cutie. When I carried her out to the cruiser, and when I carried her upstairs to bed, she never even woke up."

"Jet lag," Lissa said.

"What?"

"It's a joke the two of us have. Because the time difference is only an hour."

He hauled up a metal chair and sat beside the bed. "Are *you* okay? That's the important thing right now."

She looked at him. His face blurred, sharpened. "I'm dizzy," she said. "A dizzy blonde."

"You're a brunette," Savage said.

She sighed. Her head felt light, but now her arms and legs were leaden, impossible to move.

"I mean it," Savage said. "You have a very pretty little girl. She looks just like you."

Lissa stared at him. She imagined what she must look like—blank, as if nothing made sense to her. "This is all true, isn't it?" she said. "I really saw my father dead." She wept; the faces at the foot of the bed began moving, as if to surround her with concerned attentions.

"Yes," Savage said. "Yes, you really did."

.   .   .

So there was to be a reunion after all, and she had not come all the way from Chicago for nothing—only it was turning out not to be the fifteenth reunion of the Class of 1970, but the first reunion of Melissa Cooper Allen and Donald Savage since he had been best man at her wedding to Edwin the following summer.

"You missed the fifth reunion," Savage said. "And you didn't make it for the tenth, up at Billy Walker's camp on Square Pond."

"The fifth," Lissa said. "Edwin had just got back from the war. And the tenth—" She put her hands palms up on top of the bedsheet and sighed. "By then, he was already dead."

"I heard a little bit about that. From your dad."

"Something always seems to keep me from the reunions," she said. She turned her head away from him. How much could her father have told him? How much could he have known from such a distance, except that he was happy she was free of a crazy man?

"You look wonderful," Savage said. "You haven't changed at all."

"That's what we're all supposed to say."

"No, really. Tired but wonderful."

She looked squarely at him, trying to keep her eyes open so that she would seem to be wide-awake, and not still to be floating on whatever drug they had been jabbing her with.

"The washing machine was still running," she said. "When we got there."

"Was it?"

"We must have just missed whoever it was that killed him. He might have got Susie and me too."

"He might. But he didn't." He put his hands over hers and held them. "He didn't."

She closed her eyes. "I'm floating again."

"Pleasant dreams," Savage said.

.   .   .

The floating became a falling, the falling a slow turning, like a twig on water, and the sounds of the hospital grew fainter. She thought of Suzanne, lucky and safe. She thought of Donnie Savage, emerging from the mists of her adolescence. She thought of her mother, and the traveling toward sleep stopped abruptly; the drug could not quite master her, not quite put her out.

Afterward she could not remember if she was in a dream, watching the dream like a bystander whose disinterest is overcome by morbid curiosity, or if what she saw was a memory, pulled out of the black closet of the past and reviewed like some forgotten souvenir, a home movie to be played for the first time in nearly twenty years. Edwin, for the precious few years he was home from Vietnam, would start awake in the night, and when she sat up beside him, held his hand, stroked his face, she would see in the faint glow from the nightlight in the hall that his eyes were wide open and staring. "What do you see?" she asked, and never got an answer. The next morning he would know nothing about it. "Probably a kind of flashback," he said. "Just as well I don't remember it." She took it that whatever it was, it was awful—too awful to be saved or to be told to her.

But this—this dream, or hallucination, or whatever it was—seemed not to be awful. She was riding a bicycle, her own Chinese red one-speed with the wicker basket in front of the handlebars and the white handle grips with the red-and-white thongs trailing from the ends. She was on the outskirts of a town, the houses growing fewer and farther between, until she was facing a mansion—a large white house with blue shutters and blue slate shingles and tall brick chimneys at each end of the sharply pitched roof. A black sedan was in the half-circle of driveway, and the entire scene was shaded by the foliage of mature trees that surrounded the house. She stood across the road from this place, the bike between her knees, and she heard herself say, "This is where he lives." No sooner were the words out of her mouth than a man came out of the house—a man with extraordinary blond hair, hair so nearly white that she thought he must be old, a grandfather, an ancient spirit.

Then the image was gone, and her mother was scolding her. Lissa wasn't able to find the words to defend herself; she realized her stomach hurt and she was about to weep from frustration. She opened her eyes.

"Donnie?" she said. She turned her head on the pillow and squinted to make his face clear. "In my purse. Is it here? My purse?"

"I put it in the drawer of the nightstand."

"Someone should call Mother. She's living in Burlington; I've got her telephone number in my purse."

"It's all right," he said. "She knows. Somebody from your old neighborhood called her."

He had released her hands, and all at once—as if she were untethered—she was pushing off again, into the opaque, comforting night, knowing that for the time being Donnie would have to do for her whatever still needed to be done.

2

"IMAGINE HOW she must have felt," the blond young woman said, "coming home to find her father murdered."

"I can't," Willard Strand said. Though it was a matter of fact—which this woman could not have known—that some two and a half years earlier he had come home from a tedious afternoon conference with the Deputy Attorney-General to find his own home empty of life, its rooms as ominously silent as if death had happened in the place. Later, after he had read and re-read the note from his wife—"Remember the good times" it had said in part—and after he had sat in the front room of the house drinking brandy neat until his head throbbed, and after he had alternately blamed her and himself for a hundred misunderstandings that spanned all the years of their life together—after all that, it seemed to him that what he felt was what he might have felt if the woman had died and he had just seen her body put out of sight under the earth. *Grief,* he had said to himself, and he believed he had never felt more lost, more terribly alone—but no, he could not imagine Melissa Allen's feelings. Was her grief deeper than his had been, he still could not say.

These were the first words to pass between himself and his new assistant in nearly a half hour. They were all but strangers, had made polite but remote acquaintance at the Augusta office earlier in the day—Strand's usual partner, Frank Carey, was on vacation—and had carried on only the most minimal of conversations while the woman, Eleanor Watkins, gathered her portable computer and diskettes and quantities of manuals and notebooks and green paper into a bright orange backpack such as Strand's daughter had taken on Girl Scout camping trips twenty-odd years ago. Once in the car—a state-owned Ford without air-conditioning—Strand had driven the Turnpike south in self-absorbed silence. Nearing Portland, he had found himself moving in and out of patches of fog that filled the hollows and steamed out from under the concrete overpasses and hung back from the highway, wraithlike, in the spindly branches of the pines. He thought—the atmosphere around them so unreal—that Miss Watkins might have been dozing, or that she made a policy of not talking with elderly strangers.

Now, back on the road to Scoggin after a ninety-minute detour to the Scarborough barracks of the State Police for a briefing from Leonard Haverkamp—the man nominally in charge of the Cooper homicide—Strand had been reduced to chain-smoking, and to remembering the days when the Maine Turnpike was newly opened. He'd been a rookie in those days, when this black double ribbon of asphalt was still so lightly traveled as to seem like a waste of money. Yet even then the road had been seen by his parents in Brunswick as a threat to their way of life, an inducement to the summer people, who would spill off the Turnpike, buy up the coastline, and create a generation of natives whose lives would be scarcely better than a servitude—a dependence on the whims and tastes of wealthy strangers.

"A lot of that came sadly true," he said.

"A lot of what?"

He realized she had caught him thinking out loud, and he felt foolish. He would rather not have felt foolish beside Eleanor Watkins, who, besides being younger, was probably smarter, and had the reputation of being the sharpest newcomer in the department. "A lot of what my mother and father thought this Turnpike would do to the old-fashioned Yankee virtues. Fast-food places. A million cheap motels. Too damned much tourist traffic."

"Prosperity," Eleanor Watkins said.

Strand shook his head. "Slavery," he said, echoing his father. Christ, he thought, even my voice sounds like his. It was a voice from the grave, the old man having been dead nearly ten years. "Working for the tourist dollar."

She smiled.

"Do you know that song?" Strand said. " 'Wukking fo' de Yankee dollah?' "

"No," she said.

" 'Rum and Coca-Cola,' " he said. "The Andrews Sisters." How old was this woman, really? Thirty-five? Forty at the outside. Because she was not the assistant the office usually sent out with him, at first he had tried to veto the choice. She was inexperienced, he told Jack Henderson. He was not used to working with a woman. He was getting close to retirement, and it made more sense for her to be with the kind of younger man she would be partnered with down the road. Jack wouldn't listen, and early this morning no one else would have had the authority to alter assignments. "Before your time, I guess," he said.

"I guess."

He waited. "Not going to tell me?"

"Tell you what?"

"Just when your time is?"

She turned to face him. He stole a quick glance, and saw how amused she seemed to be. That was to the good. Perhaps she'd be all right as a partner—quick, pleasant enough, possibly just the right sort of balance for an old codger like himself.

"I'm thirty-eight," she said.

He nodded and cleared his throat—indicating, perhaps, approval.

"Too young to be useful, do you think?"

Strand had no answer to that, but attended diligently to his driving. He imagined she was flirting with him, and he wondered if he had somehow asked for it.

.   .   .

They sat in a vinyl-upholstered booth at a Howard Johnson's near the Kennebunk exit, coffee cups in front of them both, a small notebook in front of Strand, who smoked Luckies and tried not to blow the smoke in the direction of his partner.

"I could've got off at the Biddeford exit," he said, "but I wanted to show you what I meant about the way things have changed for the worse around here. I thought we'd go to the Wells turnoff, and I'd give you a look at Route One between Wells and a little past Ogunquit—or maybe all the way to Kittery." Seashell gifts, he thought, crap art of rockbound coasts and cottony waves, factory outlets for high-class labels. "We'll get to the Cooper house by three. That's time enough to get our bearings."

"I'd thought you were lost," Eleanor Watkins said.

"No, no. I've been to Scoggin many a time. Basketball tournament when I was a kid. Then used to play against the high school there, back in my coaching days."

"You were a coach?"

"Assistant coach at Thornton Academy," he said. "A brief fling, after I got out of the army."

"Hard to imagine. I'd thought police work was your life."

"What gave you that idea?"

"Talk. People in the office."

"Only after I decided there was never going to be any money in high school teaching, and that I might as well take advantage of my MP experience. I was in Germany, tail end of the war: '44, '45. That's another way I knew the Scoggin neck of the woods—and the Turnpike: for a couple of years I patrolled between Kittery and South Portland. York County. Cumberland. I used to know every pebble of this territory. Also before your time. I was assigned to the Wells barracks, which of course no longer exists."

"Maybe 'my time' hasn't arrived yet."

"I wouldn't know. I've got a daughter almost your age, but we've never talked much." He flipped open the notebook, which was small enough to be covered by his hand, and jotted a couple of lines on the first page. "Cooper," he said. "That's a good solid Yankee name. Did you put down what Haverkamp was saying?"

"Wouldn't it make more sense if you showed me places that *hadn't* changed?" She opened the cover of a legal-size notebook. "Give me some basis for comparison?"

"No such animal." He hesitated. "Where'd you go to college?"

"Holyoke," she said.

"Where'd you work before you came to Augusta?"

"The Midwest. A private agency in Minneapolis—best in the Cities, or so we claimed."

"Then you've probably got an imagination."

"I hope."

"I'll *tell* you how it used to be." She was a pretty woman, this Watkins, and now—because she bantered with him, and looked at him with alert, skeptical eyes—he began to be dead sure she was intelligent. "Your imagination can paint in the pictures, and we'll save a lot of the State's gasoline while we're at it." He drained his coffee cup; the dregs were shockingly sweet. "More coffee?"

She studied her cup. "Sure," she said.

"What sort of talk? From people at the office, I mean."

"Am I going to get someone in trouble?"

"Change the names."

"Nothing incriminating. You have a reputation." She looked at him, measuring.

"For—?"

"Cutting a solitary figure. Solo integrity, I suppose."

"I suppose I'm a loner."

She smiled. "I happen to know you worked awfully hard to keep me from being assigned to you. There's probably an office lottery."

"On what?"

"Whether I'll come back alive or not."

"I expect you will," Strand said. He poised the pencil over his notebook. "So. What's in your notes?"

She read. " 'Raymond Hussey Cooper, sixty years old. Attorney.' " She paused. "I know a lot of simple people who'd be happy to see one less lawyer in the world."

"Don't we all. Go on."

" 'Time of death, between 8:30 and 10:15 p.m., Wednesday, July 24. Collateral evidence suggests the latter end of that time range.' My words, not Haverkamp's. 'Cause of death: skull fracture, massive cerebral trauma, unacceptable loss of blood.' Also my words, but you saw all the blood in the videotape. 'Murder weapon, unknown. No suspects. Yet. No motive suggested. No sign of damage to locks or doors or windows; victim may have known his assailant.' *I* think he did. 'Survived by ex-wife, who lives in Vermont, and by daughter'—she's approximately the same age as yours too; that will add fuel to your age thing—'who discovered body approximately 10:25 p.m. Local police arrived at 10:38; State Police at 10:52.' " She looked up. "Henderson called me a little after midnight, I assume after he'd called you."

"Probably. What 'age thing'?"

"This insistence on how much history you know that happened before my time."

"Can't a man remark on the obvious?"

"Just listen," she said. She read on, skimming. " 'Available evidence at the scene sent by courier to forensics in Augusta, report expected afternoon of 7/25.' Today. 'Investigation put in charge of Scoggin Police Department, A. Michaud'—Arthur? Albert?—'chief, reporting to Haverkamp, Scarborough barracks.' "

"They were in college together at Orono," Strand said. "That's supposed to account for the locals taking things over. Friendship. I don't suppose it matters, so long as the State keeps looking over their shoulders."

"That's us," Eleanor Watkins said.

"I dread this case," he said. Finally he caught the waitress's eye, gestured for more coffee. "It's an awful thing, this business of one human beating another human to death. That tape of the scene, the corpse, that we just watched—I think I've got an okay imagination too, but I've never been able to get used to the excess of it. I try to put myself in the killer's situation: Here's a man I hate, and I know I'm stronger than he is, and I have a weapon handy, and—Christ, I honestly can't see myself doing it."

"You don't have the proper temperament," she said. "Who was it that said you should never raise your hand to a person if you aren't willing to see that person dead?"

"You think that's all it is? My temperament?" He shook his head. "No," he said, "I'm sick of it—sick and just damned tired of what people do to each other."

"Or maybe it's psychotic episodes you're tired of. You know: ' "He was always a quiet chap," neighbors said.' That's what we say about crazy killers. 'He was quiet. He was a loner. He never bothered anybody.' "

Strand smiled and stirred his coffee. "Except," he said.

"Except what?"

"This time the quiet one is the victim."

"And the investigator is the loner?"

"That too."

"Something provocative, kept out of sight," she said.

"But what?"

"We'll find out, won't we?"

"Or the locals will, and we'll all nod our heads." He started a fresh cigarette off the tip of the old one. "What if it's the only crazy moment the murderer has in his whole life?"

"And no physical evidence at the scene?"

"Yes."

"I see the difficulty," she said. "That's why you'd rather have—what? A shooting? The noise of a gun going off, and shaking the neighborhood out of bed. A slug, with rifling and scratches and unique markings that would point straight to the serial number of the killer's properly registered gun."

"A Rube Goldberg crime," Strand said. He took notice that here was another reference that meant nothing to her.

"But what you *really* want," she said, "is for an energetic assistant—I mention no names—to do all your work for you."

Strand stubbed out his cigarette. "My very first case after they promoted me to inspector was up in Aroostook County, practically wilderness. Man comes home from work at the lumber mill, gets his double-barreled twelve-gauge out of the truck, looks in the living-room window. Wife asleep on the couch with her back to the window. Man cocks the hammers and blows a hole in her back, right between the shoulder blades."

"Lovely. Another happy marriage."

"But lots of hard evidence. Buckshot rolling around in the woman's lungs. Husband's fingerprints on the shotgun. Footprints under the window. Witnesses at the mill who knew his jealousy and his short fuse. Neighbor lady the wife confided in. Finally, we find the man she was sleeping with while hubby sawed real logs."

"That's too easy; you could solve that even without me. Most shootings *are* in the family, marriage being an institution founded on frictions. Men marrying women so they can hate them better. This one won't be so easy; you'll get a chance to show off."

Strand put away his notebook. "Drink your coffee," he said. It might be true that marriage was an institution founded on frictions. Did that explain anything? And what made Eleanor Watkins so smart about it? "Let's go be the visiting professionals."

.   .   .

He'd been in Scoggin off and on over the years—the first time perhaps forty-five years ago, when he was on the Brunswick team that played here in a high school basketball tourney, then often after the war, when he coached and lived in Saco; and, more recently, when his daughter was a student at the small college north of town. Too much had changed: there was a sprawl of shopping mall on the south edge, and a fancy motel with a pool, a Ford dealership and a couple of Japanese-car showrooms; within a space of three blocks were a pair of retirement homes, brick high-rises with tiny balconies; then there was a development of frame homes crowded close against one another, pretending to be townhouses, and a McDonald's, a Burger King, a Long John Silver's, a Pizza Hut, a Chinese restaurant, a 7-Eleven. Anytown USA. *All we do in this country is eat; is that the measure of success?* A lot of trees had been taken down, and the wide main street where the old stately homes had stood—homes built by the executives of the textile mill that shut down in the Fifties— looked barren. In the town square, the statue of the mill's founder had been moved into a park to make more room for motor traffic. A lot of the retail stores in the center of town were razed, but Strand counted four banks on one block.

"Must be a wealthy area," he said.

Eleanor Watkins studied the street map open across her knees. "You could fool me," she said.

He drove on, past vacant lots, more car dealerships, more gas stations, a supermarket and drugstore. Not a bad town in its time, he thought, but made dreary by progress. He hadn't remembered it as dreary.

"Here." Eleanor pointed. "North Street."

He turned left.

"And right, onto Ridgeway."

He turned right. "What would I do without you?" he said.

"I couldn't guess."

"How come you're not married?"

"I was."

The street was narrow, and in front of the murdered man's house was a turmoil of police and civilian cars, people gawking, a couple of uniforms keeping them way from the front porch. Small-town excitement, all of it spilling across the sidewalks and onto the neat, narrow lawns.

"What kind of man was your husband?" Strand asked. He pulled smartly into a driveway across the street and turned off the ignition.

Eleanor paused, her hand on the door latch. "Which one?" she said.

"Christ, how many were there?"

"Three," she said. "So far."

Strand shook his head. What did that mean, he wondered—that she let emotion carry her away? That two celibate years after his own divorce he was actually ready to ask such a question?

"So I'm not a good judge of character," she said.

"We'll see." Strand got out of the car, looked around the neighborhood. Modest frame houses, not many trees, postage-stamp front yards. Backyards and side yards were the thing in Scoggin. High fences. Privacy. "I'll hunt up the local chief. You look around the house; see if you can make a home for us somewhere inside."

She hauled the orange backpack off the rear seat and slung it over her shoulder. "Why here?"

"The police station is in the Town Hall. I've seen it. It's a building even older than I am, and believe me, it's got no space for visitors." He closed the car door. "You want me to carry that?"

"I can manage," she said. "Nice of you to ask."

·   ·   ·

It seemed a comfortable house, roomy, with a dark but spacious hallway. The study, where Cooper had died, he'd set up as a home office: antique desk, copy machine on a metal stand, typewriter, home computer and printer arranged on an L-shaped table in one corner. The study opened off the hall; you could stand inside the room and almost reach the front doorknob. There was an odor to the house—a mix of odors. Strand could smell something that might have been garbage waiting to be thrown out, a mustiness that suggested not all the rooms of the house were used. Cooper lived alone, didn't need all this space. Daughter off in Chicago. Ex-wife up in Vermont. And the stale smell of tobacco smoke. Cooper a kindred spirit, was he? Not many cigarette smokers left in this world; it was a shame to kill one of them off.

"Police Chief Michaud—Albert." A large dark man approached, uniformed but capless. He was fortyish; a scar showed white under his left eye, a considerable paunch bulged over his belt, and his armpits were stained with damp shadows of sweat. His words carried a noticeable French-Canadian music.

They shook hands. "Pleasure," Strand said. "Bill Strand, Attorney General's office. Haverkamp told me to look you up and get on your good side."

Two other uniforms stood nearby. "Savage"; handshake. Football type in his day, Strand guessed, still wearing a crewcut even though his forehead was receding. "Putnam"; handshake. Skinny basketballer. Everybody in the place was younger than Strand by twenty or thirty years.

"Crappy business," Michaud said. He pushed the study door open wide.

Strand nodded. More smells: sweat, blood. Lord, yes: blood.

"Got a weapon yet?"

"No."

"Your medical man think he knows what it was?"

"Doc Pike," Savage said. "No, he's got guesses."

"What's he guessing?"

"Lug wrench, crowbar, piece of pipe. Metal, heavy. Pretty damned near anything you could use like a club." Michaud thrust a sheaf of photographs at him. "We took this," he said. "The state troopers made videotape."

"I've just seen it." Strand looked at the photos. Cooper was sprawled face down, pale legs splayed out from under a disarranged bathrobe, one arm flung toward the rolltop desk.

"Where's the body now?"

"Hunter's. It's a funeral home, not so far."

"He took a while dying, didn't he? Lots of blood; look what an area it covered on the carpet." He peered closely at the picture in his hand. The still camera was more cruel than television: the man's skull was astonishingly misshapen. "That's no cheap carpet," Strand said. Yet he'd seen far worse; he wondered if he was getting squeamish in his old age. Maybe it was the blood, so much of it. Maybe it was time to retire. "And that rolltop might be authentic. Is there money here?"

Michaud hadn't once taken his eyes off him. We're like two dogs sniffing at each other, Strand thought. A tired old bulldog and a fat French poodle.

"It could maybe have been robbery," Michaud said. "If that's what you asked me."

" 'Your money or your life,' " Strand said. "Not a hard choice."

"They hit him three or four times. But Doc Pike, he thinks the first blow would have been enough. He'd've bled to death just the same."

Strand handed the photographs back to Michaud and stepped over the sill into the murder room. Clutter. Smell. "Were these papers already on the floor, or did Cooper pull them down when he fell?"

"Don't know. The troopers went all over everything."

Strand retreated to the hallway. Eleanor Watkins was standing at the foot of the stairs, looking cool and feminine and not at all professional. Like a woman three men might have wanted to hang on to if they'd known how.

"The kitchen is a bachelor's mess," she said. "It needs Clorox and Comet, but there's counter space and a phone jack. It'll do fine."

"Then perhaps you could set up shop, Miss Watkins," he said.

She held her hand out to the chief. "I'm Eleanor Watkins," she said. "I'm here to assist Inspector Strand." Michaud took the hand briefly. "And," she said, looking at Strand, "to apologize for his occasional bad manners."

"Sorry," Strand said. "I forgot you hadn't been introduced."

.   .   .

Later, Strand stood on the sunporch, looking out over Ridgeway Avenue. He had a mild headache—a small fist of pain centered in his forehead just above the eyebrows—and his neck muscles hurt from tension. Both pains were dull but insistent. The inside of the Cooper house was close, airless, laced with the smells that had first come to his nostrils, now compounded by the odors of police leather and fresher tobacco smoke— his own Lucky Strikes, a fruity pipe blend that apparently identified the medical examiner. And the odor of death, imperceptible—or so he imagined—to others, but real enough to him. Where had he first smelled it? On the way out of Munich? Entering a bleak building at Dachau and finally realizing what it was he'd been smelling as he jogged alongside the churning tank treads?

He lighted a new cigarette, looked for a place to set down the spent match, found a glass ashtray on the arm of a piece of porch furniture. The ashtray was clean except for a clouded flashbulb dropped into it.

He opened the sunporch door and strolled outside to the top step. Ridgeway was a mess: cars parked every which way nearby, men and women and small children hanging about, walking by; a steady slow trickle of automobiles from both directions, gawkers hanging out of their windows.

"You," he said. He gestured to one of the uniforms he had been introduced to inside. "What's-your-name."

It was the crewcut—tall enough, stocky and big-shouldered.

"Don Savage," the footballer said.

"Right—Savage." Strand talked around the cigarette, squinting through a twist of gray smoke. "I wonder if we could do something about this damned parade. Maybe close off both ends of the street for a while—just let through the folks who live in this block."

"You bet." Savage went off to do the visitor's bidding. Takes suggestions well, Strand thought, and then felt guilty for thinking it. You had to be careful in these cases; you couldn't offend the local force, couldn't seem to be condescending to them. Judging from the chief's attitude, he'd already made his poor first impression.

He went down the steps and strolled toward one group of lookers-on. "Excuse me, folks," he said, "but there's a lot of work to be done here, and I think the police would be grateful if all of you went back to your own homes."

He got a lot of frowns, and a few mumbles. Most of the people moved off. At the same time the police chief—Michaud, was it?—appeared and began herding them away. "Move along," Michaud said. "No more to see today."

Strand examined his cigarette, split the paper with his fingernail and scattered the tobacco, burned and unburned, to the muggy summer breeze. He turned back toward the Cooper house and found himself fronted by a boy, fifteen or sixteen years old.

"I think that means you too, son," Strand said. "Nothing more to see."

"I live in the neighborhood," the boy said.

"Then you don't have far to go, do you?"

"Next door." The boy pointed across the driveway. The house overlooked the side windows of Cooper's study. "I heard her crying—Mr. Cooper's daughter—after she found him."

"Is that so? And you came over to find out what the matter was?"

"No, sir. I stayed at the window." He indicated an upstairs window at the back of the house. "I knew something was funny when the police car came and then Mrs. Adler showed up."

"You knew Cooper?"

"I knew who he was. He'd usually come outside to talk when he saw me washing my dad's car."

"What'd you talk about?"

The boy shrugged. "The weather. Things going on in town. Movies." The boy was redheaded and freckled; he looked like some comic-strip character whose name Strand couldn't quite call up.

"What's your name?"

"Ralph. Ralph Blake."

"And who's this Mrs. Adler?"

"She works for the Portland papers."

"How'd she get here so fast?"

"I don't know."

"Well, Ralph, you remember where you were, a little before you heard the woman crying? Had you gone to bed?"

"I was on my way home from downtown. I'd been playing chess with Mr. Winslow."

"Who's he?"

"My minister."

"He give you a ride?"

"No, sir. I walked home."

"See anybody on the way?"

"Yes, sir."

"On this street?"

"Yes, sir."

Strand waited. He wondered if he might have gotten lucky.

"A man," Blake said. "We passed each other."

"Somebody you knew?"

"No. I'd never seen him before."

"Your parents home?"

"No, sir. They work."

Strand put his arm lightly around Blake's shoulders and led him toward the front steps. "Come on inside," he said. "By the time we're through here, we'll have to talk with everybody on this street. I don't see why we shouldn't start with you."

.   .   .

"What do you think?" Strand said. He looked at his watch, tapped a Lucky against the crystal, put the cigarette to his lips. It was early evening. He was sitting on one side of the kitchen table, Eleanor Watkins across from him. Between them was her computer, a printer, a small tape recorder. "Do we have something?"

"From the lab, not much yet." She reached for a printout on the floor beside her. "A lot of unidentified fingerprints, a couple of palm prints— so far unidentified; it all takes time. No help from the victim—no foreign matter in his scalp that might lead to a weapon, nothing under his nails, nothing useful from the study. The stain on one of the bedspreads upstairs is semen—that could be interesting. Haverkamp's people vacuumed the whole place, emptied ashtrays, wastebaskets. So far, no revelations."

"How about this end?"

"On young Blake or on the man he passed?"

"Either." He lit the cigarette.

"I don't think Blake could kill an ant," she said. "Do you have any idea how much you smoke?"

"Are you counting?"

"We checked with the minister, Winslow. Lives across the street from his church. Congregational—the one with the clock. He and the boy play chess two or three evenings a week."

"What about this stranger?" Strand consulted his notebook. " 'Medium height, very stocky, short hair, high forehead.' " He paused. "What's 'medium' to a fourteen-year-old?" He looked back to his notes. " 'Wearing a sport shirt. Muscular upper arms that he carries away from his sides.' Ape-like." He stood up and made a clumsy circuit of the kitchen table. "Like so?" he said.

"Something like that. And featureless."

"For now. I asked the Bear to have a police artist sit down with Blake."

"The Bear?"

"That's how he pronounces his name: 'Al-Bear.' Al-the-Bear Michaud."

"And does Scoggin *have* a police artist?"

"He says he can find one," Strand said. "It's summer; this is Maine;

the number of artists per square inch must be astronomical. What does your baby computer say about faceless men?"

"Experience says there's more of them than there used to be."

"But ape-like too?" He started to make a lumbering move toward her, still playacting the man Blake had seen, raising his arms as if to catch her in a hug, just as Michaud appeared in the kitchen doorway.

"The press," Michaud said. "They say we got to have a press conference."

Strand straightened up and shook his head. "Tell them tomorrow morning—tell them around ten o'clock."

The chief looked dubious. They're yapping at him, Strand thought, pumping him full of First Amendment and morning deadlines. And here was the expert from Augusta, playacting King Kong.

"There's no news," Eleanor said. "When we know anything, we'll pass it on."

"Some of them have been hanging around all day," Michaud said. "They'll be pissed off." He looked at the woman. "Excuse me," he said.

"What are we talking about?" Strand said. "*Portland Press Herald?* The local weekly?"

"The *Globe*—Boston. The Associated Press."

Strand looked at Eleanor Watkins. "No national television?" he said. He held his hand out to her. "Shall we gather on the porch?"

Public relations, the people back in Augusta were always saying. Public relations, Strand. Make us human; make the hometown force look efficient.

In the muggy heat of the sunporch, Strand turned to Michaud. "You want me to talk?"

"Go ahead," Michaud said.

Strand cleared his throat. "We don't intend to make this a ritual," he said. There was a youngish chap in a Hawaiian shirt, with a classy-looking reflex camera hanging around his neck. A middle-aged woman with a microcassette recorder—probably this was Mrs. Adler, the *Press Herald* stringer, gray-haired and plump and palpitating with stifled importance. "We're not going to hold daily press conferences, but if there's something to tell, we'll tell it all at ten o'clock in the morning."

There was grumbling. "That gives television the break," said a florid-faced man who used a pad and a yellow pencil.

"My understanding is that the TV stations aren't even represented here."

A young woman raised her hand. "I won't have a cameraperson with me until tomorrow," she said.

Strand shrugged. "Let's get to it. Work on the case is proceeding." He looked at Michaud. "The State Police have organized the investigation, and the local police are actively following up. They're questioning anyone who might have knowledge that touches on this case, commencing with a canvass of the neighborhood. Isn't that right, Chief Michaud?"

"That's right."

"You all know Chief Michaud." Strand raised his hand in salute. "He is presently handling this case, acting on the authority of State Police Captain Leonard Haverkamp, Scarborough barracks. The A.G.'s office has sent me to assist in the investigation, inasmuch as it is the State which will carry out any prosecution, but the chief has very kindly invited me to act as spokesman."

The chief nodded slightly.

"I think he wants me to look as if I'm working," Strand said. No one chuckled. It's all right, he told himself, if the visiting fireman isn't as funny as he tries to be.

"What was the motive?" the florid man asked.

"We haven't ruled out robbery," Strand said. "More I cannot say."

"Any suspects?"

Strand smiled. "I don't know whether to say no—no suspects—or yes—everyone is a suspect." Strand lighted a cigarette and dropped the match into the ashtray he had used earlier. "Gentlemen and ladies," he said, "right now there's nothing more to say that would be of the slightest use to your editors. We thank you for your interest."

The group dispersed unhappily. On a glass-topped coffee table a newspaper was left behind. Strand picked it up—this morning's *Press Herald*. Headlines for the Cooper murder, a front page photograph: VICTIM'S DAUGHTER IN DAZED STATE. It showed a young woman being led out this very front door by two uniforms, her face blank, her hair disheveled. In the left background was Officer Savage, carrying a sleeping child, a girl, in his arms.

He held the picture up so Michaud could see it from across the porch. "Who the hell took this?" he said.

"It must've been the Adler woman."

"She was here last night in time to get a picture of Cooper's daughter and granddaughter into the morning paper?" He slapped the paper onto the table. "Jesus Christ, Michaud, look at that poor woman's face. Nobody minds if you lie down with the press, but are you guys really so fucking heartless?"

He walked away. Eleanor Watkins, standing in the front hall, laid two fingers across her mouth.

Strand took a deep breath to dilute his anger. "So, what do you think?" he said.

"I think, whatever happens, the chief of police doesn't like you much," she said. "That's what."

. . .

At the Maine Stem Motel, Strand lay awake in the dark and smoked the day's last cigarette. He thought about Raymond Cooper dead. He thought about Eleanor Watkins alive. What do I know? he asked himself.

He knew Cooper had gone to the door; the doorbell was working, so he probably responded to the bell. He knew that someone was let into the house, followed Cooper to the study and did him in. He knew Cooper was interrupted while he was doing his laundry—death calls us away from the usual. He knew that when Cooper fell, after the killer had struck him once, he went down with a sheaf of papers under him. Was Cooper fetching the papers for his visitor? Better check on any names mentioned in them. Then the killer hit him again, at least twice. Overkill. Track down the overkiller. Then the daughter showed up to find the corpse, soon enough afterward that the washing machine was still churning away in the cellar. Spooky. And the Blake kid was on his way home—from playing chess with his minister, for God's sake—and passed this no-face stranger with the muscles and the swagger. Skippy: that was who Blake reminded him of—a comic-strip character named Skippy.

What else, besides the pathetic bonus of a news photographer catching for posterity the grief and shock of Cooper's daughter?

Office computer turned off. No messages on the answering machine. Kitchen stuff: plastic container soaking in the sink, shreds of fruit floating in it. Bedtime snack. Ordinary kitchen; counters cluttered, but not with

crumbs or spills; dirty stovetop, oven a bit of a mess. Not much food in
the refrigerator. If you live alone, you eat out a lot—ask me what *that's*
like. Cooper had a sweet tooth: candy bars, soda pop—or did they still
call it "tonic" in this neck of the woods? Open box of baking soda. Ice
cream in the freezer compartment.

Tomorrow he would have to spend more time upstairs in the house.
He'd gone up there, looking around casually. Cooper's bed was stripped;
stained brown comforter on the floor at the foot. The woman Cooper
spent his time with might be helpful. If she could be found. If she wasn't
too scared to answer questions.

What else?

That daughter—poor kid, up for a reunion, finds her daddy dead. Got
to talk with her, but gently, gently. Maybe send Eleanor. What if it
were *my* daughter? What if Jackie found me beaten to death like that?
Strand felt a swift surge of fear in his guts. Be calm, he told himself;
don't ask for trouble. Then he thought: I should have got here earlier
in the day, got off to a quicker start; tomorrow I've got to bear down,
look like I know what I'm doing. Like I care. "I'd thought police work
was your life," Miss Watkins said—teasing him. But God, once it was;
once I was crackerjack. Was it only living alone that had undercut his
interest, his ambition? And Al-the-Bear Michaud did indeed have his
skeptic's eye on the team from Augusta—Miss Watkins was right: in-
truders, interlopers. Tread lightly, Strand thought.

Blake's faceless man. That looked like the best bet for the murderer,
if Michaud's artist was any good and Blake had a memory for faces. Or
maybe not; you couldn't hang a man for coincidence. Let's not have us
any false-arrest lawsuits in this litigious age.

Strand squashed out the cigarette. That's what I know, he told himself,
about the Raymond Cooper file. He drew the sheet up over his shoulders
and pulled the pillow against his face. About Eleanor Watkins he knew
a good deal less—except that she was younger and brighter than the
help they usually gave him, and better-looking, and God help him, he
wished she were here to share this bed with him.

3

THE MONDAY MORNING before he died, Edwin had parked the car across
the street from a schoolyard and sat, smoking cigarettes and watching
the children. Lissa had seen him from two cross streets away, a shadow
in the window on the passenger side. The car was idling, had never been
shut off; the exhaust on that day in October was a thin blueness in
sunlight. It was recess time, the schoolyard filled with children running,
swinging, playing with a football. She had tapped on the closed window
beside his head. Three, four times, and finally he turned his face toward
her.

She had never gotten used to his eyes after he came back from Vietnam.
They weren't vacant, not wild, but something of each, as if he saw
something that angered him without actually provoking him. That day,
recognizing her, he winked.

"Roll down the window," she had said, making the circular motion
with her right hand. He cocked his head, cigarette at the corner of his
mouth. Lissa had to point downward, meaning to direct his attention
to the window crank. She had to form *Roll down the window* with her
mouth, but didn't utter the words.

He shook his head. He had looked right through her, watching the
children beyond the low chain-link fence of the schoolyard. She had
been obliged to walk to the other side of the car, fumble in her purse
for the keys, unlock the driver's-side door and slide onto the front seat
beside him.

"Hi," she said.

"Imagine meeting you here," he said. He opened the window to throw away the consumed cigarette, closed it, lighted another.

They had called her from the place where he worked. "You better look after that man," the shop manager said. "I can't reach him." She had called a sitter for Susie, paced frantically until the woman arrived at the front door, then half-walked, half-ran in search of her unreachable husband.

"Are you okay?"

Edwin had shrugged her off, turning his mad-blank gaze toward her. "Why shouldn't I be?" he said.

She remembered the feel of her fingers tightening on the lower rim of the steering wheel. She remembered thinking: *Is this the day?* and the voice—not her own, but perhaps her father's or mother's over the long distance from Maine, perhaps the doctor's—hissed inside her head. *Is this the day?*

·   ·   ·

Donald Savage poked his head in the doorway of the room.

"Ready for a visitor?" he said.

It was Suzanne—solemn-eyed, sunsuited, a large coloring book held in her bare arms—who came warily to the side of the bed. Lissa hugged her, kissed her. This was life too; this was the other side of that ugly coin.

"What's going on anyway?" Suzanne said. "Are you all right?"

Lissa hugged harder. "Oh, Suze," she said, "everything's going to be fine."

"I think something's happened to Grampa," the child said, "but nobody tells *me* anything. It's because I'm a kid."

Lissa looked at Don—a formidable, strong figure in his uniform, a black-holstered revolver on his hip.

"I didn't know how to put it," he said. "I'm not used to dealing with eight-year-olds."

"Grampa's dead," Lissa told her. "Somebody killed him."

"I thought so. Nana Simpson was being really weird all day yesterday; she told me three different stories about where you were."

Matter-of-fact, Lissa thought. This was one way children saw the world, neutral, a simple disinterested reality.

"Did you remember Nana?"

"Sure. She was my babysitter, last time we came to Maine."

"She was weird because she wanted to protect you."

Suzanne pursed her mouth and touched the tiny bandage on her mother's arm. "What's that for?"

"I was upset. The doctor gave me a shot so I could sleep." She folded her arms so that the bandage was hidden. "Have you been officially introduced to Mr. Savage?"

The girl glanced up at him. "Sort of. He says he went to school with you a long time ago."

"I also looked in on you at Nana Simpson's house night before last. You were fast asleep, and you looked very sweet in your pretty nightie."

Suzanne rolled her eyes at Lissa. "So are you all right?" she said. "Are they going to let you come home?"

"I'm pretty sure they won't keep me here much longer." She looked at Savage. "I've really been here since night before last?"

"Really. Whatever they gave you, you were pretty spacey."

"Same old story," Lissa said. "Time means nothing to me."

.   .   .

Edwin had talked that day about one of the children, as if he had none of his own.

"You see that one," he said, "the little girl in the camel coat, the girl with the red mittens— When she grows up she's going to be a ringer for Elizabeth Taylor, a dead ringer." He looked hard at Lissa. "You know—you just know—that if you could get close to her and turn her face so you could look, you just know she'd have green eyes."

He had slumped a little in the seat.

"Irish," he said.

"A colleen," Lissa said.

He turned his head quickly, staring past her, out the window into the midmorning sun, which probably made a silhouette of her, making her face difficult to read. It was as if he were a stranger, and she had said something to offend him.

"A dead ringer," he said finally.

Yet, sitting in silence outside the fence around the school, the engine idling, the voices of the children blocked by the closed windows and smothered by the engine noise, Lissa was not so sure Elizabeth Taylor had green eyes. "Didn't we see them in a magazine once? Weren't they violet?"

He lit a fresh cigarette. "Violet," he echoed.

"Don't you remember? A close-up—the pupils were very small, and the color around them was like crushed glass, purplish and splintery."

Edwin had pondered her words. *Violet. Violent.* The similarity reminded her even then of how their lives were tainted, colored, altered by such suggestions.

For a long time, the first five years of the marriage, they had no children. It was an agreement, a contract, arrived at on their wedding night—first because they could not afford a child, later because they could not know if Edwin would survive Vietnam—and confirmed on the day she met him at the bus station and clung to him and wept the tears she had saved for the two years he was gone.

"I will never enter you," he had said that night, whispering fiercely in her ear. "Never. I will do anything else, anything you want, but never that."

At first he was compulsive about his promises. At night, in the dark, he was animal and violent, erotic and despairing. Every part of her body knew his mouth, his hands, the extraordinary heat of him. He would go without shaving, so that his beard abraded her; mornings, she stood before the mirror on the bathroom door and rubbed lotion into the rawness of her breasts, stomach, thighs. Sometimes he used his teeth; one night she had pushed him away and run into the lighted bathroom, appalled to discover in the mirror the bright glistening of her own bloodied mouth.

•   •   •

Ask me again about blood, she thought; I'm an expert.

A nurse came into the room, carrying a food tray: a patty of ground beef, mashed potatoes, peas, a carton of milk.

"You don't have to drink the milk," said the nurse. "I can get you a cup of coffee, if you'd prefer."

"Yes. I'd prefer coffee."

Lissa moved the peas around their tray compartment with a fork. She didn't know if she was ready to go back to the world, but she wanted that to happen. Susie needed normalcy—as if anything could be normal again.

"Keep the milk for your coffee," the nurse said when she came back from the corridor. "Unless you like it black."

"Thank you." She opened the milk and spilled a little into her cup. "I guess I was a problem for you, night before last."

"You were hysterical," the nurse said, "but who could blame you?"

"Yes: who?"

"But I'm sure they'll find the man who did it. I'm just positive they will."

"I'm sure you're right," Lissa said. "And that will bring Daddy straight back to me, won't it?" And here she was, weeping again, the nurse running out to find a doctor or a drug, as if the tears had never stopped.

.   .   .

Edwin said he would not have her bring children into this horrid world, but one night it was as if he had forgotten his vow. One night he turned to her in the bed, roused her and entered her. She thought he was asleep—she had been sure he was asleep—and so the act they shared might have been an act carried out in a dream. When she told him the next morning, he was at first angry, then frantic to undo what was done. She told him that if she was pregnant she would not abort the child, that she had done it once and learned all that abortion had to teach her about guilt and the betrayal of love; he argued, she shouted, but at last he was quiet and resigned to the treason of his sleep. A few nights later he told her what he had been dreaming, probably at the very moment he was inside her. It was a dream of killing, his first killing, a week after his arrival in Nam. It frightened him, this connection. He told Lissa he found something in it which was occult, impossible, as if he had planted inside her the seeds of death. He told her this was what interfered with his "rehabilitation"—the perilous angry struggle between creator and killer, which haunted his waking and sleeping. He was eloquent; he was perfectly lucid; Lissa thought these were certain signals that he was going mad.

All the while she was carrying Suzanne, she would hold Edwin, trying to keep him both from his nightmares and his wakeful fears. Some nights she sang to him, soft melodies she would later sing to the baby. When he was calm, she returned to the pleasures they shared before her impregnation, to the wildness of her own sexual imagination. In the half-light from the hall she watched him smile. She heard him call her "Mother Thumb." She cried then, knowing the child she carried was the only child he would let her have, and believing that he would never again make love to her in the only important way.

Her mother argued that she should save her tears. "The man isn't worth the expense of them" was the way she put it. This was just before her parents' divorce, and her father, when he was there to listen, made jokes about "save" and "expense" and joked that he was ashamed of his women for their mercenary way of talking. Daddy was a sergeant in the Second War; he claimed to understand perfectly what Edwin was suffering—shell shock, he had known a half-dozen men like Edwin, nothing could be done. "Just keep an eye on him." Time would diminish the problem, he told her. "But don't let him have a gun," he said. "You don't keep a gun, do you?" She told her father no, she and Edwin had never kept a gun. She remembered that she resented her father at times like that; whatever he might have been, she believed her husband was no real madman, no lunatic who would—as they said—"go berserk" in some populated place.

·   ·   ·

"But that was so hypocritical," she said to the doctor, a serious young man with a trim blond mustache and rimless glasses, who appeared at her bedside after this newest tranquilizing injection had worn off. "Mother and Daddy kept a gun themselves—a little nickel-plated revolver in the drawer between their beds. I saw it a hundred times when I was growing up. They even kept it loaded."

"But they were stable. They didn't have the kinds of problems that confronted your husband when he came back from a war—and that was a particularly frustrating war, if we're to believe what the historians say about it."

"You make it sound ancient," Lissa said. "It was only ten years ago that it ended."

"Yes, I know."

"And who knows what 'problems' my parents had? They got a divorce, after all."

"On what grounds?"

"Incompatibility. That could mean anything."

"Well," the young doctor said, "I'm not here to cope with your parents' problems; I'm here to help you come to terms with yours."

"I don't want to come to terms with them. I want them to go away."

"And you want your father back."

"That would be nice too."

"But beyond my powers as well as yours. Beyond anyone's."

"Naturally." She smoothed the sheet across her lap. "I suppose the nurse shouldn't have let me have coffee."

"I suppose not. But it didn't look as if you drank much of it."

"It doesn't seem to take much to string me out."

"I think what's upsetting you, deep down, is more than the trauma of discovering the corpse of this man you loved. It's happened twice now. Finding your father has flashed you back to the repressed memory of finding your husband. When you called for help, you kept telling the operator it was your husband you'd found. You may even project that original horror onto any men you might love in the future—perhaps you'll begin to think of yourself as a jinx."

"I certainly don't think of myself as the good fairy."

"And putting what's happened into the context of the reason for your visit to your hometown, expecting to have a happy time at your class reunion, makes matters that much worse."

"Tragedy instead of comedy," Lissa said. "I remember the masks."

"Something like that."

"Very much like it," she said. "Oh, my dear doctor. You know you are not the first man to make me say obvious things. You are not the first shrink to meddle in my life."

.   .   .

That day outside the schoolyard, the car engine idled; Edwin had never turned off the key, and she was afraid to interfere by reaching for the ignition switch. Lissa remembered thinking that eventually the gas tank would be empty, the car would stall. She imagined that the two of them would sit listening to the sounds metal makes cooling down. Their breath would cloud the windows, and the odor of tobacco be suffocating. Finally Edwin would get out of the car and walk away. A man in coveralls would appear from somewhere, carrying a red can of gasoline. She would drive home alone.

That hadn't happened.

The children reappeared at lunchtime. Most of them left the schoolyard, came past the car shouting and laughing, chasing. They paid no attention to whatever was happening inside the car. A dozen or so of their playmates remained on the schoolyard; a knot of boys gathered near the swings.

"Did I tell you about my prisoner?"

"No." she said. The truth. He had told her about killing. He had told her time and again about terror. He had told her how many fires he set to destroy how many villages.

"He'd lived in China. I'm not even sure he wasn't Chinese, some kind of advisor, a liaison. He spoke perfect English."

"How did you capture him?"

"He gave himself up to me—it wasn't anything I did. He came out of the hut alone. His hands weren't over his head; they were held away from his sides, as if he was going to embrace me. He wanted to show me he wasn't hiding anything. He was wearing a khaki uniform—that was unusual—and a belt with a leather holster at his waist. The pistol was in his right hand; he held it out to me, the grip toward me. 'Take it,' he said. 'Use it.' "

"What did you do?"

"I took it. I released the clip and emptied the chamber onto the ground. I threw the pistol off into the brush." Edwin had leaned his forehead against the window beside him. "I hope he survived all the interrogations."

"I expect he did."

"He was full of stories. About China—about old wars and about flooding and about famines and plagues. He taught history, he said. Every story he told me was like a folk tale. Not that you couldn't believe it, but that if you believed it you had to believe it was more than a story. Did I tell about the babies?"

"No." Lissa said. "I haven't heard any of this."

"There was a famine. People were dying of hunger, so when babies were born there was nothing to feed them with. The mothers were starving; they couldn't make milk. What they did was take each new baby to a ruined palace that overlooked the village from a high cliff and lay it on a windowsill. The walls were two or three feet thick, which meant there was room for several babies. Every time a new mother put her baby on the sill, it pushed the farthest child off the ledge. No mother ever killed her own baby, and no mother ever knew whose baby she killed."

He had looked at her. His eyes were blank as ever.

.   .   .

"Suze was three—almost four. I didn't take it as a threat, that crazy story about the babies. It just made me feel guilty."

"About?"

"About myself, my life."

"I don't understand."

"When I was fifteen—" She sighed. "I had an abortion. I killed a baby of my own."

"But you love Suzanne?"

"I loved the baby I killed. I loved the father who gave it to me."

"I asked if you loved Suzanne."

"Oh, yes. God, yes."

"And Edwin? He loved her, too?"

"Of course."

"He was affectionate?"

Lissa shook her head. "I can't say that," she told the doctor. "I think he didn't know how to show affection toward Suzanne."

"Why not?"

"Well— I imagine it was realizing that the way he showed affection toward me—and the way I showed it toward him—was just so . . . so perverse, that he didn't dare inflict things like that on a child. I think he was afraid he might give her pain while he was only trying to show her his love."

"He never hugged her? Kissed her? Embraced her?"

"Rarely. He was very tentative."

"Rarely. But not never?"

"Sometimes in the mornings, when Suze was up first—and she almost always was—she'd come into our bedroom and crawl into bed with us. She'd snuggle between us. Edwin didn't like that, but he tolerated it."

"Why didn't he like it?"

"He never said."

"Perhaps the girl excited him."

"Sexually? A three-year-old?"

"It's possible."

"No," Lissa said.

"Was the child affectionate to him? I mean outside the bedroom situation."

"Suze has always been a demonstrative child. A great lap-sitter, a great wet kisser."

"How did he take that?"

"I think it frightened him," Lissa said. "It was something that had to be withstood, like touching something you didn't want to touch, but you knew you had to."

"Did he act cold toward the girl?"

"It may have seemed that way to an outsider, but it was all tied to— what I said: he knew he had to accept normal behavior, even though it was a great effort for him to behave normally. *Everything* was a great effort for him, except when he and I were alone together. Dealing with Suze was an effort, dealing with his job was a terrible effort. . . ."

"What was his job?"

"He worked for a company that made paper products—boxes, paper cups, ice-cream cartons, all that kind of thing. I pushed him into it. A woman I'd gotten to be friends with while he was off in Vietnam—her father ran the company. He made a job for Edwin. It wasn't much of a job; it was boring, stupid, beneath him."

"He was overqualified."

"That's what we say nowadays. I know; I work in personnel." He was overqualified for civilian life, she thought. That was the trouble; that was what did him in.

"Then why didn't you let him wait for something better?"

"He was seeing this psychiatrist, who said that what needed to happen was to persuade Edwin out of himself, involve him in the world, coax him to talk, to 'interact'—like lancing an infection, the doctor said, letting out the poisons. I asked Ed more than once: 'Do you want to quit?' "

"And he said?"

" 'And do nothing all day?' That's what he always said. I watched him work once—one morning they let me stand behind the glass wall of the

shop manager's office. Edwin was packing those round lids for five-gallon
ice-cream containers. Behind him were two women, sitting at the machines that crimped aluminum rings onto the lids. There were these great
silver skeins of metal for the rims hanging behind them; they looked like
an endless shiny chain of wreaths, and the finished lids got dropped into
huge boxes—two, four, six, eight—forever and ever. He couldn't keep
up with them. The plant manager told me the women were on piecework.

"When they stopped for the midmorning break, Edwin went on packing. He had to seal the full cartons and stack them on skids; then a
forklift came to carry them off to the loading dock, five cartons high.
By the time the women finished their cigarettes and came back to the
machines, he had caught up. He'd catch up again at lunch, again at the
afternoon break, again in fifteen or twenty minutes past the end of his
shift."

"Tedious," the young doctor said.

"He liked not having the time to think about anything complicated.
I think he liked the pain of it too. He would cut his hands over and
over again on the sharp edges of the rims and on the sealing tape. He
used to make a big joke about all the smears of blood he left on the
cardboard lids. 'Raspberry flavoring,' he called it."

It turned out she'd always been a whiz on blood.

.   .   .   .

It was the suspended quality of their lives, that ominous stasis, that
perplexed her more and more as time passed. When Edwin first came
home from the army, they had shared hours of activity: talking, traveling
about, lovemaking in their curious fashions. Then the job came oddly
between them, and the child, and the troubled stories about a past that
seemed more and more vivid to him. Now they communicated less,
moved about less, loved each other across spaces of extraordinary silence.
She grew increasingly fearful of what such spaces might mean. She
thought that one day he would be so distant as to be faceless, that she
would cease to recognize him as the man she had married.

That day, the last full day of his life, a commotion near the schoolyard
swings had drawn them away from their preoccupations, their awful
visions. It was a fight; two boys were squared off, their small fists clenched,
their faces angry. The others—all boys but one—made a rough circle

around them. Punches were being thrown; the bystanders encouraged the fighting.

"What do they think they're doing?" Edwin had said. He flung the car door open angrily; rather than running to the schoolyard entrance he went straight to the chain-link fence and vaulted it. He confronted the children. Lissa drew the car door closed to keep out the cold, to watch from her safe distance.

He had stepped between the two adversaries, one hand on the shoulder of the smaller, the other against the chest of the taller. He talked to them by turns. Once or twice he seemed to be addressing the onlookers. She saw on all their faces petulance, disgust. Some of them wandered away from the swings, hands in pockets, feet kicking at schoolyard rocks.

He persuaded the two fighters to shake hands; the gesture may have been grudging, but it sufficed. For the first time Lissa noticed a cut on the face of one of the boys.

.   .   .

"When the group broke up, only the girl stayed behind, and of course it was the girl in the camel coat, who probably looks more like Elizabeth Taylor today than she did then. She said something to him; I don't know what, but he reached and brushed her hair away from her face and over her shoulders. They had quite a conversation, and then a man—a teacher? the principal?—appeared in the schoolhouse doorway. He and my husband exchanged a few words, then they separated."

"Did the teacher think your husband was molesting the girl?"

"I don't know. Possibly. It's that kind of world."

"He didn't tell you?"

" 'A little nosebleed,' was all he told me. Then I asked him if her eyes were really green, and the next moment he was weeping. He just collapsed against me. I knew better than to show concern, or affection, or pity. I understood he wouldn't want me to say anything to comfort him. I just looked out the car windshield and thought of all sorts of things: the colors of blood and broken glass, the story of those children dying from great height, the helplessness of the mothers too hollow to make milk or keep their babies. You can imagine how I felt for them.

"You know, as Ed had gotten stranger—sicker—I'd wake up in the morning and say to myself: Is this the day? It was like a voice inside my head: *Is this the day?* Now when I think about it, I see that, in a funny way, every day was the day. That what was happening was a lot like the stuff they sprayed to kill the jungles, that Agent Orange chemical—that its effects were supposed to fade, but really it was turning lethal, cell by cell, inside the muscle and bone of the men we were all married to."

"And the next day he was dead?"

"I told Suze he was killed in a car accident—that he'd gone walking along the highway and gotten run down. The truth was that he'd gone into the bathroom and stuck a gun in his mouth. That's where I found him. I tried not to find him, but I knew he was there, when the house was so quiet and that was the door that was shut." She turned away from the serious young doctor and hugged the pillows against her cheek. In a frenzy, she had thrown away the shower curtain, the towels, the bath mat, the window blinds. "The very last thing he'd done that morning was persuade me to make love to him. Real love. Wide-awake. Real fucking."

"What do you think about that?"

"I'm relieved not to have gotten pregnant again—not to have had a child who would be cursed by Edwin's self-hate. Or whatever it was." She shook her head. "Imagine," she said, "his hiding that pistol from me for five years, going on six. I used to wonder if it was the one that belonged to the Chinaman who surrendered to him, if he hadn't really flung it away into the trees after all."

4

STRAND WAS UP at first light. He showered, dressed, and put on his wristwatch. It was barely 5:30; he wondered what he should do until, at some more decent hour, he could walk across the motel parking area and knock on Eleanor Watkins's door. He turned on the television set; there was a test pattern on Channel 6, snow everywhere else. He opened the drawers of the motel-room dresser, the desk, the single thin drawer in the round table under the window. A Bible. A phone book. He wondered why he hadn't had the foresight to bring a paperback, a magazine, anything. He had heard that traveling salesmen hid copies of magazines—girlie magazines—under the mattresses of motel beds, so that their solitary colleagues, caught as Strand was with nothing to do and no reading matter, might find and enjoy them. He tried it, getting down on his knees, lifting the edge of the mattress he had slept on— you were supposed to reach far under, he recalled, to the very center of the bed, where a chambermaid would not easily discover the offensive material—but his hand encountered nothing.

He looked again at his watch: 5:45.

Strand switched the TV back to Channel 6, propped himself against the bed's two pillows, and while he sat, waiting for a program to take the place of the test picture, he nodded off.

He woke up again a little after seven, turned off the set's morning news show, splashed cold water on his face. He made sure the room key was in his pocket, closed the door behind him, and strolled across to Eleanor's unit. He knocked, got no answer, knocked again. He tried the door, which was locked. He tried to peep in through the window, but the curtains were drawn tightly. It surprised him that she was such a sound sleeper. I'd wake her up if she were mine, he told himself. I'll say I would.

.   .   .

The side door of the Cooper house was open when he pulled into the driveway. One of the garage doors was half-opened, and a black car sat inside. He made a detour toward the garage, pulled both doors open for light, went in and made an admiring circuit of the sedan. It was a Buick, not new—late Sixties?—but well kept and with no sign of rust, as if Cooper had never driven it in the winter. The outside of the car was immaculately clean, its chrome brilliant and uncorroded. The tires were good, but the fronts were scuffed, as if the alignment needed seeing to. He peered in through the driver's window; low mileage. Cherry. A cream puff. Not quite old enough to be a classic. He opened the car door, using his folded handkerchief to work the handle, and sat, briefly, behind the wheel, which he did not touch. The ashtray was half full, and stank. He got out and knelt to peer under the front seat; in the shadow he could see a root-beer can that had rolled out of sight, and what looked like a crumpled Kleenex. Nice machine, Strand thought. Worth taking care of. Leaving the garage, he closed both doors behind him.

When he climbed the four steps to the kitchen, he found Eleanor Watkins, in an electric-green jogging outfit and white running shoes, standing at the stove, pouring hot water into a glass coffee maker. The water through the filter made a sound like a leaky faucet.

"Good morning," she said.

"I thought you were still in the Land of Nod," Strand said. "That you were the world's heaviest sleeper."

"Just a compulsive jogger. I did five miles—or what I estimate to be about five miles—and decided to end up here." She looked at him, eyebrows slightly raised, as if he were a person somewhat below her standards. "Coffee?"

"Please," he said. He lit a Lucky and sat at the kitchen table.

"How nicely we complement each other." She set the cup before him, held the coffee filter slightly out of the pot while she filled it. "Good cop, bad cop—healthwise, I mean."

He turned the coffee cup between his hands. "I suppose Haverkamp's team went over Cooper's Buick for prints or whatever."

"I seem to recall some reference to it. Shall I give him a call?"

"You might. You do five miles every day?"

"Almost."

"Almost five miles, or almost every day?"

"Both." She sat across from him. "Actually, I got more exercise than I bargained for. When I walked across the kitchen floor yesterday, I noticed my shoes wanted to stick to the floor, so this morning I said what the hell—I'll wash it."

"Woman's work," he said.

"Screw you," Eleanor said. "And you didn't even notice."

"It looks fine. You needn't have taken the trouble."

"I also threw away some of the stuff in the refrigerator. I hate filth more than I hate waste," she said. "Speaking of which, would there be any objection if I took a shower in the crime-scene bathroom? I've got a change of clothes; I can smell a lot better."

"You want to shower in a house full of cops?"

"Nobody else is here yet. When they do show up, they'll be in the parlor, interviewing the neighbors." She frowned over her coffee. "Are you afraid I'll compromise myself by bathing?"

"I just never heard of such a thing," he said. That was true. "This is a crime scene; not a bed-and-breakfast."

"Whatever you say."

"Why don't you wait and have one of Michaud's people take you back to your motel room?"

She raised an eyebrow. "Speaking of compromise?"

"What if something vital got washed down the drain?"

"What if your cigarette ash got mixed up with the killer's?"

Strand sighed. It was like sitting down to a meal with his daughter. "Just let me have a look around," he said. "See what's to be seen." He took a careful swallow of the black coffee and stood up. He wanted to ask why she was arranging scenes of domesticity—Mr. and Mrs. Visitor at breakfast, Mrs. Visitor showering in the host's bathroom—and how cozy were the two of them supposed to be? Walking behind her chair on his way to the hall, he stopped in the doorway. "You smell fine," he told her.

•   •   •

The atmosphere of Cooper's bedroom was gamy—it had a smell, a humidity that was partly yesterday's warm day closed into the house, partly and unmistakably the freight of sexual shenanigans. The bedspread was where Strand had left it yesterday when he picked it up from the floor and laid it across the unmade bed. He was looking into bureau drawers—socks, handkerchiefs, leather belts, collar stays—when Eleanor came into the room behind him.

"The lab wouldn't say exactly how long the stains had been on the bedspread, but they thought not long."

"Cooper was not a very neat character," Strand said. "But he washed his sheets. Last act of his life. Cleanliness must really be next to godliness." He closed a drawer and picked up the silver-framed photo of a middle-aged woman. "Who is this, do you suppose?"

"Wife."

He glanced at her. "Special expertise?" he said.

"Takes one to know one," she said.

He sat on the bare mattress. "His car was fresh-washed too, but the inside was a mess. What do you suppose his priorities were? Appearances first? I was thinking—that chaos in his office *might* have been made by whoever killed him—somebody ransacking the place for anything valuable, pawnable—or it might have been his ordinary sloppy housekeeping." He looked under the bed. "What were those papers he was lying on?"

"Foolscap," Eleanor said. "Sheets from a legal pad with notes and numbers."

"Names?"

"No names."

"Phone numbers?"

"Figures. Monthly budget, something of that sort. A few notes—truncated into a funny kind of shorthand Cooper must have invented for himself. It looked like he was working up a divorce action for somebody."

"Speaking of expertise," Strand said. He opened the drawer of the nightstand, studied it, began taking things out of it and setting them on the surface of the stand. "Pills," he said.

"What kind?"

"Aspirin. Cold capsules—or maybe they're for allergies, this not being a usual season for the common cold, even in Maine. Here's Librium. That's mild, isn't it?"

"It comes in various strengths. It's not usually one of the abused—not like Valium."

"None of that here."

"Good news," she said.

"Nose drops. Eye drops. Tube of that white jelly gunk—K-Y. This is an eclectic character we're dealing with."

"It's an eclectic universe."

"Nail clippers." Strand leaned to peer into the back of the drawer. "Two more items." He reached in. "Condoms, one of the fancy brand, packaged in hard plastic so you need your partner's help to get one open. And— What have we here?"

"What?"

"Ammunition." He opened a small yellow box. "Cute; twenty-five caliber."

"Nothing to put them in?"

"No weapon." He replaced everything except the box of cartridges, which he slipped into a pocket of his jacket, and closed the drawer. "I'm going to browse through the dressers and the closets," Strand said. "I suppose there's no harm in your showering if you're swift about it—but lock the door, to be sure none of Michaud's people walk in on you." He lit a fresh cigarette.

"You do smoke too much," Eleanor said.

"Keep telling me," he said. "It makes me feel reckless."

·   ·   ·

Nothing special turned up in the closets—neither the closet in Cooper's room nor the closets in the other two bedrooms, though one of the two rooms appeared to have been recently occupied. The room nearest the master bedroom contained a bed that was partly unmade; a wastebasket in one corner had a couple of candy-bar wrappers in it; a hand towel hung from a hook on the closet door. A copy of *Penthouse*—I could have used that this morning, Strand thought—was hidden under several comic books on the lower shelf of that room's night table; it was a recent issue, dog-eared at a lesbian feature near the back of the book. The comic books were perhaps significant. He wondered if things were adding up. When he opened the top drawer of the dresser he found toilet articles: a toothbrush and toothpaste, a bottle of shampoo, a small black hair dryer. Strand closed the drawer without handling anything inside it. The other drawers were empty.

The other room seemed entirely unused; there was dust on the dresser top and around the edges of the carpet where the floorboards showed. Nothing in any drawers except sheets of old newspapers and a faint smell of mothballs.

Back in the upstairs hall he opened what he took to be a closet and found stairs leading upward. Crawl space? No, in a house of this vintage it would be a genuine attic.

He climbed. The smell of dust was dry and strong; the air was ponderously hot: he could feel sweat breaking out under his clothes and on his forehead. Yesterday's heat, last week's heat. The attic was a gerrymandering of space into a large central room filled with old furniture and trunks and cartons, and three or four smaller areas under the slant of the roof. More cartons. Bookcases with old titles: The Rover Boys, the Boy Allies, Tom Swift. College pillows covered with metal buttons: Sweet Sixteen, Kiss Me I'm Sterilized, McKinley. My father's generation, Strand thought. Cooper's father's.

Enough dust, he told himself. Enough heat.

By the time he started down the front stairs, Eleanor—should he still be thinking of her as "Miss Watkins"?—was in the shower. He could hear the water running and splashing, and he tried to imagine what she looked like. Younger, he had never understood the notion that a man could look at a fully clothed woman and undress her with his eyes. He'd never managed that successfully—any more than, in high school, he'd been able actually to undress that girl in the rumble seat of Bill Quint's Ford. He had to imagine the thing mechanically, one piece of clothing at a time, and was never sure what the sequence ought to be. Was it a skill or a talent? If a skill, he should have known more women to learn from. Shouldn't have married young. Shouldn't have picked a wife who'd finally give up on him, who'd leave him alone.

He paused at the foot of the stairs to light another cigarette. I ought to have lived up to what she wanted of me before she gave up and left.

It was all unjust deserts. Or was the thought only one more too-late gesture of love? And what was the name of that sweet girl in the rumble seat?

.   .   .

He smoked the cigarette on the sunporch, pacing from one end of it to the other, using the ashtray that held yesterday's ashes, yesterday's flash-bulb—no doubt the one that lit the picture on page one of yesterday's *Press Herald.* The police cruisers were gone, but now a blue sedan was parked up the street—Chevrolet? Pontiac? Christ, you couldn't tell one make from another these days—with two plainclothesmen sitting in the front seat. There was far less traffic, a few gawkers driving by on a street that ought to be deserted most of the day; no harm in the locals taking down a few license numbers. He turned away, sat in the chair with the ashtray on its arm, took an inventory of the porch: catch-all—snow shovel, pair of rubbers, pair of overshoes, half-full bag of rock salt, bag of cat litter. Cat? Not likely; this was all winter stuff, left over from the last ice and ready for the first ice, the first snow, four or five months from now. Fear of falling. Strand understood Cooper's fear, shared it; how much stronger it got as the years piled up.

He crushed out the cigarette, stood, strolled to the other end of the porch. Out this window: the driveway, narrow strip of lawn, the Blake house. Ralph Blake's bedroom window was the one farthest back, over-looking the Cooper kitchen. No way he could look down into the room where Cooper died; if only little Skippy could have witnessed the actual murder. Strand considered the boy's description of the stocky man with no face. Whatever we see, he thought, we see imperfectly. In this case—Strand had walked it with Blake—the streetlamp was behind the man, his features shadowed; he'd have seen the boy's face clearly, but not vice versa. Carried his arms so. . . . How come? Upper arm muscles too well developed, were they? Kind of thing you see in wrestlers, weight lifters, barroom bouncers? Ape-like—that's how he'd illustrated the man for Eleanor Watkins, prancing around the kitchen table like a ninny when Michaud caught him.

He went back inside the house; he would go down to the cellar, see what there was to be seen at the bottom as he had at the top, then come back to the first floor to hear what Michaud had for him. You never knew what a small-town constabulary might turn up; they were like salesmen who knew the territory.

At the foot of the front stairs he glanced up toward the sound of a door opening. He had, just for an instant, a glimpse of Eleanor Watkins crossing to the master bedroom. The green jogging suit was draped over her right arm and covered her lower body. If she had been naked, her skin would have shown vividly white against the color; he had a momentary vision of long legs, small breasts, the wet, blond hair streaming down her back, and then she was gone.

·   ·   ·

The cellar was ordinary, but blemished by its single touch of horror: the double track of dried blood that had seeped from the study up above and dripped onto the cement floor. Blood had incredible penetrating power. It had soaked through the carpet, then the wax and varnish of the hardwood floor, then between boards to the subflooring and past those rougher boards to the cellar. Hot stuff. Strand tried to imagine the irresistible force of it, the relentless, insidious pressure of the dying man's life, his blood going about the serious business of driving whatever there was to be driven, going wherever there was to go. Nothing distracts it, he thought; nothing obstructs it. Now it was congealed, its energies suspended into tiny stalactites and stalagmites of dark red. It might still be sticky, Strand imagined, but he was not about to touch it to find out.

The rest of the place was of ordinary interest. It was everyman's cellar, one end of it finished with paneling, a sofa, ping-pong table, vintage jukebox; the other end—the business end—with washer and dryer, freezer, out-of-date refrigerator. Oil furnace in the middle of things, its tank a few yards away, looking like some kind of black beast huddling against the wall. Off in a corner: my God—Indian clubs, punching bag, assorted weights, what used to be called "dumbbells." Strand wondered who was the health nut.

He took a swipe at the punching bag; it was deflated, and its leather was hard and cracked. The Indian clubs, four of them, showed a thick layer of dust in the light from the cellar bulbs. Ideal murder weapons, any one of them. Too bad they looked like they hadn't been touched in months, maybe years. He took out his handkerchief and used it to heft one of the dusty weights without actually putting his hand on it; it was lead, old-fashioned and brutally heavy. In a corner was a set of golf clubs, small; kid's or woman's. What is all this? he thought: if they'd killed him in the cellar we'd have weapons galore. Even the clothesline strung between the rafters, to strangle him with. Strand replaced the weight and moved on.

Here was something covered up with an old bedsheet: suitcases, four sizes. Cardboard boxes, most of them empty, a couple of them full of junk—stuff you had to weed out periodically, have a yard sale for. He opened the freezer and looked in. Ice cream, two or three pint cartons; candy bars; Sara Lee pastries. Somebody—maybe Cooper, but maybe not—was really fond of desserts. The refrigerator held Coca-Cola, Orange Crush, ginger ale, two bottles of lowbrow champagne, a six-pack of Narragansett beer. Why am I floundering around down here, Strand thought, when I could be upstairs leering at Eleanor Watkins?

·   ·   ·

In the parlor, Michaud and one of his uniforms were taping an interview with a blue-haired woman in a flowered dress. Michaud's cap was on top of a console piano near the window, and he sat on the edge of a pale blue sofa with a notebook in his left hand, a stubby pencil in his right. The uniformed policeman was the one named Savage. Strand stood for a moment in the doorway.

"You should hear this," Michaud said.

"I'll come in when you've got the case all wrapped up." Strand smiled at the woman. Now what the hell? he asked himself. What *did* Michaud have? "We appreciate your help," he said.

He found Eleanor in the Cooper study, dressed for work in a plain white blouse, jeans, loafers, moving gingerly about the room with a sheaf of papers in her hand, avoiding the pattern of blood that marked the carpet. Not much build, he noted, but nice hips, very nice ankle to her; her hair was still damp, tied back with a thin red ribbon.

"This will interest you," she said. "I haven't had time to get through the whole thing, but these seem to be the most interesting features of the lab reports so far."

Strand bent beside her to look. On the wall opposite the desk, three or four feet up from the floor and about four feet apart, were two marks that looked like leaves, the veins pointing upward and out from each other.

"Handprints," he said. He put on his half-glasses and leaned for a closer look. Palms, the incomplete design of the fingers, more like an animal's track than he would have expected. He measured his own hand against one of the prints.

"Woman's," he said.

"Or a man smaller than you."

"A boy." He straightened up and tucked his glasses away.

"But we're still waiting for an ID."

Strand gazed thoughtfully at the small palm prints. Possibly this Raymond Hussey Cooper had gotten what he deserved—if anyone ever deserved a violent death.

•   •   •

In the back of a filing cabinet—one of four in the victim's office—Strand found more magazines. They were tucked in behind several files of letters, and he had to pull the drawer nearly all the way out before he was able to get at them. There were perhaps two dozen different issues of a dozen magazines—*Oui*, *Hustler*, *Men*, a couple of gay magazines, two or three more pornographic titles he had never heard of. The bulk of them were muscle magazines, through whose pages men paraded their physiques and wore wrestling costumes of fishnet tops and bikini briefs. Most of the magazines were months or years old; only one or two were current.

Eleanor looked over her shoulder. "A treasure trove," she said.

"A lot of flesh," Strand said. "I found a *Penthouse* in one of the upstairs bedrooms."

"The old man spent a lot of time alone," she said.

He turned to face her. " 'Old man'?" he said.

She colored. "Sorry."

"I should hope."

"I meant he could have gone in for self-abuse—or whatever you call it in this part of the world."

"I wouldn't know," Strand said. "A man of my restrained and mature years. We used to call it 'dubbing off.' "

Eleanor turned pages in one of the magazines. "Look how these boys glisten," she said. "Ready for the oven."

Strand dumped the magazines back into the drawer and closed it. "Let's reheat some of that coffee of yours."

"I'll make fresh."

"Suit yourself." He followed her to the kitchen; pretty woman with a pretty walk. "Is this the state of Maine's coffee, or the old man's?"

"It's mine," she said. "Bureaucracies drink a lot of it, but they don't fathom reimbursing employees for it."

Strand sat at the table and watched her filling a teakettle with water from the cold-water tap. Graceful but not self-conscious. Didn't she know he couldn't take his eyes off her?

"I found a carton of Pall Malls in a hall table," Eleanor said. "Is it ethical for you to smoke them? Or is it like using the dead man's shower?"

"It's not *unethical*," he said, "but not quite my brand."

"There's something quaint and old-fashioned about you mature men and your unfiltered cigarettes."

This time he ignored the bait. "About these three husbands," he said. "They all die natural deaths?"

She smiled. "They're all alive and well, so far as I know. Maybe I don't have an especially high regard for men, but I never thought they were worth risking the gallows for."

"No gallows in this part of the world," he said.

"You know what I mean."

"Probably."

Eleanor turned on the unit under the kettle. "This'll be slow," she warned him. "It's electricity."

"Tell me something," Strand said. "Tell me if you notice any evidence at all of a woman's touch around this place."

"Such as?"

"I don't know. That's why I'm asking." He smoked. "A stray lacy article. A fancy soap in the soap dish. A bottle of perfume, a satin slipper—"

"A diaphragm in a dresser drawer?"

Strand sat straighter. "You found such a thing?"

"No. Just trying to define your 'woman's touch.' "

Teasing me, Strand thought. "You mind if I call you Eleanor?" he said.

"It's about time," she said.

"Eleanor," Strand said, "I'm having more than one unkind thought about our dead friend Cooper."

"And that's about time, too."

"That he was a very unstraight gentleman?"

"Hasn't it seemed likely? I wondered what was taking you so long to figure it out."

"I suppose I don't want to be hasty," he said. "Or, as you remarked earlier, it takes one to know one."

She dropped the printout on the table before him. "Try this," she said. "The dried semen on that bedspread belongs to two different men."

·   ·   ·

"Sure, this Cooper was queer," Michaud said. "You bet he was. A three-dollar bill."

They were on the sunporch, Strand and Michaud, facing each other across the glass-topped table with its wrought-iron legs painted white. On the table was a small cassette recorder, a Sony micro, the kind you took onto a plane if you were a businessman with letters to dictate. Strand drew the ashtray closer, got settled in the chair. He wished he'd brought along one of the A.G.'s Nakamichi units—longer tape, better sound quality. Not to mention who would retain physical possession of the tapes.

"A string of teenage boys," Michaud said. He leaned forward to set the tape in motion. "This is an old lady named Alice Briggs. Lives across the street." He twisted in his chair and pointed toward a blue clapboarded house with white trim, archaic lightning rods set at each end of the ridgepole. "Get this."

There was a disorder of noise on the tape—the machine sliding on hard surface, a background of male voices—then Michaud saying, "You just say us your name and where you live."

"My name is Alice Mary Briggs." It was a voice cracked with age, but positive, its positiveness reinforced by the woman's habit of accenting every noun and putting space between each word. "I live at 26 Ridgeway Avenue, Scoggin, Maine."

"Did you know a man named Raymond Cooper?"

"Oh, yes. I did. We've been neighbors for twenty years."

"You're friends?"

A hesitation. "We speak. Sometimes in the winter he shovels my front walk."

"You aren't friends?"

"We're neighbors."

"Skip all this irrelevant stuff," Strand said. "Get to it."

Michaud ran the tape forward. "You don't like the background," he said.

"I didn't think I needed it."

The tape resumed.

"Did you see anything unusual across the street that evening?"

"In the evening? You mean after supper?"

"Or later."

"I don't stay up very late, you know. I need my beauty sleep." Alice Briggs made a small dry chuckling noise. "But no; I didn't see anything unusual in the evening."

"Not at the Cooper house, or near it?"

"Not in the evening."

Christ, Strand thought, what am I supposed to be listening for? He blew smoke across a shaft of light from the midafternoon sun.

"But earlier," the Briggs woman was saying, "one of the boys was there."

"One of the boys?"

"Yes. Mr. Cooper has two or three boys who come and do work for him. Wash the car. Trim the bushes. You know."

"What do you mean by 'boys'?"

"Young fellows. Twelve, fourteen. Those sweet-faced children who haven't started yet to look like little men." Hesitation. "Lord, I don't know how to describe the young people—not at my age."

"But one of them was there in the afternoon?"

"Washed Mr. Cooper's car for him. Mr. Cooper helped. He was out in the driveway with the boy. One soaped, one rinsed. They got water on each other. Mr. Cooper was sometimes quite kittenish."

"When the car was washed, did the boy leave?"

"No. He went into the house with Mr. Cooper. He gives them tonic, you know, to help them cool off. I see them walking away, eating candy or those fancy ice-cream bars."

"How long did the boy stay?"

"This time . . . quite a while. I suppose I was just getting ready to sit down to supper—Mrs. Haywood brought over a casserole she'd made—when I saw him come out the side door and get on his wheel."

"His bicycle?"

"Bicycle. Yes."

"So what time do you think the boy came to Cooper's house?"

"Oh . . . I expect it was two or two-thirty."

"And he left the house when?"

"I always sit down to eat at six, sharp." She cleared her throat softly. "That wasn't unusual," Alice Briggs said. "The boys often stayed after they'd finished Mr. Cooper's chores."

Michaud leaned forward and stopped the tape. "Interesting?" he said.

Strand poked out his cigarette. "That's one possible word," he said. "I imagine we'll think of better."

"You don't need to hear more. You know where it's going to lead to."

"You ask this Briggs lady if she ever saw a woman go into the house with Cooper?"

"I asked."

"And?"

"She never saw the subject with a woman since the wife left."

"Have you talked to any of the boys?"

"We will," Michaud said. "We know who they are."

Strand stood. "Go to it," he said. Maybe we're on the same team after all, he thought; maybe he's learning to trust us. "When you finish up today, I'd like to take the tapes back to the room with me. Play through them tonight. Catch up with what you know."

"We'll make transcripts." Michaud picked up the tape machine. "You let us hold the tapes."

"Whatever you say," Strand said. So much for trust.

5

LATE SATURDAY MORNING, Lissa had begun packing the few things Donnie brought her from Nana Simpson's, folding the clothes she had worn from Chicago and was already sick of, padding about the hospital room in stockinged feet and catching glimpses of herself in the mirror of some sort of chifforobe built into the wall beside the bathroom door. You look like death warmed over, her mother might have said. And feel like it, she would surely have answered.

They had kept her in the hospital for a third night—the young psychiatrist down from Maine Medical reluctant to let her out into the world until he felt she would not disintegrate at every word spoken to her. She had slept fitfully, dreaming and waking—faces and places appearing like random pictures in a family album. The morning light had brought her up from sleep, but she felt as if she had not rested at all. For a while she had lain quietly, letting the night fade, until there were no pictures left except two: the image of her daughter, alive and asleep and needing a mother, and of a man who was sometimes her father, sometimes her husband, dead and needing no one. Then she had sat on the bed, rung for a nurse, been allowed to eat and dress.

Now she combed her hair, forcing herself to pretend she cared about how she looked. She was near the window, the comb held rigidly in her hand, as if it were something to cling to while she waited to be released. As if this room were a haven, and the outside world all threat.

Down below her, on the walk leading up to the main entrance, two people appeared: a rumpled middle-aged man in a light brown suit who stopped halfway to light a cigarette, and a blond, rather young woman in seersucker who, when the man threw his match onto the lawn, spoke to him, possibly saying something critical. Like a schoolboy made conscious of doing something not allowed, the man went after the match and picked it up. Finally he paused to take the cigarette apart with his fingers and threw the paper and shreds of tobacco aside as he led the way into the building.

.   .   .

She was not surprised when the two of them stood in the doorway to the room. The man introduced himself as Willard Strand.

"This is Eleanor Watkins, my assistant," he said. His was an awkward presence in the room, as if he wasn't sure what to say, as if he would have preferred to be somewhere else. "We're sorry to disturb you." Hesitant. "I know this has all been an awful shock, and that you'd rather not have the intrusion."

"It's all right," Lissa lied. "I'm already disturbed."

"We're down from Augusta," he began.

She interrupted him. "I wonder if you know how funny that is."

"Funny?"

"I say I'm 'disturbed.' You tell me you're from Augusta. When we were in school, we joked about Augusta. It's where they sent the crazy people— the State Hospital for the Insane."

"AMHI," he said. "Different name, but they still send them there. I can't speak for Miss Watkins"—he looked at the woman in seersucker— "but I'm not one of the crazies."

"I'll have to take your word for it."

Strand seemed to smile. "We're both with the Attorney General's office," he said. "We're looking into your father's death."

"His murder," Lissa said. She gripped the comb in both hands. "What have you found out?"

"A number of things," Strand said, "but not enough. That's why we're here."

Lissa closed her eyes for a moment, gathered her energies. She thought she could survive an interview if she concentrated strictly on the words being said to her. "I can't imagine how to help you," she said. "I don't know anything. I don't live here anymore."

"We have several questions," the woman said, "but only if you're up to answering."

Lissa gave up the comb, putting it on the small surface in front of the mirror, and seated herself in the molded plastic chair under the window. She wanted not to be rude, but wasn't certain she could avoid the rudeness. What did they imagine she could possibly know about this horror? Even if she could collect all her wits, what could she say?

"You have to know that I've lived in the Midwest for the past dozen years. I haven't kept in touch with my hometown—not noticeably, anyway."

"A few friends, still?"

"Very few. Not even friends. Acquaintances."

"You write? They write? You get some news of Scoggin?"

"Precious little."

"No gossip about your father?"

"None." A settling truth; she saw—or thought she saw—where the man wanted to go. "If you mean women in his life, jealous husbands who would want to beat him to death . . . no; no gossip at all."

"We're looking for motive," the Watkins woman said. "You see that."

"Yes, I see that."

"May I smoke?" Strand asked.

"I wish you wouldn't." He had taken the pack out of his shirt pocket; she saw the bright red bull's-eye. "That was the brand my husband smoked."

She wanted to go on, quickly, and explain that the brand of cigarette was not the reason for her objection—that she was mildly allergic to the smoke, that whenever she visited her father she spent as much time outside the house as possible, for the sake of herself and her daughter—but Strand had already put the pack away.

"Nobody likes to make guesses at motive," he said. "When we guess, we run the risk of painting ourselves into corners. I told the press people yesterday afternoon that we hadn't ruled out robbery as a motive for the murder. At the time, nobody that I know of had found a reason even to suggest such a thing, but when you're talking to the ladies and gentlemen of the press, any motive will do, I suppose. One of the things I need to find out—from you, as one of the more knowledgeable persons available to me—is what your father might have owned that was especially valuable, especially worth stealing."

He waited. Lissa kept her gaze fastened on his face, knowing her eyes told nothing, betrayed nothing, promised nothing. What did she care about the press people? For that matter, what difference did *motive* make?

"Or I could ask the Scoggin authorities to put together an inventory, a list of the contents of the house. I could show it to you. You might notice if something in particular was omitted."

She knew that her silence was making Strand uncomfortable. She knew he wanted to smoke. He probably knew she wanted him to leave her alone. She looked up at this Miss Watkins; at least the woman's expression was sympathetic.

"Anything at all," Miss Watkins said.

"Perhaps something unusual, but not necessarily of much monetary value." He tamped the end of an unlighted cigarette against the back of his hand. "Something that might have attracted a thief's attention."

"His life," Lissa said flatly. "His life was especially valuable—though not unusual."

Strand was watching her. He was less uneasy now, and his attention oppressed her—the waiting, the emerging cat-and-mouse flavor of this interview, this stupid visit home. He saw into her, saw that she was vulnerable, and now he was deciding if he should press, push, pry. But she had come for a reunion; nothing else. The suitcase Nana Simpson had sent over lay open on the bed, half unpacked. The clothes she had worn driving up from Logan were beside the case, waiting to be shoved in and hidden under the lid. She would throw them away, burn them, anything to be rid of them. They reeked of death and blood, and even if they didn't, she would always imagine they did. *Why didn't this man let her get on with it?*

Eleanor Watkins sat on the end of the bed nearest her. "Would you rather we talked another time? Tomorrow?"

But Strand broke his cigarette in two and stood to drop it into a wastebasket in a corner of the room. "Look," he said, "I know this isn't pleasant for you, and it isn't a lot of fun for me. I've got a daughter, her name is Jacqueline, who's about your age, and your father was about *my* age. I'm not disinterested in all this; I do have feelings. So: was there anything else, any material thing, that might have been worth—what somebody did to him?"

Lissa gave up. Her gaze went to the sunstruck floor, saw the scrawled grime rubbed off the bottoms of shoes, the scars made by hard-rubber heels in the wax, saw a bobby pin she must have dropped when she tried to put order into her hair. The poor man is trying to do a job, she told herself. And the poor woman assistant is caught in gender politics— doesn't know whose side to take.

"My father had a lot of passions, a lot of enthusiasms," Lissa said. "They never lasted long. He collected things—different things for different enthusiasms. For a long time, when I was little, it was stamps, foreign stamps. He'd hold up different stamps with tweezers and show them to me—usually big, diamond-shaped ones, or triangular ones, with bright-colored birds and animals on them. When I was in junior high, it was coins. He had Chinese coins with square holes in the middle of them, and coins made out of bronze, so heavy you wondered how men could carry them in their pockets. In high school, I'd come home and he'd be in the garage making bookshelves or end tables or God knows what; he spent hundreds and hundreds of dollars on power tools. He had jigsaws and lathes and—I don't even know the names of all the wood-working machines he owned. There was barely room for the car. Things. He was passionate about *things*."

She felt dizzy, and sat on the edge of the bed.

"And now *he*'s a thing," she said. A thing in a box.

"Where are they all?" Strand said. "The stamps? The coins?"

"I suppose they were sold. I told you: the enthusiasms never lasted— a year at the most. Then my mother would make him weed everything out. That was her word: 'weed.' "

"No enthusiasms lately?" He had a new cigarette to play with. Nerves. Habit. She couldn't know which. Could he give up smoking if he had to? "No new passions?"

"Not that I know of," she said. She looked again at Miss Watkins. "Forgive me, but yes, why don't we talk about this some other time? I feel dreadful. I haven't seen my daughter since yesterday, or the day before yesterday—whenever they woke me up to keep me awake; God knows when that was. I have to get out of this hospital before the disinfectants and bells and bedpans and sweetie-voiced nurses drive me out of what's left of my mind." She stopped. Was she as hysterical as she thought she sounded? Was that a measure of how divided she felt? How she wanted to be with Susie, but was terrified of everything else?

"That's fine with us," the woman said.

Strand was watching; now he was doing to Lissa what she had at first tried to do to him: being blank with her, looking through her, waiting for her tantrum to be over, ignoring his partner. Daughter of his own or not, what did he care about a woman's personal problems? What did he know about a mother's concerns? He had put on his glasses and now he wrote a few lines in a small green notebook.

"Please, I'd like to finish packing."

He closed the notebook. "Your late father owned a handgun."

It wasn't a question. She weighed the statement. "I remember it," she said. "It really belonged to my mother. Daddy bought it for her so she'd be protected whenever he was out of town. It was nickel-plated. Or chrome. Something very shiny."

"And small," Strand said. "Twenty-five caliber. It would have been small enough to fit in a man's palm."

"Yes," she said. "He let me hold it once. I was sick and home from school. Measles, I think. Daddy was desperate to keep me entertained— I don't remember where my mother was—and finally he brought in this silver gun. I thought it was huge. Of course he'd unloaded it." And when she was fifteen and knew she was pregnant—and knew that she was never going to be allowed to have the baby, no matter what she said or how hard she pleaded—she had gone one afternoon into the bedroom and gotten that pistol out of the drawer. It was loaded then; she had thought long and hard about killing herself. You hear of people dying for love, she had told herself, and this is one way to do it. Then she had put the gun back, fear, she had decided—or was it hope?—being stronger than despair.

"We found ammunition for it, but not the weapon itself," the woman said. "Where do you think it might have been put?"

"I don't have any idea."

"Do you think your mother took it when she left your father?"

"Can we talk about something else?" Lissa said. "If you don't already know it, my husband shot himself, about five years ago."

Strand took the pack from his shirt pocket and put his unlighted cigarette back into it. "Sorry," he said. "I *didn't* know. We don't mean to rake up all the miseries of your life."

"I've had a few," she said.

"What about this? We found a lot of magazines."

"Bill." Miss Watkins had stiffened; she put out her hand as if to stop him from talking.

"Just a second," Strand said. "Soft-porn stuff. A few naked ladies, a lot of naked men, showing off, or doing you know what—"

"It's all right," Lissa said. "I found some of those the last time I visited. It was because he lived alone. We kidded about it, about his centerfold sweethearts. I said I thought he must be a real swinger, and he said he was just an ordinary dirty old man." God, if only she could have found those before the police did, she could have saved her dead father some embarrassment, some damned silly smirks from the people who were turning his house, his life, inside out.

"Did he do health things?"

"Like what?"

"You know—jogging, working out, that kind of thing."

"I doubt it."

"Because we also found muscle magazines. These pretty boys in bikinis, huge pectorals, biceps like loaves of bread, thighs like tree trunks." He paused. "And magazines . . . similar to those."

Lissa shook her head. "Dad was not one for exercise," she said.

Strand smiled. "A man after my own heart," he said. "But there did seem to be exercise apparatus in the cellar of the house: weights, punching bag, that sort of thing."

"My grandfather's generation," Lissa said. "When Dad closed up his father's house, the exercise stuff went into our cellar. Gramps didn't want to sell it."

"Is your grandfather alive?" the woman asked.

"Oh, yes." She put her hands up over her face. "God," she said, "it's so unfair." That his father should have outlived him, she meant.

"Well," Strand said awkwardly, "we'll talk again. With your permission."

She raised her head. "Did they kill him with one of those stupid Indian clubs?"

"No, no," he said. "No, we don't know what they used."

"Find them," she said. "Find the ones who did it."

"We will," he said. "I promise."

Miss Watkins paused, put an arm around Lissa's shoulders. "He means it," she said. "We *will* find whoever it was."

Strand waited in the doorway. "The night you found him—do you remember somebody taking your picture?"

"No." Lissa tried to think. "No, I don't know if anyone did."

"I wondered," he said. "You were on the front page of the paper."

"You won't tell the whole world about Daddy's magazines, will you?"

"Of course not," the woman said. "We won't embarrass you."

When they were gone, Lissa wiped away the tears with the backs of her hands. For a long time she sat by the window, thinking what a failure she was, how careless with lives. I lost a child, she thought. I lost Edwin. Now I've lost Daddy. She watched Miss Watkins and Strand leave the hospital grounds, the gray cloud of Strand's smoking following him like a wake. She wondered if the pattern of her life's losses was something she had inadvertently designed for herself all those years ago when she let herself be taken to Boston for the abortion. Perhaps people filled in their own destinies without realizing it; perhaps they chose the tragic mask over the comic, saying unintentionally, *Who wants to be happy all the time?*

.   .   .   .

When they discharged her from the hospital, Donnie was waiting for her in the lobby. He carried her suitcase in one hand and took her elbow in the other, steering her out across the parking lot.

"You okay?" he said.

"Yes. Fine."

"You want to go someplace for a drink?"

"I don't think so." She was quite sure she couldn't handle a drink right now. "I don't know what they've given me—what medication—but I don't think I'd better take a chance."

"Strand upset you?"

"What do you think?" She pushed his hand away, gently, to tell him that she could walk without his help. "I'm sure he means well—the woman tried to be sweet—but I didn't like him. I suppose I came back for the reunion expecting to find everything the same—never mind time, never mind accident, never mind geography."

He stopped her by putting his free hand back against her arm. "Here's the car."

It was a police car, and she shrank from it.

"Relax," Donnie said. He put her bag in the backseat, and held the passenger door open for her. "You're not under arrest."

She sat stiffly inside the car. "I've never ridden in a police car," she said.

"I won't run the siren. Nobody'll notice you."

"Everybody notices me. I'm a curiosity. Widowed daughter of a dead father."

He sighed and started the car. She felt grief welling up in her belly, waited for it to sweep her away again. She closed her eyes; the grief backed off.

"How could it happen?" she said. "How in hell could it happen?"

"It's how the world is," he said. "You live in a big city; you know what the crime rate's like."

"This isn't Chicago. This is a little town."

"Then it's changed."

Lissa rested her head against the window beside her. One of the air-conditioning louvers threw a steady draft that cooled her skin and disarranged her hair. Now they were passing the new shopping center— once it had been three blocks of frame houses she barely recalled from her childhood, all of them flattened for a parking lot rimmed with stores, a discount house at one end, a supermarket at the other, two gas stations flanking the entrance. The vanished houses had been generous: three-storied, with wide verandas and turrets with huge mullioned windows, and flagpoles in the front yards. Pendletons, Kimballs, Elliotts—the town's wealthy families. The houses had gardeners who cut the lawns with hand mowers and trimmed the hedges with long-handled clippers. They had been houses like the one in her dream at the hospital. Flowers climbed trellises; lilacs and hydrangeas smothered the porch railings in summer.

"I don't suppose I'd said more than ten words to your old man in the last five years," Donnie said as they drove up Main Street. "I'd see him once in a great while at the green front, always buying something fancy like Napoleon brandy or Glenlivet Scotch. You'd see his picture in the *Sentinel* when he'd gone to some conference of lawyers in Boston. He was never *with* anybody—I mean he never seemed to have dates with the town's eligible widows; he didn't hang out with the big shots at the City Club. Was he in Rotary or Kiwanis?"

"I don't think so. He didn't use to be a joiner."

"He was in the American Legion, though."

"Yes, I guess he was in the Legion."

"Because when we were kids, I can remember him wearing the dark blue cap with the Legion gold star on it, every Memorial Day. He used to make a big deal out of it—saluting us, giving us orders."

"He was in a parachute division—the 82nd—in the war," she said. "He used to brag about it." And used to think it licensed him to give her advice about poor Edwin.

"A really tough old bird. That's what I always thought when I was a kid."

"But he wasn't," Lissa said. "My mother complained about what a milktoast he was, how she always had to stand up to the plumber and the TV repairman or else Dad would let himself be cheated, taken advantage of." Mother. She still hadn't talked to her mother. Damn. Thoughtless, thankless child. "I wonder what my mother said when she found out he was dead."

"I called her the next day. She wanted to talk about me. She remembered the names of all the kids that hung out around your house."

"Who told her about Daddy?"

"I didn't ask."

"Did she seem upset?"

"I suppose that's why she talked about everything but. She remembered that we used to steal for your father."

"Hubcaps," Lissa said. "For that old car of his."

"You remember. He paid us two dollars for each one. We thought we were big stuff. We must have been how old?"

"Eleven or twelve. Junior high school."

"Embarked on a life of crime at an early age," Donald said. "Your father the mastermind."

"Fagin," she said. If that was the worst he'd ever done, did they have to murder him for it?

"He had a way with kids, your old man. Sometimes I wondered why he didn't get into scouting."

"Sissies," she said. "That's what he called scoutmaster types." She looked at him. "You aren't a scoutmaster, are you?"

"Once in a while I get sent to a troop meeting to talk about law and order, and how the police are your friends." He chuckled. "If I was a Boy Scout leader, would you feel safer with me?"

"I feel safe now," she said. "How could I feel safer?"

He shrugged. "Here's Grove Street."

"Let's not stop at Nana's right now," Lissa said. "Let's drive to the house."

"What in the world for?"

"I just feel like it. A whim." And so it was; she had no reason for wanting to see the house—not to go inside, God knew, but only to sit outside for a few minutes, to stare at it, to ponder what it contained. "Humor me. I'm trying to make sense out of it all."

"So are we," Don said. "So are the State Police. That's why they got this Strand down here from Augusta."

Lissa looked down at her hands. "Why does the Attorney General have to be involved?"

"I don't know, but that's the way it works. I think we know what we're doing; as much as the State Police do. For damned sure, we're as professional as the guy from Augusta. Especially since he's so hot for that assistant of his."

"How do you know that?"

"You watch them; he can't take his eyes off her."

He stopped in front of the Cooper house and shut off the ignition. Across the street and fifty yards away sat a dark blue sedan, two men in the front seat. Don gestured toward it. "That's our vehicle," he said. "Surveilling."

She smiled.

"What's funny?"

"Is that really a verb? To surveil?"

He said nothing, looked at her appraisingly.

"And what's the difference between a vehicle and a car?" she said.

"Not much," he said. "The words are just habit."

Lissa stared out the window. Ridgeway was narrower than she had thought it was; there was barely enough room for two cars to pass without running onto the walk on one side of the street or the other. The space between the houses was slight, and the front yards simply didn't exist, yet she had never felt they—she and her mother and father—had lived hemmed in. She looked at the house set off from the street by a strip of vivid yellow ribbon, at the sunporch where she had grown geraniums and played house, where she had slept on hot summer nights.

"When do you suppose they'll let me back inside?" she said softly.

"Inside to stay? Do you want to do that?"

"I'm not sure. I just think I ought to have the choice—either of moving into the house or closing it up for good."

"I'll ask old Strand; they've got a computer set up in the kitchen, tied in to Augusta by phone, and Michaud's got us doing interviews in the front parlor."

"I don't think I like that," Lissa said. Why would they do that? she wondered. How dare they? This was a home, not some kind of institutional building you could take over for professional reasons. The *family* wasn't dead, was it?

"We don't have much choice. Michaud keeps bugging the selectmen for a bond issue to build a new town hall, so we can have some room, but nothing happens."

"I don't care about that. The house is mine now—or Mother's. I'm not sure which. But it doesn't belong to you or him or the damned Attorney General."

"I'll find out how much longer we have to stay there," he said.

"*I'm* not a corpse," she said, her objection seeming to gain momentum. "You people better not treat me as if I am."

"Hey, we won't," Savage said. "We don't mean to."

The afternoon sunlight slanting against the house made the yellow clapboards seem darker, almost copper; there were clouds building; the dark light was a threat of a thunderstorm, and the harder greenness of the lawns meant rain to come. How many afternoons had she stood at the windows of that sunporch and watched the rain streaming down the glass? How many years lay between this day and every one of her other days?

"Do you know anything?" she said. "You police?"

The question seemed to trouble him. "Some things. Not who."

"Or why?"

"Not why."

"What I most remember," she said, "is blood. It may be the only thing I remember for the rest of my life. All that blood—that enormous shape of the blood soaked into the carpet in front of his desk. Isn't it Lady Macbeth who says something about 'Who'd have thought the old man had so much blood in him?' Shakespeare must have seen somebody beaten to death, to know about the blood."

She glanced at Savage; he was staring ahead, trying not to see her.

"I have to get in there to clean it up," she said. "The carpet's useless; I imagine the floor will have to be scrubbed."

"Sanded," he said.

"Maybe," she said. She pondered the blood. It smelled; it had an odor of its own, like something incredibly rotten, oppressive against the sense of smell. "Lye soap," she said abruptly. "My Grandmother Ross would have scrubbed the floor with homemade lye soap."

"Strong stuff."

She watched the dark car down the street. "Do you people really believe the criminal returns to the scene of the crime? Isn't that why they're watching?"

"We want to see who comes by, who's curious. Maybe not every gawker's just a gawker."

"It was someone he knew," she said. Such a nice man, my father. She rested her arms on the back of the seat and laid her cheek against her arms. "All your surveilling," she said softly, "and not a clue in sight."

"Time," Donnie said. "Just give it time. You'll survive this."

"Survive," she said. "That's all I can expect?" She turned in the seat abruptly and opened the car door. She got out and headed straight for the corner of the house where one end of the yellow ribbon marking the boundaries of the crime scene was attached. As she got close to it, she could see it was printed, in black, with the words SCOGGIN POLICE, the two words repeated over and over along the length of the tape. She ripped the tape away from the house, then followed it around the front of the porch, tearing it down as she went, wadding it in her left hand until at the other side of the house she flung the whole ball of ribbon under one of the hydrangeas. When she turned back to the police car, she felt better; she noticed that Donnie was watching her carefully, that he hadn't moved at all.

·   ·   ·   ·   ·

At Nana Simpson's, he put his hand out to stop her, just as she was opening the door of the police car and getting out.

"What are you going to do about the reunion?"

"Jesus, don't ask," she said. "I'm certainly not going to go."

"I think you ought to." He reached for her hand. "Listen," he said. "You can't drown in this thing. You can't let it stop your life."

"I'm not letting it stop my life. I have funerals to plan. I have caskets to buy. I have cemetery plots to look at. I have a busy, busy life."

She wished her mother could be here. Mother would be panicky about clothes, would be telling her how she had nothing appropriate to wear. That was Mother's favorite word: "appropriate." Never "proper" or "right" or "necessary." "Appropriate." "Is Donald Savage an appropriate friend?" Mother would make the services for the murdered man—her own husband, the man she had borne Lissa for—into something trivial. I'd like that, Lissa thought. I'd like this to be a trivial event; I'd like to be fretting about appropriate clothes. Does one wear black to a summer funeral? Mother would ask that question, and Mother would find the answer.

"But after that," Donald said. "You aren't going to spend all night at the cemetery, are you?"

She looked at him—at the intense concern on that still-boyish face of his, at the short, out-of-style haircut, and at the wilted uniform collar with its almost military insignia that didn't quite cancel the boyishness— and the question struck her as funny. She laughed, and the laughter— though it was brief, though she quickly caught herself and suppressed it—lit a shy smile on his features.

"We've done that," she said.

Because just then she remembered that they had done that, sixteen years ago. They had stayed all night in the cemetery in the field beside the Methodist church, on a warm Saturday in July, lying together behind a granite monument wrapped in each other's arms, kissing and kissing. Donnie had wanted to do more, had tried to touch between her thighs— not once, but time after time, as if she might forget from one moment to the next what she had forbidden, what she had allowed. She had only allowed him her breasts, first through the cotton brassiere and then, because his hands insisted and would not stop teasing the tender nipples, by letting out her breath to permit him to slide his hand inside the brassiere, to free one breast and then the other. She remembered what a conflict of feelings, of emotions, swam through her, how she could hear her own voice saying over and over again, "Please don't love me, please don't love me."

My God, she thought now, I was only seventeen; I'd been with only one man—one darling, irresistible man—in my life. Yet all the while she had been realizing pleasures, sensations, glitters of small electricity all over her body, and with one part of her mind she thought how she did not want Donald Savage to take this . . . this wrestling, this "heavy breathing," as something meaningful, while with another part of the same mind she was thinking how small her breasts were and that if she turned onto her side they would seem to be larger, and he would be more excited by her. But he was not the boy she wanted; he was rougher than she thought she deserved—this boy whose interests were in shop and football and drinking beer on Saturday nights with his cronies.

"I remember," Donald said.

Please-don't-love-me, please-don't-love-me—she had murmured it over and over like a chant, an accompaniment to his feverish exploration of her, and his own chant had answered hers: Why-not? Why-not? Why-not? The grass underneath her was cool and damp, the weight of the boy on top of her like an animal force she very well knew she was not so foolish to fear. And this time the fear had won out; she had held her thighs closed, she had kept on pushing away his hands, she had made him be satisfied with her womanness above the waist only—necking, not petting.

"If you'd known more about me then," she said.

"I knew enough."

"Knew what?"

"About your being pregnant, and then not being pregnant. We all knew; you were a celebrity."

"God," Lissa said.

And was that why he had tested her? Lying beside and half under Donnie Savage, all her clothes on, even if in disarray, trying breathlessly to slow the growth of his unexpected passion—was that only a formality, not even personal? *All the important things, we experience before we're twenty*—she had read that somewhere. Pregnancy—that dry fact cut short. All right: she had thought then that if she confessed to him, he would be turned off. Now she saw that just the opposite had been true—now, when she was thirty-three and a mother and bereft of all the men who were important to her.

She opened the car door. Donnie got out on his side and brought her suitcase to her.

"There's a clambake tomorrow afternoon at Jean Goddard's camp, starting at two," he said. "You ought to go."

"I can't," she said. "I wouldn't be any company."

"It might be good therapy," Donnie said.

"I've had enough therapy to last me."

"Then will I see you before your father's funeral?" he said.

"Jesus, Donnie—" She felt tears coming. "Jesus Christ, will you stop making dates? We're not meeting outside the Capitol Theater so we can hold hands in the balcony."

He tried to take her wrist, but she yanked it away and picked up the suitcase.

"No," she said, and went up the walk to the house. Not right, she thought. Not "appropriate."

6

When strand came out to the Cooper sunporch that afternoon, Eleanor was sitting in one of its wrought-iron chairs with a large notebook in her lap. Papers—her inevitable green-shaded computer printouts—were scattered on the floor around her feet. A glass of iced coffee sweated on a windowsill. He sat, heavily, across from her.

"What's going on?" she said.

"I give up. What?"

"Michaud turned the place upside down and inside out while we were at the hospital."

"Looking for?"

"Motive. He claims Cooper had a valuable coin collection that's come up missing; he wants to make sure it's not somewhere in the house."

"Who told him about a coin collection?"

"Not me."

"I'll be damned." Strand pulled the cigarette pack out of his shirt pocket; it was empty. "It doesn't exist, does it? Didn't the daughter tell us the coins were one of the enthusiasms that faded away?"

"I told that to Michaud," Eleanor said. "He ignored me. I swear he covered every square centimeter of Cooper's office. He even looked for a floor safe. The carpet was stuck to the floor; it made a dreadful noise when he pulled it up."

"Motive," Strand repeated. He looked at the crumpled cigarette package in his hand, squeezed it into a ball, dropped it into the ashtray beside him. "I thought we'd found motive aplenty."

"He doesn't like that one."

"And who can blame him?" He wondered if he'd put a spare pack in his suit coat, now hanging on the back of a chair in the dining room. "Not a very pleasant thing in a nice town like this."

She turned a page in her lap. "Not very pleasant, the visit to the nice daughter."

"No."

"I don't think she has a clue about her father."

"Probably not."

"I thought perhaps you were the least bit unkind."

"I tried not to be."

"That was *trying?*"

Sarcasm. What was this about? He was too old to be taking lessons in professional tact from this woman. Perhaps she was warning him.

"Would you have pressed your own daughter so hard?"

"I don't know," he said. "Maybe harder." But then he thought that wasn't likely—not if Jackie'd just lost her father. Hell, he thought, that's *me.*

"Asking about stealable stuff—that's one thing. Asking what she knows about her father's dirty magazines is something else again. And what's going to happen when she finds out the real truth about the man?"

"I can't imagine."

"Maybe she won't have to."

"How do you hide such a thing?" Strand said.

"You keep your mouth shut?"

He shook his head.

"Think about it. Call it tact."

"Dream on," he said.

She scowled and dropped the printout to the floor. "Meanwhile, I've made a few calls home. Bart Anson—you know him?—Bart's doing a search for us. Gay-bashers. Anti-porn types. You know."

"He won't find anything we can use."

"Men have this reputation for not finding things that are right in front of them," she said. "And for not listening to bright women."

"Spare me," he said. "Cooper was still in the closet. Only his closest friends knew for sure. And the friends never told on him—not even to their own daddies."

"Except one."

"Except, possibly, one."

"I also called Eloise Adler."

"Who the hell is that?"

"You remember. She's the *Press Herald* stringer, the one who got here almost ahead of the police."

"Ah."

"It was Michaud who called her. I was curious, so I asked. It seems the two of them go way back together. I thought you'd like to know."

"Something current?"

"Maybe."

"Kind of an odd couple, if you ask me. I'd have given Michaud more credit."

"She's not so dumb," Eleanor said, "and she's a handsome woman who'd have been a beauty when she was younger. Good bone structure."

"If you say so."

"Which reminds me—" She rummaged under the printouts beside her chair and came up with a single sheet of white paper. "The artist's sketch of the faceless man."

Strand put on his glasses and took the sketch. The man who looked up at him from the page was broad-faced, dimple-jawed, had huge ears and narrowed eyes with heavy brows.

"Looks like somebody from a TV horror show," he said.

"It's going to be in all the papers, and on the television news shows."

" 'Take no action yourself'? That kind of thing?"

"I guess."

He handed it back to her. "Can't hurt, I suppose."

Eleanor studied him—sizing him up again? "I was thinking—this isn't a business matter—that I might ask you to make good on your dinner invitation. Tonight, I mean, it being a Saturday. If you're not too worn down by the chief's funny business. If things work out."

"Things will," Strand said. You bet they will, he told himself. "Right now I have to buy cigarettes, and I think I'll try to find the Bear, ask him what's going on. Then perhaps we could drive down to Ogunquit. We could have dinner at the Cliff House, if it's still there, and I could tell you what the place was like back in the Fifties."

"And will you please stop flaunting your age? I'm no longer impressed."

.   .   .

The Scoggin Town Hall was a brick pile with dark halls whose wood floors had warped and buckled under a hundred years of traffic and humidity into a pale brown tide that sparkled with nailheads worn silver. Michaud sat at a steel desk in a tiny office that opened behind a glassed-in counter. His cap and uniform coat and a black-holstered .38 hung from a hook behind his chair. He tapped nervously across his opened left hand with a yellow pencil held in his right.

"Don Savage says the Cooper woman wants us to vacate her premises," Michaud said.

"So to speak," Strand said.

"I phoned up the superintendent of schools. He says we can use Edison School; it's got plenty of space."

"That's fine with me. What's happening with your investigation?"

Michaud smiled. "It's—how do you say it?—going on."

"Ongoing."

"That's the saying."

"We'd also better decide how we're going to handle the press people," Strand said. "Now that we've got a fair idea of the real motive, we can't talk about robbery with a straight face, can we?" He flicked ashes into the wastebasket alongside the desk. Michaud sat straighter. "I looked first," Strand said. "It's empty."

"I never seen a man who smokes so much," Michaud said. "Your lungs are going to kill you dead." His voice carried his accent without a trace of real concern for Strand's health. "Doesn't your doctor talk to you about cancer?"

"So what do we say?"

"We don't say."

Strand studied Michaud through blue smoke. "We can't say that it might have been an outraged father, or that Cooper sodomized young boys, but we have to say something."

"Why do we?"

"They'll push. The rummy from the *Globe* will push hard. He'll want the truth, even if he can't print it."

"The truth, it might never come out," Michaud said.

"Not a town where gays are appreciated," Strand said. "That's what you're saying? You're not going to admit there are such people?"

"Except the weirdos—clowns, people who couldn't keep it secret." He laid the pencil on the desk so it was exactly parallel with the outside edge of his blotter. "La-de-dah types. Guys who manage summer theaters."

"It's got to be faced sometime."

"The man's got survivors. A widow. A daughter. And you got to think of the town. A lot of people could get hurt."

"Come on, Al-Bear," Strand said. "This is 1985."

"This is Scoggin," Michaud said. "I got to live here. Everybody's got to live here, except you and your woman."

Strand sat back. Point taken, he thought; town of six thousand souls, no industry to speak of for thirty years, no tourist attractions except a couple of lakes. A bedroom for the shipyard in Kittery, Pease airbase, seasonal beach businesses. A backwater. A make-believe ostrich in a real sandpile.

"That's why you're pushing robbery."

"Who says it wasn't?"

"You already have a suspect or two?" Strand said.

"Not yet."

"But you have a hunch."

"I don't hunch," Michaud said. He turned the pencil so it made a right angle to the blotter's edge. "How'd you get to be in the Attorney General's office? Luck? Hard work?"

"Bribery," Strand said.

"I'm asking a serious question. Don't fuck with me."

"A little of both." How much was Strand obliged to tell him in the name of public relations? "But mostly work. I was a trooper—first in the Wells barracks, then the Thomaston barracks—for seventeen years; I finally got asked if I'd like to be in the Augusta office."

"You've been with the state almost forty years?"

"Thirty-some. I coached for a while. Basketball. Track." He raised one eyebrow at Michaud. "You trying to decide if you can trust me?" he said.

"Why shouldn't I trust you?"

"That's what *I* would say. Why shouldn't you?"

"Mister Inspector Strand," Michaud said, "you're a stranger in my town. That's all."

Strand stubbed out the cigarette. "You know I'm not planning to tell you how to proceed," Strand said. "Haverkamp's a friend of yours, and Haverkamp put you in charge. It's your case, your show. You tell the media people whatever you want them to know; whatever you don't want them to know—keep it under your hat. That's okay with me."

"That's what I plan doing."

"Just don't keep it from *me.*"

"You got access; you and your lady friend—your partner," Michaud said. "You watch us do our job. I don't have a problem with that." He slid some sheets of paper out from under the blotter, turned them so Strand could see the top sheet: a list, several short paragraphs. Michaud passed the papers across the desk for Strand to look at. "Since Wednesday morning," Michaud said. "Nine crimes solved, dating back to last winter. Assault, breaking and entering, a stolen car; we even got leads to a hit-and-run from New Year's Eve."

"Impressive," Strand said. "Worth calling your friend Mrs. Adler—putting it in the paper."

"Keep looking."

Strand exposed the second sheet. "What is it?"

"Read."

He read. It was an insurance company appraisal of Cooper's coin collection. He looked for the bottom line: *Appraised value: $4800.* "Where'd you come up with this?"

"It was in Cooper's desk."

Strand studied the appraisal. "It's a couple of years old."

"Which means the collection is maybe worth more today."

"What if it turns out Cooper sold the collection two years ago? That he got the appraisal to satisfy the buyer?"

"Bring me the buyer."

Strand smoked. "His daughter says his hobbies didn't last. She says he got excited about collecting things, then went on to something new. Sold the old hobby to finance the new."

"Bring me the buyer."

"Where's the policy itself? Or the rider on his homeowner's?"

Michaud shook his head. "Don't have it."

"Safe-deposit box," Strand said.

"Not there." Michaud took back the papers and dropped them into the middle desk drawer. "Don't tell me it can't be robbery."

"And the sex stuff?"

"Man gets robbed," Michaud said. "So what if it also happens he's a pervert?"

"Sure," Strand said. "You're right. It's a free country."

.   .   .

While Eleanor dressed for dinner, Strand sat alone in his room, smoking and staring at the television. The picture was on, the sound off; what he was watching seemed to be a game show devoted to pairing up single men and women. It was a hilarious business, if the faces were any clue to the proceedings, and it had nothing to do with his own state of mind. He was still hearing the tapes Eleanor had played when he got back from the Town Hall; a couple of twelve- and thirteen-year-old boys admitting to acts involving themselves and the murdered man. Sodomy: that was the generic term. Were they forced? No. Coerced? Not really. Was there a phrase "consenting children"? Really they had been seduced—by money, by pictures, probably not by sweets. Or maybe it was the attention—any attention—that seduced them. Attention impure and simple. Maybe they had father problems, or the problem of no father at all.

So. Whose father killed Raymond Cooper? Whose older brother? Whose beefy uncle? Whose self-appointed guardian angel?

Next question: And now what? The Bear wanted to do it his way; he'd said as much. This was his town, his jurisdiction, his responsibility. He knew the people; the people knew him. What would they tell a stranger like Strand about "perverts"? How much more pronounced Michaud's French-Canadian accent had gotten as his indignation surfaced. Defensive and proud at the same time, waving that list of solved crimes; criminals tripping over each other to confess the small stuff—nobody going to pin a murder on *them*. And evasive about publicity, as if there were things Strand ought not to concern himself with. Public relations. *My town. I got to live here. A lot of people could get hurt.* What people? And never mind what the town would tell Michaud; what was Strand eventually going to tell the state of Maine. In the end, he reminded himself, no matter how tired I am, it's up to me.

Eleanor knocked at his door, came in before he could get up to let her in. The room was transformed into a garden of fragrant flowers whose name eluded him.

" 'Dating Game,' " she said. "How appropriate."

"I wasn't watching."

"My second husband loved that show. I remember standing in the doorway once, and realizing that he was really and truly *engrossed* in it— he looked like Einstein figuring out relativity. What a revelation that was."

"I was thinking about those young kids Cooper played with. If somebody hadn't done him in—"

"Nobody would ever have found out," she finished. "They could have put the whole thing behind them." Then, as if she had heard the echo of what she said, she put her hands up to her face to cancel the words. "God, I'm sorry," she said. "I only meant that if he hadn't gotten killed, the boys might have grown up to ordinary lives."

"Might. Or they might have chosen the other life and put themselves even more at risk."

"I meant at least their secret would have been safe."

"Some secrets aren't ever safe," Strand said. "Not where the police call the press before the body's cold."

"Will this spoil your dinner?"

"Not mine, not yours." He looked at his watch: nearly 7:30. He got up, straightened his tie in front of the mirror, shrugged himself into his sport jacket. "That perfume of yours will sweep all ugliness right out of my head."

"Roses," she said. "The sweetest, smallest buds."

•   •   •

He had suggested the Cliff House because it was a resort he remembered, a site that retained associations for him—though he discovered much of it had changed, and not necessarily, he thought, for the better.

"At least they couldn't wreck the geography," he told Eleanor. He stood with her as close to the edge of Bald Head Cliff as circumstances permitted; a double strand of rusty barbed wire held them back from looking straight down to the cove and its waves, an act he recalled from more years earlier than he wanted to count—the breathtaking quality of it, the sense of near-vertigo. "Nearly a hundred feet of sheer rock."

"You'd think they could have carved it out," she said. "Mount Rushmore East. Or quarry possibilities. Immense profits in the construction of public buildings."

"They used to call this path the Marginal Way. Maybe they still do. You could walk alongside the ocean all the way to York. It was a very narrow track, but we did it."

"We?"

"This is where Harriet and I spent our honeymoon." He lit a cigarette, cupping his hands against the onshore breeze. "Happy memories," he said.

"We don't really retain the unhappy ones," she said. "Psychological self-defense. The chemical miracle of the human brain."

Strand steered her toward the hotel. "I'm beginning to appreciate your talent for the sentimental comment," he said. "It's a rare talent nowadays."

At some time in the recent past the old hotel had been remodeled. The lobby was wider, deeper, surrounded with French doors. What Strand remembered as the cocktail lounge—he and Harriet had hung out there after a couple of performances at the nearby Playhouse, rubbing shoulders with the stars—had been added to, extended, had become a dining room twice the size of its predecessor. There were windows all around, a sense of urgency he immediately found disheartening, a clatter and bustle that suggested turnover—getting guests and transients in and out and in again—rather than the unhurried pleasures of good company and good food. It was like seeing an unwelcome extension of his work, talking to the daughter, listening to the tapes of the Cooper neighbors and lovers, having words with Michaud—the sense that everyone had spent the week piling up details that would turn out to be mostly unusable, mostly irrelevant, if the chief had his way.

"Not what I expected," he said. He unfolded the white napkin into his lap, rearranged the silverware so he could lean his elbows on the table. "This place has grown and gone all modern."

"But it's nice," she said. "Nice lighting, nice view, nice crystal goblets for the water."

"How about a nice Martini," Strand said, "in a nice stemmed glass with a nice twist?"

"That would be—how should I say it?—very nice."

And it was after a second Martini, after the lobster and wine had been ordered, that he decided to chance being seriously personal—to put the work truly aside and float on the gin and the sense of well-being that had grown all evening each time he noticed men at other tables admiring Eleanor.

"May I ask a question that's none of my business?"

"It's one of the things you seem to do best," she said.

"Where are your three husbands now?"

She looked amused. "All three?"

"Or any one of them."

"I haven't the slightest idea," she said.

"You never saw any of them after you were divorced from them?"

"The fact is, I hadn't seen any of them for quite a while *before* I was divorced from them." She took a sip of her drink and set the glass between her hands, twirling the stem very slowly, surveying him with the same amused expression on her face. "It sounds like you've never come to terms with your own divorce," she said. "Apparently because you were married such a long time, and you think 'time' is an important consideration."

"Thirty-one years," Strand said. "My marriage."

"But time is just what's *not* important in a divorce. You didn't pay attention. A divorce doesn't have that dimension. *Getting* it is nothing but time—you think it's going to drag on for ever and ever—but once you've got it, it occupies neither duration nor interval. God knows, the fact of it cuts deep, but timewise it's simply an interruption."

Strand nodded as if he understood. "Maybe you have to do it more than once before you get the point of it."

"Think of it as being like death," she said. "The same sense of loss; the same sense of grief." And then she shook her head and looked away from him. When she turned back, she looked sheepish. "Sorry," she said.

"I was thinking," Strand said, "that if I had been one of your husbands, I'd have tried to figure out what it was that went wrong, and I'd have tried to correct that fault—if indeed the fault was in me—and then I'd have tracked you down and asked you to remarry me."

"Did you go after your own wife?"

"I thought about it."

"But you see," she said, "that's you. You're a tracker-down; it's your calling. None of my husbands had such a vocation."

"A vocation which seems to have stopped exciting my own tired interests."

She put out one hand and covered his—the hand not holding a cigarette—and gave him a wan smile. "Enough," she said. "Enough for one day."

"Enough talk?"

"Enough self-deprecation. Enough loss, old age, frustration."

"We ain't seen nothin' yet," he said. "Of frustration, I mean."

"Maybe. Put on your bib. Eat your lobster."

"No bib," he said. "That's for the tourists."

"Don't pick on me." Eleanor let the waitress tie the bib at the nape of her neck. "This is the only decent party dress I brought with me."

Strand stubbed out the cigarette and shook his head sadly. "No comment," he said.

"But what about you? What about deliberately coming here to confront your happy memories. Was that wise?"

"Ask me later."

"You think I'm unsentimental. Are you the other side of that emotional coin?"

"I never thought I was." He plied a lobster claw and slid out the meat.

"Ghosts," she said. "A lot of people don't like ghosts—don't like coming back to be haunted by them."

"I suppose I don't believe in them. If I did, I'd have taken you to Long John Silver's." He lifted the wine bottle out of its nest of ice and refilled her glass. "Bought you a Diet Pepsi."

"Not mentioned your wife?"

"Oh, I might have. Like you, I haven't any idea where she is today, but I trust she's happier where she is, who she's with—not sitting around worrying about me."

"It couldn't have been a bad marriage."

"It was good as marriages go. I never knew any better. You know: got married right out of the army, went to Springfield College on the GI Bill, coached a few years."

"You said. The daughter your only child?"

"Yes. And not because we didn't want more. We just never thought we could afford more. I had college debts, and coaching paid less than peanuts. I was always getting second notices—with those awful red stickers—from this or that place. It was embarrassing; it humiliated Harriet."

"So you joined the department."

"Like the Beatles song says."

Eleanor smiled. "That's *my* generation," she said.

"I wasn't *dead* in the Sixties. Just in the State Police."

"You liked it?"

"Yes," he said. "I confess, that for a long time I liked it very much indeed."

He thought about liking police work, and hating police work—how it was at the bottom of Harriet's giving up on him—and trying to imagine a retired life without it. Outside the wide windows of the dining room the day was almost gone; the cottage lights down the coast toward Kennebunkport had begun their twinkling. Here I am, he thought, free, white, and twenty-one, relaxing on the Maine coast with a beautiful and bright young woman, sipping expensive wine, envied by all, and tomorrow I'll go back to being nagged at by a dead fairy—no, a dead pederast. A deaderast. He gazed across the table at Eleanor Watkins. With such women in the world, why would any man prefer boys?

"What was that fat notebook you had this afternoon on the sunporch—the one with the green cover?"

"Ah," she said. "Family album. I found it on top of the piano and wasted a little time going through it."

"Interesting?"

"Only to me. Lots of father-daughter clichés I never learned—Mother must have been the photographic talent in the family. Baby carriage scenes. Seashore scenes. Front lawn scenes. Birthday party scenes."

"Should I look through it?"

Eleanor laughed. "It's not a mug book. It wouldn't help *you* solve anything. Besides, if it was useful, Michaud would already have it."

He nodded. "Michaud's an odd duck," he said. "You think?"

"Maybe he's just being normal," she said. "How would you like some muckety-muck from Augusta breathing down your neck?"

"I'd feel insulted."

"There you are." She rested her chin on her hands and seemed to study him. "Anyway, maybe it's *you* who's the odd duck."

"Meaning?"

"That you're right, what you said about 'vocation.' You're not really *in* this investigation. You're—I don't know: disinterested? Is that the right word? If you weren't the same age as Ray Cooper, and if you didn't have a daughter who's the same age as Melissa Cooper Allen, I don't think you'd stay around at all; you'd go home and turn in your expense account and curl up with a good mystery that wouldn't challenge your brain. I think in your heart of hearts you're perfectly content to let Michaud run things, even when you're unhappy about the way it's all going to turn out. Whether or not Scoggin really wants to find the murderer—I think that bothers your head; you're still on the side of the law, and you still want justice. But it doesn't bother your gut. 'Looking over Michaud's shoulder.' You said it the first day we got here. That's precisely what you're doing. And my shoulder . . . "

"Especially," Strand said.

"And everybody else's shoulder. You're like the worst kind of foreman, who stands around with his hands in his pockets and takes credit for what the workers do."

"I'll take the blame as well."

"Maybe you'll have to. Between your ennui and Michaud's willfulness, God knows who's going to get the blame for this case. You're right: I think we *should* fear for the cause of justice, on every count."

Strand smoked. It wasn't that he felt found out, he told himself. What was there for him to hide? "Everything you say is probably the truth," he said. "I just feel over the hill."

"You're three months and two weeks past your sixtieth birthday," she said. "I looked it up before we left Augusta."

"That strikes you as young?"

"It strikes me as *not old,*" Eleanor said. She reached to touch his hand. A soft warmth that arrested his thoughts. "Pay the tab and let's head back to the motel."

"I don't know," he said. "All poses aside, I'm going to be sorry to say goodnight to you."

"Maybe you don't have to," she said. "That's the rest of it—of your public failure of interest."

"What is?"

"Good lord, do you honestly believe everybody around you can't see where your mind is? What you're thinking about?" She lifted his hand to her lips and kissed it. "Do you honestly believe *I* can't?"

"I don't know what I believe about you. I haven't solved you."

"I'll help." She laid her hands over his and leaned toward him. "I'm very self-conscious with you. You see that, I'm sure. This word game we play, this flirty little dance. That's me, trying to decide who I am when I'm with you."

"Who do you want to be?"

"I haven't found out yet. I'm just beginning to separate the man from the reputation—and I'm starting to see that you aren't necessarily what you're perceived to be. You certainly don't see the world as clearly as I'd been told."

"How so?" Her hands on his were like an energy source, sending their pulses through the backs of his fingers and into his bloodstream, exciting and warming him. Or it might have been the alcohol. "Why is my world view fuzzy?'

"Because everything falls short—short of what you remember, short of what you expect. Who on earth could please you?"

"You?"

"That's the trap I'm looking at, isn't it? You're attractive to a woman who can't even remember her own father. That old mortality you harp on so is like a weird aphrodisiac, because we love things that we know will die."

"Thanks."

"No, really. I wondered the first time I saw you—it was my second day on the job—if you were accessible. It was just an idle thing, a notion. I liked your slouch, I fretted over your chain-smoking. When I found out I was going to be assigned here with you, I thought it might be a kind of destiny. When I heard that you didn't want me, it turned into a test. I wonder if I can catch him, I thought. I wonder if I can get him into bed."

"Can you?"

She took her hands away, a gesture that felt like genuine loss.

"Let's see," she said.

.   .   .

"What makes me marvel," Strand said, "is that no matter how much you want a thing, and no matter how much you've rehearsed it in your head, the reality is never the same." He was in bed with Eleanor Watkins, under her, part of her, having made love slowly and delectably, feeling like an ocean that bore her weight as easily as if passion had made her buoyant.

"Are you disappointed?"

"Dear heaven, no."

"Then pretty soon you must come for me," she said. "You've given me one orgasm after another."

"I think once will be my limit," he said. "Let me postpone the novelty as long as I can."

"Novelty?" She raised herself onto her elbows. In the half-dark of the room he could scarcely discern her features, the fall of her hair that brushed his face.

"Remember that I've been without a woman for two years." He sighed, held Eleanor hard against him, moved inside her and against her as if he wanted in that moment to carry her endlessly upward. "Sometimes I think I really am a wasted old man, but this," he said, "this is magical."

"Do come for me," she whispered. "Stop being a wasted old man."

Later, when she rested over him, leaning on her elbows, she punctuated her words with light kisses on his mouth and eyes.

"You see? Some things can be realized."

"And have you done this often?"

She hesitated. "Done what?"

"Done *whom*. Done your partners because you wondered if you could. Seduced them, I mean. Is it part of your *modus operandi?*"

"No; you were special, and you know it. What about you?"

"Do *I* go to bed with every assistant that comes down the pike?" He shook his head. "Not usually."

"Sometimes you have scruples?"

Strand sighed. "My last assistant before Frank—it was that shooting behind the restaurant in Biddeford, the souvenir Luger—was a twenty-seven-year-old graduate student at MIT, a chap who'd have made two of me and probably wouldn't have taken kindly to being molested."

"One does have to draw the line," Eleanor said.

"But how did you get into this?"

"Into this bed?"

"Into this line of work."

"Oh," she said. "I see: speaking of seducing partners." She sat up beside him. "I was headed for a nursing career, I thought. Then I got all politically wound up and made a habit of getting myself arrested at peace marches, and then finally it dawned on me that my humanitarianism was too abstract for the hospital ward, but my brains were okay for labs and computers and all-around curiosity. That's it in a nutshell. In another age, I might have been Madame Curie."

"I wonder if *she* would have seduced me?"

"Are you feeling aggrieved?"

"Possibly."

"Please don't."

"I was never unfaithful to my wife. I didn't go out looking for a replacement."

Eleanor looked at him—a steady, probing sort of look.

"It's true," he said.

Eleanor drew up her knees and pushed herself upright. "You're telling me I'm the first since your wife walked out?"

"I am," he said. "Yes."

"Two years?"

"And longer. I swear it."

"Am I supposed to feel guilty?"

He reached up to caress her neck, let the back of his hand slide self-consciously down over her breasts. "You're nearsighted, aren't you?" he said.

"Yes. Why?"

"The closer you get, the more flaws you see."

"My God," Eleanor said. She slid away from him and sat on the edge of the bed. Not looking at him, she pushed the hair away from her face and seemed preoccupied with the fingernails of her left hand.

"I, to the contrary, am farsighted," Strand said. "The years may be unkind to me, but mirrors are not. I don't see wear and tear—but I see ahead, to the conclusions of things."

"So what are you saying? What shall we do? Call it off? Or shall we love each other from opposite sides of whatever bedroom we're in, far enough apart so I won't see your years, but you can enjoy mine?"

He was surprised by her vehemence. He wondered what else he should have said.

"I'm a pessimist," he said. "It cuts my losses."

She lay beside him, her back turned toward him. "I'm going to sleep. You may hold me if you want."

And he did, his face in the perfume of her long hair, left arm around her waist, thighs and belly pressed against her warm buttocks. He thought about her lecturing him, about the dilemma of Michaud's loyalties, about growing old and making so much of it that it got in the way of his work. He thought about the fears of his life that had begun to catch up with him. He thought about a young boy bare below the waist, spread-legged, with sweaty hands splayed against Cooper's office wall—a vision that made him shiver, and kept him from being further aroused by the willful woman he held.

7

LATE THAT AFTERNOON, standing at Nana Simpson's parlor window and watching through the lace of the curtains as any number of cars drove slowly past the house, Lissa wished she could stop them and ask what kind of people these were. What kind of people lived in Scoggin, Maine, in this violent day and age? What did we think, believe, want? No; *they*. She was just a visitor from Chicago. *They* seemed to have this curiosity that was indecent, almost obscene, about *her*. As much curiosity about the daughter of the dead man as about his murderer. Perhaps more, the way things were going. Why? she wondered. What did *they*, the locals, think and believe and want from their small-town, tourist-distrusting, new-shopping-mall lives? What were their values, now that all the old houses were torn down, the old lawns paved over, the old men and women dead or shut up in fancy brick nursing homes? There must still be values. "The right thing"—that must be a pronounceable phrase in this part of the world—so that even though nothing could call her father back to life, at least there would be an abiding interest not just in catching a glimpse of the dead man's survivors, but in bringing his murderer to justice. The state of Maine wouldn't spend its money on sending a team of investigators to town if there wasn't at least a concern for truth, for justice. And revenge. In the old days, great attention would have been paid to revenge.

She turned away from the window. Now, dialing the Vermont number, Lissa had no idea what, really, she had to say to her mother—if she should apologize for not phoning sooner, then fill in details that would shock Mother and provoke her own fresh pain—or should she begin with some innocent topic, some chitchat about Susie, about how the old town had changed, about the July heat? How to deal discreetly with death: someone ought to write a book.

Blessedly, Mother was Mother.

"Alice Briggs called me in the wee hours, the morning after it happened. You remember her? She must be in her seventies now. She lived next door to us on Grove Street, before we moved to Ridgeway. Then she lived—lives—across the street from the Ridgeway house. Do you suppose she followed us? At any rate, she told me. 'A commotion.' That's what she called it. 'What a commotion we're having.' "

"It was awful," Lissa said. She thought Alice Briggs must have been in spinster heaven with her news. "I found him. There was blood all over the place."

"It's dreadful," her mother said. "After Alice phoned, I wanted to call you, talk to you, but I knew you wouldn't be up to it. The Savage boy called later in the day. He said you were in the hospital."

"I was. I didn't handle it too well. After Edwin—"

"Are you apologizing because you were devastated? My dear, *don't*."

"And the people," Lissa said. "The people in Scoggin are so strange about it. They know I'm at Nana's, and they drive by at all hours. It's like I was a celebrity, or a criminal."

"That's Scoggin, dear. Not much happens in Scoggin. I can't say I miss the place. I thought about driving over for the funeral, but really— between its being such a dreary drive, and the roads so narrow, and seeing that town again . . . It isn't as if he'd notice my not being there."

"Mother—"

"Oh, Melissa. Now don't get *after* me. There was a time when I adored your father, and I'll always be proud that the two of us produced *you*, but it had been so very long since we had any real feelings for one another. I know you think I'm callous, and that I ought to show a little more feeling for the man, but Ray had changed so much toward the end of the marriage, I hardly knew him as the sweet boy I met after the war."

"Well, I'm going to the funeral," Lissa said. "I have to. If I didn't, I'd feel—I don't know what I'd feel."

"And you should go, dear. He always cared for you. He loved you, I think, instead of loving me. After your trouble—" her mother didn't dwell on the word, or give it any special stress, and yet Lissa felt the force of *trouble*—"I think you became the only woman that really mattered to him. And then when you were with Edwin, especially after he came home from that pointless war, Ray was totally preoccupied with you."

"I didn't get an abortion, or marry a madman, because I wanted to compete with you."

"Oh, dear Melissa, what a thing to say. I didn't mean to imply anything of the sort—not any of that deep psychological nonsense. I only meant—"

"I'm sorry." Lissa curled the phone cord around her wrist and shifted the phone to her other ear. "I guess I'm sensitive about my luck with men. I'm really sorry."

"But isn't this your reunion weekend?"

"It was supposed to be."

"Oh, Melissa, do go. You'll have a lovely time; it will take your mind off all this—this mess. And you've come all that way to see your old friends."

"I don't think I could bear it," Lissa said. "Everybody would be feeling sad for me. I'd break down and be really pitiful."

"Is there a visitation at the home? Are they opening the casket?"

"No." They wouldn't dare, Lissa thought. "No, the casket is supposed to be shut. There's just the funeral on Monday. Mother, good God, nobody would know him."

"That's a relief," Mother said. "I mean the closed casket. It's the idea of displaying the dead. It always makes my skin crawl."

"Don't worry. And I thought I'd go see Gramps."

Her mother sighed loudly, meaningfully. "I wouldn't do that," she said. "He's too senile to comprehend anything simple, let alone something important."

"Even the death of his only son?"

"Anything. Truly, dear. He's mostly deaf and blind, and he occupies a world no one can penetrate. He's millions of miles from reality. Don't waste your time."

"It seems cruel not to tell him," Lissa said.

"It would be more cruel if he understood you. Think about that."

"All right, Mother."

But she knew she would disobey; it didn't seem reasonable not to tell her grandfather about the murder—perhaps not that awful word, "murder," itself, but something that surely would connect with the old man's consciousness.

"Has anyone *said* anything about your father?" The question was broken, tentative. "Anything unusual?"

"Such as?"

"Alice Briggs told me she thought your father was doing a little gallivanting in his old age. Have you heard that? Anything like it?"

"Nothing," Lissa said. "What did she tell you?"

"Just that Ray seemed to be 'keeping a lot of company.' That was how she put it."

"I don't know anything about that," Lissa said. "I doubt old Miss Briggs understands half of what she sees. He's a very private man. Was."

"I don't put anything past your father, God rest him. He was also a very complex man." Mother paused. "I have to run, dear. You and I will have a long talk soon. Why don't you stop off in Burlington on your way back home?"

"I think I will. I only took the week's vacation, but I've got to call the office and stretch it to two. I'll plan to stop—but let's make it tentative. A lot depends on what happens here."

"Like what, dear?"

Lissa thought. "On what the police find out. About who did it—who killed Daddy."

"Oh, Melissa," her mother said, "what's done is done."

"I know that, Mother."

"I mean, you can't bring him back."

"I know that too. Don't you want to punish whoever killed him?"

"Yes, of course I do. What did you think?" There was a confused pause. "I *must* run, Melissa. If something comes up, if you can't stop for a day or two, then call me as soon as you get back to Chicago."

"I will, Mother. I'll let you know, either way."

"Goodbye, dear. Don't wear jewelry."

"Goodbye, Mother." Mother hung up first. Lissa held the phone for a few seconds, thinking about jewelry and about her father's love, and about how it was after all true that finding the murderer couldn't bring him back—that perhaps solving a murder was like a formality without a reason. Then she hung up.

.   .   .

The nursing home—Birch Manor—was at Scoggin's south end. It was new, flat-roofed, made of unembellished red brick broken by aluminum-tiered windows. It sat in a clearing surrounded by pines and a few token birch trees, and its asphalt-paved parking lot extended deep into the woods. The lot was full; cars were ranged around the semicircular drive, and the only open parking space carried a painted "Handicapped" insignia. Lissa thought about taking it—bereavement was not a handicap, she decided—then drove back out to the street and parked on the shoulder.

Her walk to the Manor took her past a dining room: a greenish room filled with round blond wood tables mostly unoccupied. At a table close to the windows sat two old women, white-haired, wearing similar flower-print dresses, bent over dishes of what appeared to be applesauce. One of the women looked up at Lissa as she passed their window. The woman smiled; she had no teeth. Lissa felt guilty, smiled back and waved.

The hall where she found herself when she came through the front door smelled vaguely of turnips and something that might have been perfume or talcum powder. It was not a hospital smell, at least, but it was not a pleasant atmosphere—not an air she would have wanted to breathe for very long. Age, she thought. This was the age smell.

"It's supper time," said the young woman at the desk when Lissa asked after Frank Cooper. "If you'd like, you can bring him to the dining room. He's in 144-B."

She set out down the corridor. It was no easy trip; tiny old ladies, sitting in wheelchairs or making slow progress with spindly chrome-legged walkers, were like obstacles—or landmarks—on her way, nodding or grinning or only staring at her as she passed. This was in some sense a grotesque fairy tale, and these were ancient elves placed to point her the direction to her grandfather.

At the entrance to the room, she hesitated. How long since she'd seen Grandpa Cooper? Since Grandma died, twelve years ago? Since Daddy's divorce? Since she moved to Chicago? She couldn't for the life of her remember the last time, and, when she looked in, she was not even sure the man in the wheelchair by the window *was* her grandfather. But there were only two beds in the room, and one of them was stripped of its linens.

"Grandpa Cooper," she said, louder than her normal speaking voice. She walked into the room and bent toward him. "How are you, Gramps?"

The old man raised his head, like an animal listening to a new sound, testing the wind for threat. His eyes looked past her. "Who is it?" he said.

"It's Melissa," she said. "It's your granddaughter."

"Who?"

She raised her voice. "It's Melissa."

A smile flickered at the corners of his mouth, then faded. It might not even have been a smile, but only, as with infants, a small muscular reflex whose source could have been anywhere in the nervous system. "Melissa," he said. "My son has a daughter named Melissa."

"That's me," she shouted.

He lowered his head. "Oh," he said. "I'm glad you came." His hands trembled in his lap. "Sometimes my son comes. A lawyer. He's very well thought of."

"I hear it's time for supper," she said.

The old man seemed to take the statement under advisement. "Yes," he said.

"Would you like me to wheel you to the dining room?"

Another considered pause. "Yes, if you want."

She slid herself behind the chair and started to push. The wheelchair resisted. She found the brake mechanism, released it and moved forward.

"I see you have the room all to yourself," she said into her grandfather's left ear. She steered him through the door and into the hallway. "There's no one in the other bed."

"He died," he said.

"Oh. That's too bad." Now she didn't know what else to say, so she attended to her chauffeuring: past the nurses' station, past any number of the little old women—all of them in flowered dresses—who watched her curiously as she went by them a second time.

"He was number six," Frank Cooper said.

"And what number are you?" she said.

"Six different people have died in that bed. Since they put me in that room."

God, Lissa thought.

"I don't have a number," her grandfather said.

"I know," she said. She drove the wheelchair into the dining room. "I misunderstood."

"Not yet, I don't."

When she turned the wheelchair and locked it in front of the table,

Lissa saw that he had what looked like a real smile on his face, and she thought she might have said something right. She thought, too, that, after all, there was no point in abusing the old man with the news of his son's death—Mother was right, and what difference would it make? She sat watching him eat only cornbread and milk from a tray that also held coleslaw, baked beans, a wizened hot dog, and a small dish of fresh strawberries and cream. He ate with excruciating slowness and spilled everything he touched. Milk dribbled down his chin and his shirtfront. Dry chunks of cornbread dropped into his lap and onto the floor.

After about a half hour, she gave him a good-bye kiss on the forehead, found a candy-striper who promised to return the old man to his room, and drove back to the Simpson house. She knew in her heart how pleased the old man would have been to learn that he had outlived his son, if only she had known how to tell him.

·   ·   ·

She asked Donnie to go with her to the funeral home that evening— not so much because she *needed* him with her, but to have someone, afterward, to talk with, someone to take her mind away from whatever "arrangements" needed still to be made.

"It's all so weird," she said to him when he stopped for her, still driving the police car. "It was weird when Edwin died and I had to go through the rigmarole with the Veterans Administration. I had papers and papers to sign. I wanted him cremated, and that seemed un-American to everybody. I just wanted to scatter his ashes on Lake Michigan, off Jarvis Beach, because it was the only place he ever went where he seemed to relax. You'd think I'd desecrated the flag or something. And I still had to pay for a casket; don't ask me why."

"Some stupid law," Donnie said.

"I imagine," she said. "But the law shouldn't be stupid."

The funeral home parking lot was nearly empty; far at the back of the lot were two Cadillac hearses, side by side like a pair of matched gray carriage horses waiting to be harnessed. Out in front was a large blue signboard with HUNTER MORTUARY in sunken gold lettering; silver floodlights grew discreetly out of the lawn, one on each side of the sign. Donnie parked at the curb.

"You don't have to come in with me," Lissa said. "Really."

"Whatever you say."

PLEASE RING, a small card above the doorbell invited. She rang. A young woman in a cool white dress opened the door to her.

"I'm Raymond Cooper's daughter," Lissa said.

The young woman held out her hand—slender-fingered, a thin gold bracelet on her wrist—to touch Lissa's sleeve. "Please," she said. "We'll just go down to the office."

The foyer of the home was like the lobby of a hotel—carpeted in tones of deep red, a modest crystal chandelier hanging from a high ceiling, a mahogany desk standing to one side, and on it a guest book waiting to be signed with a filigreed gold-filled pen on a thin chain. Lissa followed the woman, wondering who she was.

"Is Mr. Hunter still active?" Lissa said.

"Not so much." The woman ushered Lissa into a small, square room and gestured for her to sit in a straight chair beside a steel desk. The woman seated herself behind the desk. "He plays a lot of golf nowadays. He's not officially retired, but he does leave most arrangements up to his son, and to me."

"I wondered," Lissa said.

"I'm Katherine with a K," the young woman said. "I'm the daughter-in-law. I married Bill Hunter."

Lissa nodded.

"I know," Katherine Hunter said, "you're surprised I'm so young. I'm Bill's second wife."

"No, I wasn't surprised. Nothing surprises me in Scoggin."

Katherine opened a folder and brought out a thin sheaf of papers. "Your father had foresight, Melissa. The casket, the cemetery arrangements, the service. He did this several years ago—set up a funeral trust for himself. He seems to have known exactly what he wanted." She handed a sheaf of papers to Lissa. "This is the contract, and the list of items."

Lissa took it. *Nonrevocable Mortuary Trust Agreement* said the top sheet; it was dated two weeks after Edwin's suicide. She turned the page, then another and another. The agreement was five pages long, the last signed by William Hunter and by her father and witnessed by someone whose name she couldn't read. A sixth page was attached; it spelled out details, and the cost of each. *Transfer of remains to funeral home: $75. Embalming: $165. Other preparations of the body: $50.* What were "other preparations"? she wondered. She did not ask. The casket price was $1,240; something called a "burial container" was $600. A footnote told her that the cemetery "required" the burial container. She felt slightly giddy as she read the items. *Hearse. Other automotive equipment. Services of funeral director and staff. Newspaper notices.* The page blurred, and she handed the agreement back to Katherine Hunter. "It seems very complete," she said.

·   ·   ·

Donnie leaned across to open the car door for her, and she slid in beside him. "You okay?"

"I'm fine," Lissa said.

"You look a little pale."

"It was as odd as I'd expected, but I'm fine."

"I care about you, you know."

She turned her head to look at him. One of his eyebrows was raised, and his brow was slightly furrowed, as if he half-expected her to say something cruel or critical. "I appreciate that," she said. Then she felt obliged not to pursue his appreciation, not knowing where in the world he wanted it to take the two of them. "It's just that they have a way of spelling everything out. It's a little much."

"I want—" He broke off.

Lissa sat forward uneasily. "Want what?" she said. "What do you want?"

"I guess I want you to get over your father. Be happy. Go to the reunion stuff." He looked down at his hands, which were clasped in his lap.

"I couldn't handle the reunion," she said. "I'd be miserable."

He nodded. "Why don't you come home with me? At least have a drink."

"What about Cheryl?"

"Cheryl would be happy to see you," he said.

She looked at him. "I wonder."

He started the car. "You're right," he said. "I wonder too. But let's give it a try."

"I don't know," she said. "It's already been a bad enough day—these arrangements, all those people driving by Nana's house."

"People love to gawk."

"How do they even know I'm there?"

Donnie shrugged.

"Gossip," Lissa said. "Plain gossip."

"Anyway, all these years have gone by. Cheryl's not an ogre, you know."

"Really?"

He smiled. "Only to me."

"Well— All right."

She settled herself against the passenger door and watched the town go by. She wondered what shape Donnie's attentiveness to her would take in his own home, in front of his wife. This small reunion—the three of them—seemed filled with traps she could not have taken into consideration when she thought about the reunion she no longer felt brave enough to attend. What she had always thought of Cheryl, what Cheryl thought of her. The cemetery night Lissa had spent with Donnie— surely Cheryl knew about it, and might even have known about it then— and the "want" he had stopped short of expressing. There was no way to know if the years had softened everyone's feelings or hardened them.

"But this is going to be uncomfortable," she said, almost to herself.

He pulled the car into the driveway of a white Cape Cod on Maple Street. Maple was narrow, well away from Main, and there was no traffic—scarcely even the distant sigh of traffic. They sat for a few moments in silence. Lissa heard the soft wind in the leaves, felt the evening warm on her face through the opened windows.

"You're quiet," she said.

"I was thinking: this is a hell of a way for you to start celebrating your fifteenth reunion."

She almost laughed. "Oh, Donnie," she said, "it's a hell of a way to start anything."

"You keep calling me 'Donnie.' "

"You don't like me to?"

"It's just that nobody ever calls me that nowadays. Cheryl, once in a great while—but even she's gotten into the habit of calling me Donald."

"Sorry."

"Maybe you think I've never grown up."

Lissa smiled. Except for his hairline, it was true that he looked only a little older than she remembered him from their school days. Donnie

Savage, football hero and class heller. She knew all the stories of his driving to York Beach and getting drunk, and of the State Police arresting him for speeding—more than once—on his way back to town. Then he had married Cheryl Shoemaker, who calmed him, reformed him.

"What's Cheryl doing now?" she said.

"Real estate. She's got her own agency—bought the old Wiggin house a couple of years ago, remodeled it. She's got her office downstairs, rents out an apartment up."

"How's business?"

"Good. She's gotten into oceanfront property—Wells and Moody and Ogunquit—and lake cottages. She's a smart lady; a good businesswoman."

"She's energetic," Lissa said. *Cheryl Cheermaker*, said her memory, and conjured up a doll-faced blonde in short red skirt and red panties. She looked at Donnie, who seemed to be studying her.

"You always were something," he said. "You do look terrific."

She couldn't think what to say, not even for old times' sake. Either she had given up trying to find responses to his flattery, or by now she realized that when men said such things the words were like bait: if you took it, you had to follow to places you might rather not go.

"I mean it," he said.

She shook her head. "I don't know how you do it," she said. "You men. I feel like hell, I hurt like hell, I couldn't possibly look like anything except hell. How can you tell me I look terrific? And what would Cheryl think?"

"It doesn't matter what she thinks."

He put out his hand to touch hers. She moved her hand away.

"I wonder if it isn't because you see me as a victim," she said. "You feel sympathy and pity, and somehow it turns you on." She looked toward the house. She thought one of the curtains moved in the front window. "But I'm not the victim. I'm the victim's daughter."

"I know that."

"We'd better go in," Lissa said. "And the first thing to remember is that what Cheryl thinks *does* matter."

.   .   .

"I hardly recognize the old hometown," Lissa said. She sat at one end of a gold couch in the Savages' living room, sipping Scotch and water;

Cheryl, blonde and blush-cheeked and sitting with her head high—so the pouchiness under her chin wouldn't show, Lissa had decided—sat at the other, nursing a rum and Coke. Donnie had poured himself a beer, and sat across from the couch in a brown recliner.

"It's not Chicago. That's for sure," Donnie said.

"Don't be embarrassed that you stayed here," Lissa said. "Heaven knows, sometimes I've wished *I* had."

"What do you do there?" Cheryl said.

"I headhunt."

Donnie seemed startled. "You what?"

"Oh, Donald, don't be dumb." Cheryl sipped at her drink. "Who do you work for?"

"A company called ExecuFind."

"What's headhunting?" Donnie said.

"We place corporation types—vice-presidents, comptrollers, people high enough up in the business world that they don't go to ordinary employment agencies."

"I never heard of such a thing."

"I'm not making this up," she said. "Take my word for it."

"Are you good at it?" Cheryl gave Lissa a wide-eyed look.

"What kind of a question is that?" Donnie said.

"What's wrong with it?"

Oh, God, Lissa thought, please don't let Donnie defend my imagined honor in another woman's house. "I think I'm pretty good at it. I do all right."

"These executives come to you?"

"Or I go to them, offer them better jobs, better salaries."

"So you steal people," Cheryl said.

"Yes. That's what I do," Lissa said. "I steal them." She looked across at Donnie, knowing that the expression on her face was probably saying to him, in spite of herself, "You see how awful this is?"

"Anyone ready for another drink?" he said.

"I'm fine," Lissa said.

"Well, I'm ready," Donnie said. "Excuse my thirst."

He launched himself from the recliner and went out to the kitchen, leaving the two women contemplating the ice in their glasses.

"We're all so devastated about your father," Cheryl said. "Donald keeps me posted on how things are progressing. It must be awful for you."

"I'm surviving," Lissa said.

"If there's anything I can do, call on me."

Lissa cleared her throat. "I hear you're quite the real estate tycoon."

"I've been lucky," Cheryl said. "In fact, I'd just barely gotten home when you and Donald pulled in. I had a closing in Kennebunk. Donald?" She held her glass up to him as he came back into the room. "I'm sorry. Would you get me another?"

Lissa settled back. Cheryl smoothed her skirt over her knees.

"It was a nice little cottage at Cape Porpoise. A neurologist from New York City bought it for his wife."

"Thoughtful husband."

"Have you seen many old friends?"

"Not really. I probably wouldn't recognize anybody at the reunion. Faces and names slip away after fifteen years."

"Although you were never much of a joiner," Cheryl said. "You didn't run with any particular clique, especially after the trauma of your sophomore year."

"I'm surprised you noticed." God, this was deadly. If Cheryl still disliked her so much, how had Donnie dared invite her here? "Donnie says things are going very well for you. Today wasn't unusual."

"The market for vacation property is always strong, even when ordinary residential is down."

"That's nice," Lissa said.

"I wondered," Cheryl said, "what you were going to do about the house. Your father's house."

"What do you mean?"

"Now that he's gone— You'll be selling it, won't you?" Cheryl took the drink Donnie handed her and sipped it. "I mean you're not planning to live there, are you?"

"I work in Chicago," Lissa said. "It wouldn't make sense to keep a house in Scoggin."

"Then you'll need an agent. A good realtor."

"I suppose I will."

Cheryl sighed and compressed her lips. "Melissa, dear, I'm offering to take it off your hands."

"You'll sell it for me?"

"Or another possibility—to save time and trouble—is for you simply to sell it to me, and then I'll hold it until the right buyer comes along."

"I'll think about it." She looked at Donnie, who averted his eyes.

"And his car," Cheryl said. "You can get good money for that gorgeous old car of his. He hardly ever drove it in the wintertime; there's no rust on it."

"Donnie didn't tell me you sold cars too," Lissa said.

Cheryl smiled. "What a sketch you are," she said.

"I've been trying to persuade Lissa to go to the reunion clambake tomorrow," Donnie said—rather too loudly, Lissa thought. "It seems a shame for her to miss everything after coming all this way."

"I'd say that's up to her," Cheryl said.

"How come you two didn't go to the banquet tonight?"

Donnie looked at Cheryl; Cheryl looked at the floor. "Cheryl had a falling-out with the reunion committee. She's boycotting."

"I'm not exactly 'boycotting.' I simply chose not to participate."

"Well, I'm not boycotting, but I can't go," Lissa said. "For one thing, everybody will be couples. It's not just that I'll be the odd fish because Daddy is dead—everybody curious, everybody trying to be kind even though we've all forgotten each other's names—but because I'm not part of a couple."

"I'm sure Donald would be pleased as punch to squire you."

"No, it's more than being alone. I hadn't thought about missing Edwin, but now all of a sudden here he is in my head."

From the direction of the kitchen, a telephone rang. Cheryl stood quickly and moved toward the sound.

"Excuse me," she said. "I'm expecting this."

Alone with Donnie, Lissa realized that she had started to feel weightless, cloudlike, a little bit woozy. From the Scotch, yes, and from the awkwardness of this visit; it was the first drink she had taken since the hospital, and now her cheeks had begun to tingle and she felt a thin tickle of sweat under each arm. She could not remember how long it had been since she was politely drunk. She could only remember, at first, the kind of drinking she had done after Edwin's suicide, shutting Suze into the bedroom and sitting at the kitchen table in front of a bottle of gin—gin and lime juice at the start, and then gin by itself, because the lime juice never lasted.

"This is the first time in years having a drink has made me feel just sad," she said. She looked sheepishly at Donnie and wiped away what she realized were tears on both her cheeks. "Which is very strange.

Strange that in a couple of days I'm burying my father, and tonight my very first drink makes me remember Edwin. I shouldn't put alcohol on top of pills."

"I won't offer you a refill."

"Please don't."

"Maybe I ought to drive you home," Donnie said.

"Yes, why don't you do that?" Cheryl was in the doorway, both hands cradling a pale blue telephone. "This is Todd Brady, from Realty Partners; it's about that easement across the Thayer property. I'm going to be a while."

"That's Cheryl's life," Donnie said. "One damned phone call after another."

Lissa tried to take it all in—the tone of his voice, the look Cheryl shot at him. She found herself finishing her own thought: "Until I found my father, I hadn't thought about Eddie's suicide in years. I'd almost forgotten him."

"Let's go," Donnie said.

He was standing, holding his hand out to her. Lissa set her empty glass aside and brushed the hair back from her face.

"Sorry," she said. "I didn't mean to get maudlin." She let Donnie help her to stand, then gave Cheryl a smile she knew was blank. "I appreciate your hospitality."

"Nice to see you after all this time," Cheryl said. "Do think about the house."

.   .   .

If Lissa felt a certain awkwardness at leaving with Donnie, it was tempered by the way Cheryl had treated her. She insisted that he drive her straight to her father's house, and in the car she kept doggedly silent—about what she felt, what she planned—although when they arrived Donnie said, "You aren't really going to stay here, are you?" and she compressed her lips, hard, and answered, "I don't know."

The porch light was on, just as it had been on the night of the murder. The endless yellow ribbon she had torn down in her earlier anger was a tangled heap of light that glowed under one of the hydrangeas. For a long time she sat in front of the house with Donnie—looking for courage, she thought, that would lift her through the outside door, across the porch, into the silent hallway where the ornate chandelier put down its insufficient light. The whiskey was wearing off, and at the back of her mind, or perhaps now at the very front of her mind, was the notion— the vengeful notion—that she and Donnie might spend the night in the house, and God damn Cheryl anyway. It was not as if the place were haunted, after all; what had happened was perfectly real, perfectly of this world, and anyway the house was not storied enough for ghosts. There had never been any histories of events in this or that bedroom, no famous overnight guests, no scandals. Only now was there murder, to make "the old Cooper place" famous.

Was she afraid to go inside it? Here she was, telling herself what her father's house was not, avoiding what it was.

"Well," she said. "It looks ordinary enough from here."

They left the car. With Donnie at her side, she climbed the wooden front steps, unlocked the porch door. The sunporch was still stuffy from the heat of the day.

"I wonder who turned the porch light on."

"I don't think anyone ever noticed it," Donnie said. "I think it's been on the whole time."

"That's *my* light bill." Black humor, she told herself.

She stood at the front door—the killer had stood just here—and put the brass key in the lock. This was the key her father had had made for her when she was a sophomore, when she badgered him without mercy for freedom—or the appearance of it. I'm too old to be waited up for, she had argued. You and Mom need your sleep. I'm perfectly able.

She pushed at the door with her hip, and then she was inside. Donnie closed the door and stood beside her in the dark. Now she wondered what she should do. Put her arms around him? Kiss him? How long had it been since she had loved a man, gone to bed with a man because she wanted to? And how long since she had been to bed with a man whose lovemaking didn't fill her with terror—as if terror were the real excite- ment of sex, and simple lustful passion a childish foreplay. What lessons had Edwin taught her in the few years they shared? None she could use in another man's arms, unless the man was mad.

"Quiet," Donnie said. "Everybody cleared out this afternoon."

"Truly?"

"It's all yours. If you want it."

All hers. And Cheryl wanted it.

"I told you Cheryl wouldn't be happy to see me."

He put his hand against her right shoulder and squeezed. "That's not your problem."

"Not much," she said.

She pressed one of the wall switches and the small round bulbs of the chandelier came on. The living-room door was open at her left, at the foot of the stairs that led to the bedrooms. The study door was shut. But what was different here? Something. She closed her eyes, tried to rebuild from memory the experience of entering this house to discover death.

"The clock," she said. "It's stopped. I thought I missed the ticking."

"Run down," he said. "Shall I wind it?"

"Stopped when the old man died. How appropriate."

She went to the grandfather clock; it was tall, taller than she was, and the figures 7 and 5 were at eye level. She pressed the tiny catch and opened the clock-face door. The key nestled on the ledge at the right-hand corner of the face; Donnie took it and wound the clock and the chime, moved the hands to match the time shown by his wristwatch, and reclosed the door.

"It's still not ticking."

"You have to give it a nudge." She reopened the door. When the clock did not begin its solemn tick-tock she had felt a momentary chill, and for an odd instant she imagined she and Donnie were on the verge of discovering the missing murder weapon—it would be tucked inside the clock case, stained orange with rust and blood, interfering with the movement of the pendulum—but when she remembered and gave the shaft of the pendulum a nudge, the ticking commenced. No matted hair. No blood, with the killer's prints congealed and plain. Television scenarios, Lissa thought. Detective films. Mystery novels. *We do not live in fictions.*

Yet she was nagged by the idea that the weapon, whatever it was, would eventually be found in the house, and that she, having lived here, knowing its geographies from attic to cellar, might very well be its discoverer. If you wanted something done right, you had to do it yourself; she supposed that was partly the reason she had wanted the police to leave.

"I want to look around," she said.

They went down the hall to the kitchen. The room was clean, and smelled strongly of bleach and, less strongly, of stale cigarette smoke. The counters were bare. The table was set for one person: a straw place mat, cup and saucer, utensils. The top of the sugar bowl was held open by the handle of a spoon. Salt and pepper—the saltshaker needed filling—stood beside the sugar. Eerie. This was scarcely her father's kitchen. She knew his habits, his indifference to neatness, his persistent failure to plan or organize or look ahead. She'd married his opposite. Every evening Edwin set his table for the next day's breakfast, plugged the coffeepot into a timer, put out the next morning's cereal box. Neatness didn't save you.

The people from Augusta had put everything in its place. The double sink was spotless. The floor shone as if the linoleum had been washed. She opened the refrigerator: it held nothing easily perishable—only a box of baking soda, cans of Coca-Cola, her father's inevitable candy bars. In the freezer compartments were ice cubes, a half-empty carton of ice-cream bars. Somebody lived here, she thought. Nobody lives here now.

"Looks all right," Donnie said.

Lissa pulled out one of the kitchen chairs and sat down. "I don't know what I'm doing here," she said. "It's spooky, and it makes me wonder about myself."

"How so?"

"I mean, what do I think? Am I really going to spend a night here?" Then she decided to say it: "Do I really think I can persuade you to stay with me?"

He sat across from her. "If you want," he said solemnly.

"But you're very married."

"I'm sorry for that," he said.

"God." She pushed herself back from the table. "Let's not stay."

When they left the kitchen, Lissa closed and latched the door behind her. From the hallway she looked into the parlor—someone had put coverings over the furniture, so that the room seemed to be filled with pale eyeless animals gathered around the coffee table. An ashtray on the table hadn't been emptied—that must have been an oversight; she would clean it up whenever she did screw up her courage to stay here.

"That man smokes cigarettes constantly, doesn't he?" she said. "The Attorney General's person."

"Strand's quite a smoker. True."

"He's killing himself." She closed the door to the parlor. "What would you say to Cheryl?"

"About what?"

"If you stayed out all night."

"I haven't thought about it."

When she switched off the hall light, the curtain over the beveled glass of the front door let in a hazy version of the porch bulb; the varnished balustrade glowed, and the corner of the first step, and the near side of the clock, but everything else was dark. My God, Lissa thought, I don't know if I can even imagine being in this place. I don't know if this was ever my home.

"I want to look in here," she said. She propped her purse between two balusters of the staircase railing and put her hand on the doorknob that would let her into her father's study. Donnie put his arm out to prevent her.

"No," he said.

"Yes. I have to."

Entering chilled her; even the light, when she turned it on, was cold. Whoever had come to cover the furniture, to scour the kitchen, had not come into this room. It still carried the odor of death, of her father's blood, of violence. Here was the phone she had used to call for help; she knew if she picked it up, examined it, she would see the lines of her palm, sweat-etched across stipples of blood; heartline, lifeline. What would her father's hand have revealed? A lifeline coming abruptly to a stop. And there, in front of the rolltop desk he took such pride in, was where he had lain, in the swamp of his own precious blood. In the overhead light the stain was every bit as dark and clear as she remembered. It was shaped like a country on a map—Finland, possibly; East Germany; perhaps the Vietnam where Edwin had first conceived the idea of death. A stain longer than it was wide, with an irregular separation at one end like the petals of a flower.

She turned away. For the rest of my life, she thought, I will be turning away from all of this. The whole rest of my life.

"Let's get out of here," Donnie said.

She put her arms up and embraced him. "Dear Christ," she said. "My whole life is blood and death and losing men I love."

Donnie lifted his hands to her hips. "Come on," he said. "This is a terrible place for you."

"Take me upstairs."

"Lissa—"

"Please take me upstairs. Make love to me. Please." She pushed him out of the death room, turned him toward the staircase. "Please, Donnie."

Now they held each other, standing at the foot of the stairs. "This is crazy," he said.

"Please." She kissed him, hard, forcing her mouth against his. It *was* crazy. It was the way she began with Edwin—an assault of fervency, a depth of ardor that had something to do with love, but in a way so oblique she could never have explained it, never had been able to explain it to the doctors of the mind who probed her past with men. Like Donnie, Edwin was slow to respond, slow to rise to her hunger, and only when he was at the pitch of excitement, out of control and careering into the blind caves of his own skewed desires, would he be able to meet her halfway. "Please, Donnie."

They went up to her father's bedroom side by side, the man a little behind and to her left, ascending into the dark of the second floor with no words and with sharp explosions of breath as if they had been running for miles. This was the end of the night in the cemetery, the end of high school, the finish of her passion and Donnie's. At the top landing Lissa was already unbuttoning her blouse, kicking off her shoes—for a moment limping into the room, until she kicked the second shoe aside—turning as she reached the bed to fall on her back and pull Donnie on top of her. Her hands were at his belt, and it was only now, his weight portentous against her, that she could feel him tugging at the zipper of the narrow skirt and heard the fabric tear around the button. Now she had pushed his trousers down his thighs; now in frustration he had shoved the skirt above her waist and brought down her hose and underpants. "I don't have any way to protect you," he began, but she stopped him with her hand over his mouth. "It's all right," she said. "Don't worry. Don't worry." All their motions, hers especially, seemed to take an eternity. It was as if the circumstances were allowing time for her body to catch up with her intentions, until at last Donnie was making love to her, blindly, avidly, on her father's bare mattress.

8

AT THREE IN THE MORNING the tuneless rattle of the telephone dragged Strand up from mixed dreams. Eleanor stirred; unaccustomed to having her beside him, he didn't know if she was actually awake.

"We think we got a break," said a voice in his ear. "Chief Michaud wanted me to call you."

"What kind of break?" He hauled himself up on one elbow and groped for the switch on the base of the lamp. He tried to focus in the motel room's sudden garish light—the alarm clock, the maple dresser, the television, the chocolate-colored cube of the refrigerator on the floor of the open closet. "What are you talking about?"

"The Cooper thing. We picked up Roland Thibodeau; we think he's the guy your witness saw the night of the murder."

"Who is this?" Strand said. "Is this Savage?"

"It's Putnam."

Strand found his reading glasses and fumbled in the nightstand drawer for his notebook. "Which one are you?" he said.

"Putnam," the voice said. "I was the one with Savage the first day you got here."

"Okay, yes. I got you now: the skinny geek."

"Yes, sir."

"When you say *my witness*—" Strand turned over the small pages until he found one that carried a list of names and times. "This is the Blake boy? The next-door neighbor Miss Watkins and I talked to on Thursday?"

"That's right."

"The chess player."

"Yes, sir."

"Blake identified this Thibodeau?"

"No, sir. We haven't brought Blake down here yet."

"Who is Thibodeau? Should I know the name?"

"He's a professional boxer—also he's got a record of robbery and assault long as your arm."

Strand flipped the notebook back onto the nightstand and swung his legs out of bed. "Thanks, Putnam. I'll be ready in twenty minutes." He wondered if he should roust Eleanor out of this lovely bed, then decided not to. "Have somebody pick me up at the motel."

"And something else," Putnam said.

"What's that?"

"Something we found on Thibodeau that's very, very interesting."

Strand reached for his cigarette pack and waited. Putnam seemed also to be waiting.

"What is it—a fucking secret?" Strand said. "Do I get three guesses?"

"It's a weapon."

"The murder weapon?" He sat up, put his feet on the floor.

"The missing gun."

"Twenty-five caliber?"

"Yes, sir."

"Registered to Cooper?"

"To his wife, yes, sir. The numbers checked."

"Twenty minutes," Strand repeated.

He hung up the phone and lit the cigarette. He sat on the edge of the mattress and felt the raw smoke abrading his throat, filling his lungs.

"I suppose I'd better shower," he said.

"What was that about a weapon?" Eleanor was awake, watching him. She slid her free hand under his T-shirt to stroke the center of his back, her fingers tracing his vertebrae, making him shiver like a cat.

"I don't know if God is giving me another chance to be professional or if He's making a miracle for Al-the-Bear."

"How?"

"Putnam—" He twisted to catch her hand and bring it to the side of his face. He rubbed the stubble of his beard against it, then kissed her fingers. "You remember which one is Putnam?"

"Yes. He's the sweet, quiet one."

"Oh?"

"He's the baby on the force. That's what they call him. 'Babe.' "

"Putnam says they've turned up the little handgun that belonged to Cooper. Don't ask me anything else about it. Putnam is stingy with his facts."

"Does that really shed light? You thought it might, the day we found the cartridges."

"Don't ask me that, either." Strand took off the undershirt, careful as he pulled it over his head not to knock the cigarette out of his mouth. "What do you think? They've arrested some prizefighter named Thibodeau. Apparently he had the gun on his person."

"Is it going to be robbery after all? Murder with no perverse sexual overtones?"

"The question for today is: Does God make things that convenient?"

"Wasn't there something about omnipotence? Then the response is: He *can*."

"So He can—but you remember that deeper theological question: Is it God, or is it Michaud in disguise?"

"Shall I come with you?" Eleanor sat up in bed and hugged her knees. "I don't mean into the shower; I mean to the little red schoolhouse to help you decide your spiritual dilemma. Shall I get dressed and be official?"

"No, no," he said. He stubbed out the cigarette. "You can be official when I find out what Michaud thinks he's up to." He circled the end of the bed, naked, and bent to kiss her face; she put her arms around his neck and kissed back. "That's why I'm leaving you the car keys."

"I'll be anxious for your call."

"What's this sudden interest in Putnam?" he said.

"He's just a sweet baby—I told you."

"Aren't I sweet?"

"You're sour. I love the smell of you," she said. "I love you up close."

"Tobacco," he said. "Foul breath." He disengaged himself from her embrace. "The stench of old age. I don't see how you can prefer it."

"Aphrodisia," Eleanor said. "We flower children are suckers for all that chemical stuff."

.   .   .   .

So what, Strand wondered, was going on in that frenchified little mind of Al-Bear's? Did he really want the world to believe that the killer bludgeoned Cooper and left him to bleed to death, then went upstairs and happened to find a woman's pistol and stole it from the nightstand drawer? How did he know he didn't have blood all over his shoes? How did he know he wouldn't leave footprints upstairs and downstairs and in my lady's chamber? And if that's really what he did, then why didn't he take the bullets that went with the revolver? They must have been side by side, for God's sake. And who the hell *was* Thibodeau? Common enough name in this neck of the woods. Toweling dry, Strand thought he should have pushed Putnam harder for answers. Damn Putnam anyway—gawky youngster with too much Adam's apple—talking as if he was writing a detective novel, holding back, whetting Strand's interest. Jesus H. Christ, I'm interested, he told his mirrored face, lathered and ready to be shaved, and I better prove my interest to Eleanor. How did she know Putnam's nickname is "Babe"? What did she want to do? Mother him? What the hell am I being jealous about?

What kind of case was it when you prayed to God you'd find a club, and then you were disappointed when you found a revolver? If somebody'd put a bullet into Cooper, Strand said to himself, by now we'd have blunt instruments coming out our ears.

He wiped away the last scraps of lather, climbed into trousers and yesterday's sport shirt, sat on the edge of the bed to pull on his loafers.

"I was wondering," he said, "exactly where last night's discussion left us."

Eleanor turned over to face him. The light from the bedside lamp made her squint, and she put up one hand to shield her eyes. "Perhaps it's self-evident," she said. "Didn't I spend the night? Did you think I was only humoring you?"

"I was afraid we were both just distracting ourselves."

"Postponing, maybe. Speak for yourself. You probably ought to be ready to alienate me again."

"Because of your sexual motives?"

"That, too."

"Why else?"

"I don't know. Maybe you just like to play your pessimistic true-blue-betrayed-husband character. And maybe I'll play too. I'll insist on my knack for picking the wrong man."

Strand stood into his second shoe. "I don't know what to make of you."

"I thought you told Putnam you'd be ready in twenty minutes."

"I'm ready."

"We aren't supposed to reach conclusions," she said. "We're just supposed to sort out the questions."

A car stopped outside. The drum of the engine reverberated against the walls; the room began dancing to a rhythm of vivid blue light.

"That's it, Putnam," Strand said. "Wake everybody up."

"Be kind. He might have decided to turn the siren on."

"Go back to sleep." He kissed her forehead lightly. "The car keys are on the dresser."

"Maybe you're right," she said. "That we were only distracting ourselves."

"Dream on that," he said.

•   •   •

The Edison School was a few blocks from the center of town, a red brick building, two stories only, built between a gully and a residential neighborhood. It had two entrances, BOYS and GIRLS molded into the concrete above the doors, and sat in the center of, roughly, three grassless acres—the ground worn bare by generations of children—bounded on two sides by a chain-link fence. Because it was relatively isolated, and had no function during the summer months, the school board had been easily impressed by the glamor of letting it be used as headquarters for a homicide investigation.

"If things are still hanging fire after Labor Day," Strand had said to Michaud, "then I suppose we'll have to find an empty summer camp up at that lake of yours."

His driver—not Putnam, but a rabbity little uniform new to Strand—parked on the street in front of the building and let him out. He entered through the boys' entrance. The conversation with Michaud was yesterday; even now, Labor Day seemed somewhat too close, especially if this Thibodeau was more than just an interesting suspect caught in the indiscriminate net of the investigation. Michaud craved a robbery motive—downright needed it. Michaud clearly didn't want, or truly didn't dare, to go public with the homosexual business. *People could get hurt.* Sooner or later, Michaud's problem was going to be the State's problem, and Strand's. Then what?

"Where'd you pick this guy up?" he asked Putnam, who met him at the head of the first flight of worn stairs. "And better still, *why*'d you pick him up?"

"West Scoggin. A poolroom over toward the New Hampshire line."

"And the crime?"

"He was trying to sell this revolver to the owner."

"The owner called you?"

"And stalled till we got there."

"This Thibodeau give you any shit?"

"Always. I bet I've busted Thibodeau five times this year—just me. Don's brought him in a couple of other times. Same stuff. Drunk and disorderly. Public nuisance. Suspicion of B and E. And worse things."

"What's the worst of it?"

"Assault; robbery. He beat up an old man in Shapleigh, runs a gas station, general store."

"Beat him? What'd he beat him with?"

"Fists."

"No weapon."

"Huh-uh."

Damn and hell. "He a big man?"

Putnam squinted at him. Strand had followed him to the principal's office—calendars on the wall, attendance sheets stacked on the corner of a metal desk.

"You don't know who Flash Thibodeau is?" Putnam said.

"Flash?"

"That's what they used to call him on the posters: Roland 'Flash' Thibodeau."

"All I know is that he sounds like a bad apple."

"He used to be heavyweight champion of the state of Maine."

"So the answer to my question is: 'Yes, he's a big man.' " Strand lit a fresh cigarette. "I'll be damned, Putnam, you ought to go on 'What's My Line.' You don't give away a thing."

"Yeah," Putnam said, "he's big. He's a fucking animal." He grinned at Strand. "My uncle took me to see him fight once. He's built like a bus stop. About five ten by five ten."

"Stocky," Strand said.

"Nobody ever knocked him down. Anyway, he's a fighter, but he's no boxer; he's a one-punch type. If he doesn't get it in, he's a loser on points—but he used to almost always get it in. Fuck, it was awesome, like he just lays his fist on the canvas and brings it straight up into the other guy's jaw. Murderous. I came home, my aunt went out of her gourd. I looked like I had measles. I was all covered with blood from whoever Thibodeau was fighting. It spattered all over the place. All over me. She could've killed my uncle for taking me to the fights."

"So what about this weapon—this revolver?"

Putnam opened the top desk drawer and held up a plastic bag. "Nickel-plated, twenty-five caliber. Nice little piece—if you're a girl."

"And Thibodeau had it on him?"

"Yeah. Had it tucked in his back pocket when I got there."

"He threaten you with it?"

"No way. Besides, it wasn't loaded."

Strand took the revolver.

"They say it was the wife's. The ex-wife's. She forgot to take it with her when she got the divorce and moved to Vermont."

Strand turned the bag in his hands. The gun was small, almost pretty. A bit of the plate was peeling off the underside of the short barrel. "Let's take a look at this pugilist," he said. "And where's the Blake boy? We need him to make an ID." The Bear especially needs him, he added, the words addressed strictly to himself.

.   .   .

Thibodeau was in a classroom, sitting at a child's desk in the front seat of the row nearest the windows. He was a burly man, black-haired, with a high forehead, and his arms bulged from the short sleeves of a striped round-necked sport shirt. He wore blue jeans and soiled tennis shoes. He sat perfectly still, big hands resting on the tiny desk top, gazing straight ahead as if he were reading something written on the blackboard. Hanging from a wire above the blackboard along the side of the room was a row of children's crayon drawings—American flags, parade scenes—left over from Patriot's Day, Memorial Day, Flag Day, some holiday not long before the start of summer vacation. The board itself was clean; the chalk rail was empty. Except for the fact that the teacher's desk was cleared and unoccupied, Thibodeau might have been an overgrown teenager serving out his detention for, say, roughhousing at recess—staying in school out of duty, waiting for his sixteenth birthday so he could drop out forever.

Strand paused in the hallway and studied the boxer through the classroom door's round window. Late thirties, early forties, hair getting thin. Thibodeau's was a small face set in a large man's head; it was a face cramped into an expression of chronic anger and disappointment. The eyebrows were prominent and close together, nose blunted and misshapen from the man's ring encounters, mouth full-lipped or swollen, jaw weak, cheeks and chin stubbled bluish-gray. Was this the face in the sketch broadcast to the world? Right shape, wrong features. Not enough hair. No manly dimple in his jaw. But ape-like? No doubt. He scarcely fitted the desk; if he got up to walk, the desk would probably stay with him. Strand contemplated Thibodeau's hands—enormous hands, closed but not clenched. Certainly they could break bones—ribs, jaws—but crush a skull the way Cooper's was crushed? Not so likely.

"When was he champion?"

"Ten, twelve years ago. Not for long."

"Didn't take care of himself?"

Putnam nodded. "That, and he got cocky. He started getting beat by younger guys, guys who stayed in shape and laid off the beer. They wore him down."

"Michaud think he's our man?"

"As good as any," Putnam said.

Strand paused in the middle of lighting a cigarette. "What's that supposed to mean?"

"Figure of speech," Putnam said.

"What's he got to say for himself?"

"We haven't talked to him. We called his girlfriend. She says the two of them were at Old Orchard the night it happened."

"Old Orchard Beach? The amusement-park place?"

"She says they rode the Ferris wheel and necked all night."

"Does he have his rights?"

"Yeah."

Strand opened the door into the classroom. "Then let's ask him."

Thibodeau looked up, no change of expression touching his eyes or mouth. He was sullen, and only as articulate as he needed to be. No, he had not murdered anybody. Yes, he and the girlfriend, Theresa, had gone to Old Orchard Beach.

"Kid stuff," he said. "Theresa likes that kid stuff."

"And you were there all night?"

"All night. We rode the rides till one or two in the morning."

"Then what?"

"We walked on the beach. We screwed."

"On the beach?"

"Yeah."

"Anybody see you at the beach?"

"Screwing?"

"No," Strand said. "Walking. Or on the pier, earlier. Or on the rides."

"Lots of people."

"I mean anybody you knew, or anybody who knew you."

"Shit, I don't know. I wasn't looking for nobody."

Thibodeau shifted in the tiny seat. Strand smoked and scribbled in his notebook. Sitting at the same kind of student desk, he felt large and awkward; he could imagine how Thibodeau felt, the man's bulk dwarfing the desk.

"How long I got to stay here?"

"Here, not long. In the lockup, I don't know."

"You can't lock me up. I haven't done nothing."

Putnam, sitting at the teacher's desk, held up the plastic bag. "The gun you stole."

Thibodeau shook his head. "I bought it," he said. "I told you that."

"From who?" Strand held his pen poised.

"Some kid."

"What kid?"

"Just a kid hanging around. A young kid. I don't know his name."

"How young is 'young'?"

"Shit, I don't know. Twelve, thirteen? A kid."

"How much you pay for it?"

Thibodeau looked at his hands. "Five bucks."

"Good deal," Putnam said.

Thibodeau raised his eyes toward Putnam. "I didn't cheat him. That's what he asked me for. Five bucks."

"What were you going to do with it?" Strand said.

"Nothing special."

"Were you going to rob another grocery store? Like the one in Shapleigh where you beat up the clerk?"

"That was three years ago." Thibodeau glared at Putnam, who was dangling the revolver in its transparent bag like a pendulum. "I did my time for that."

"How come you wanted to sell the gun at all?"

"It was no good to me, a lady's gun like that. You can't hunt with it. You can't even shoot targets. I was just doing the kid a favor when I give him five for it."

"Some favor," Putnam said. "You figured you could peddle it for a lot more than five bucks."

"I'm not stupid," Thibodeau said. "That's capitalism."

"This kid," Strand said, "he didn't have any name? Not even a first name? A nickname?"

"I never heard anybody call him anything."

"Just 'Hey, you'?" Putnam said.

"He didn't have a name I heard."

Strand put up his hand to make Putnam be quiet. "Had you seen this kid before?"

"No."

"Seen him since?"

"No."

"Where was this? This capitalist transaction?"

"Wells Beach. The arcade."

"When?"

"Couple of months ago."

The answer jolted Strand. *"Months?"*

"Yeah. April or May."

"I'll be damned." Strand got to his feet, tucking the notebook into his shirt pocket. "After you get Blake here," he told Putnam, "see if you can't bring in the girlfriend. An alibi over the phone doesn't convince me."

"What do I tell her?"

"That she's a material witness. That we want to count the grains of sand on her fanny. I don't much care what you say to her."

"No problem. Savage is already picking up the Blake kid. I'll send him out after the girl."

"You get any prints off that revolver?"

"Michaud had it dusted. He didn't tell me what was on it."

Strand sighed. "He's like you, Babe. He's stingy with his facts."

.   .   .

"Sorry to wake you up again," he said to Eleanor. "None of this is the way I'd planned the morning."

He was in the principal's office, the phone tucked into his shoulder while he put match to cigarette. Out the single window he could see the lights of a police cruiser—Savage?—as it swung across the bare schoolyard to the side of the building.

"I was reading," she said. "It's all right."

"Put yourself together. Clothes, makeup, running shoes—whatever you need to play cops and robbers on short notice."

"Where is this school we've adopted?"

"If you go to the center of town and turn left at the monument, you'll see it in about five blocks. Institutional red brick."

"Something interesting must be happening."

"Or not happening." He opened desk drawers, looking for something to use as an ashtray. "It seems to be the right gun—the one we missed in the bedroom nightstand. Nobody seems to know anything about prints."

"We'll have to wait for Augusta."

"Not that I lack faith in Michaud."

"Heaven forbid. How had you planned the morning?"

"What?"

"You said this wasn't the way you'd planned it. How had you planned it?"

"Use your imagination," he said.

He hung up and went out to the hallway. Savage and young Blake were coming out of the far stairwell.

"We appreciate your coming down here at this ungodly hour," Strand said. He put his arm on Ralph Blake's shoulder, then immediately dropped it to his side. "We want you to look at somebody—tell us if you've seen him before."

"Will he see me?"

"No, no. He won't see you." He steered Blake to the door of the classroom. "He's in room three here. Just take a look through the window and tell us if this is the man you saw when you came home that night— the night of the murder."

Blake stood on tiptoe and peered into the room. Strand looked over his shoulder. Thibodeau hadn't moved. Putnam was sitting on the teacher's desk, the heels of his shoes bumping rhythmically against the front of it. Putnam was talking; it was hard to tell if Thibodeau was listening.

"I'm not sure," Blake said. "He's got big arms, but I don't know about the face."

Strand tapped at the window. Putnam slid down from the desk and came to open the door a few inches.

"Ask him to walk around a little," Strand said. "Ask him to walk to the rear of the room a couple of times and come back to his seat."

Blake watched. "Could be," he said. "He holds his arms out from his sides the same way. But I think the man I saw had more hair, and his face wasn't so round. And maybe this man is bigger."

"Maybe he got a haircut," Savage said.

"So you can't *positively* identify him as the man you saw?" Strand said.

"I can't."

"Do it again." The voice was Michaud's, and it carried—or so Strand imagined—a faint undertone of threat. "Take a long good look at this guy."

Blake stared through the window, then shook his head. "I can't be sure," he said.

"What's not sure?" said Michaud. He stood behind the boy, peered over his shoulder into the room.

"The man I saw wasn't so big around the middle—and was maybe taller. And he had more hair."

"You're positive this isn't the man?"

"I'm saying I'm not positive he *is*," Blake said. He looked at Strand, as if for help.

"If the boy isn't sure," Strand said, "you can't make it stick."

"*If* I need an eyewitness," Michaud said. "Maybe I might not need one."

"What's on the gun?"

Michaud turned up his palms and shrugged. "When I know, you'll know," he said.

"Damn it," Strand said.

Michaud pushed a forefinger against Strand's chest. "And one thing before I forget: when we want Thibodeau's snatch brought in, I'm the one who'll give the order."

Strand looked at his shoes, then at Savage, then at Blake. "Okay," he said to Blake. "Thanks. The chief and I appreciate your trying to help."

"Give him a ride home," Michaud told Savage, "and bring the woman for questions." To Strand he said, "You and me, maybe we need to talk about jurisdictions."

.   .   .

Thibodeau's girlfriend was chunky, nearly as tall as her man; she was black-haired and pale-skinned, and she was dressed, apparently, in whatever was in the nearest closet. She was in her middle forties. If she had been younger and thinner, she might have been beautiful. As it was, she was attractive in an intimidating way—something in her brown eyes, a light, an edge of color, that acted as a warning. " 'Don't come on to me' is what she's saying," Eleanor proposed, " 'unless you can stand the gaff.' "

"Thibodeau can stand it," Strand said. "Wait till you see him."

"I peeked," she said. "I saw the build of him."

"The ideal couple?"

"Maybe. It would be a kick to see them in bed together."

Strand was startled and showed it. "You're something," he said.

"Sorry," she said. "I forget what a Puritan you are."

"In any case, it can't be arranged."

"I have to decide if I'll take next best." She touched the back of her right hand to the back of his left, then quickly drew it away. "You should come out and admire the sunrise," she said.

"I saw it before you did. Sorry."

"Is Thibodeau the one?"

"Skippy doesn't think so."

"Then do you want to hear the other bad news?"

Strand took a breath. "What?"

"No one seems to know where the interview tapes are."

"The ones you played me yesterday afternoon?"

"Those, yes. And all the rest of them."

"They're probably being transcribed; some typist has them."

"Huh-uh. I asked. And they're not in the stuff that was moved here from the Cooper house. That's all in the teachers' lounge where it's supposed to be. But no tapes."

"What the hell is going on?" Strand said.

"Territorial imperative?"

Sure enough, Strand thought. Sure enough. Albert Michaud, pretending to be so helpful in the beginning, had slowly but surely—over what? the past two days?—withdrawn more and more from what the A.G.'s office would have called "host cooperation." He was putting the case together in a way that suited him—never mind Strand, never mind the State. Never mind the truth? That, too? Touchy business, this. Getting touchier.

Savage emerged from the third-grade room.

"She backs him up," he said. "Says they were together all night. She remembers every ride they took."

"No shit," Strand said, then was immediately sorry for the word. "Forget that," he said to Savage. "I'm tired, I'm hungry, I'm not in what you'd call a terrific mood."

"Don't apologize."

"You and I should talk sometime. We might have a lot in common."

Savage smiled, a boyish smile. "Maybe," he said.

Strand glanced at Eleanor. She tilted her head slightly, turned and walked away. He watched the restrained movement of her hips, the straight line her ankles described as she walked down the hall. Her perfume lingered in the air like an undeserved promise.

.   .   .

While Putnam took Thibodeau to the town jail, and Savage took the Blake boy home, Strand went across the hall into the classroom—room five—Michaud had chosen for himself.

"I don't like to see the State placed in an adversarial relationship to the local authorities," Strand said. He winced to hear the pompous echo of the words. "I thought we'd hashed this over," he said, "and come to an understanding—that you and I are not going to work at cross-purposes, that you're the boss, but you don't keep me in the dark."

"And ditto," Michaud said.

Strand pushed aside a stack of bright red spelling books and sat on the teacher's desk in the grade five classroom. In his left hand he held an ashtray made of folded notebook paper, flicking his ashes as he talked. Michaud leaned against a radiator under a pair of opened windows. Eleanor—dear Eleanor—came in and stood nearby, balanced against the back of another chair.

"I'm starting to feel a real lack of communication," Strand said. "I trust I'm not being unfair."

"You said from the beginning, this case is the Scoggin department's case," Michaud said. "Haverkamp told it to me. You backed him up. I took your word for it."

"That's true. I said that Miss Watkins and I were on the scene only to consult, to be of whatever assistance we can."

"I think we got the man who did it," Michaud said. "Simple as that."

Eleanor coughed, turning the cough into a ladylike throat clearing. Strand got off the desk and flicked his cigarette out through one of the open windows.

"*Possibly* he did it," Strand said. "Blake couldn't identify him."

"Maybe Blake's one of Cooper's 'friends,' " Michaud said. "Maybe he doesn't want to get involved. Maybe he's just scared by Thibodeau."

"You have evidence for any of that?"

Michaud ignored the question. "Thibodeau has a history of assault. A long history. He is a brutal man. He was caught with the victim's gun." Michaud held his hands out, palms up. "What the fuck else do you want?"

"Do you already know whose prints are on the gun?"

"I told you: when I know, you'll know. The State does the lab work." Michaud went to the desk; from under the stack of books he slid out a manila folder and opened it. "*Your* people. I won't be surprised the prints belong to Thibodeau."

"I'd be surprised if they didn't," Strand said.

Michaud shrugged. "I'm not going to argue with Augusta. It looks to me like Thibodeau went to the Cooper house, killed the man, stole money, a handgun, valuable coins—"

"Does this mean you found the coins?"

"We know they're missing. The daughter told us."

"She told us she didn't even know if he still *owned* the collection."

"How do I know what she told you?" Michaud said. "Your investigation is one thing. Mine is something else. Why don't you share information with me, you're so hot for cooperation?"

"You think a pair of fists could do that much damage to a man's skull? There has to be a weapon."

"So you say."

"So the damned medical examiner says." Old Al-Bear, he was really stonewalling, Strand thought, and what was there to be done about it? "He says the first blow—one blow—would have killed him." He looked at Eleanor; she was quiet, watching him and listening. "Thibodeau have a punch like that?"

"Thibodeau has a temper," Michaud said. "He's strong, like a horse kick."

"So I hear." Strand studied an unlighted cigarette in his hand. "You're going to do this, aren't you? You're going to railroad this poor punch-drunk jerk."

"Nobody's railroading nobody. He's a menace. Maybe we do society a favor."

"Who did it?" Strand said.

Michaud sat behind the teacher's desk and straightened the pile of red spellers. "Thibodeau looks like our man," he said. "Period."

"Who? Who really did it?"

"Period," Michaud said.

"Where are the interview tapes?"

"Period," Michaud repeated. "Period, period, period."

9

WHEN THE TELEPHONE RANG in the upstairs hall, at a time she later worked out to be between two o'clock and three o'clock in the morning, Lissa sat up in bed, panicky, sweating. She knew where she was. She knew what had happened in this house. She could not imagine that anyone would guess she was here, in a dead man's room, lying beside a friend who was married to someone else—which meant that the call was for her father. It was a ghostly thought, awful and unfathomable. She shook Donnie with both hands, her fingers digging into his shoulders.

"Donnie! God, Donnie! The phone." She let go of him and got out of bed and turned on the light from the wall switch. She saw the bare mattress, the uncased pillows, the man in his white undershirt and navy blue socks struggling awake. The telephone kept ringing.

"Where is it?" Donnie said.

"In the hall." She was shaking, hugging against her breasts the un-buttoned blouse, only this moment realizing she was still wearing it. "They want Daddy."

Donnie went to the hall, one hand brushing her hip as he went past her. She heard the phone picked up, its ringing stopped, and Donnie saying "Yes?" Not "Hello"; "Yes."

"All right," Donnie said. "I'm on my way."

She heard the phone fall into its cradle.

"Who is it?" she said.

He came back into the room. "I have to get going," he said. "Something's up. They want me at the school."

"How did they know you were here?" She felt her breathing resume a normal rhythm; her heart slowed its pounding. Now the room seemed like a stark sort of painting, primitive, with unreal shadows cast downward by the ceiling light. Here was Donnie looking like a cheap film; here she was, naked except for the blouse, and her bra hanging foolishly under it from one shoulder.

"The surveillance team," he said. "They saw us come in."

"And never come out." She watched him dress. "Well. That takes care of your reputation," she said.

"And yours. Are you going to stay here?"

"I don't know." It dawned on her that if Donnie went to work she would be alone in this house whose atmosphere was *sordid* no matter how you defined the word. She began gathering up the rest of her clothes. "No, not a chance. You can take me to Nana's. If I'm there when Suze wakes up, at least she'll remember she has a mother."

Outside in the car, Donnie took her left hand and kissed the knuckles. "I'm sorry to have to leave."

"It's okay," she said.

"It was wonderful," he said.

"No, it wasn't," she said. "It was just something that happened." The blue car was still parked across the street, the two men in it, she knew, watching and watching. What do they think of me now? she wondered. What does this whole damned town think?

.   .   .

Waking up in the bed at Nana's—beginning her day a second time and with more propriety—the first truth was that Lissa felt calmer than she had in a week. It was more than just enough alcohol to make her light-headed the night before. It was as if the mad, the desperate lovemaking, Donnie's earnest attentiveness to her poor starved body—or so she thought of it—had been one step toward dispelling the cold shadow of her father's death. If it was contradictory, still it was all right; it had just gotten out of hand, gone too far. She imagined she would pay for the night, somehow, and at some time in the future—in guilt, in remorse, thinking: how could she have done such a thing to Cheryl, never mind her dislike of the woman; how could she have given way to her own baser *want*, especially knowing that Donnie was only an object she had taken to herself in place of a dead love; how could she, in her father's bed, the man not even in the ground yet, so defile his memory, his name? Calm? Hardly. But alive, sensitized, energized—that she certainly was.

She sat up in bed, stretched, swung her feet to the floor. She smelled sharply of sex; the coarse hair between her legs was matted; her thighs high up carried the faint orange cast, like a sunset, marking the last traces of her period. She put on her robe and went lightly to Nana's bathroom, to shower away all that was left of the perverse passion she had deliberately imposed on Donnie.

·   ·   ·

When she left the shower, the alarm clock in her room showed shortly after eight, and silence was still hollow throughout the house. Let them all sleep, she thought. It was not until she had put on jeans and a T-shirt, and left the house for a morning walk to settle her new restlessness, that she was reminded it was Sunday by the well-dressed families going home from Ste. Anne's church. The day of the week would give her an errand: she would buy a newspaper at the Corner Pharmacy, or whatever its name was now, and she would take it home to Nana Simpson and Susie. The three of them would sit in Nana's living room and share out the sections. Susie could have the comics first, and Nana the homemaker pages, and Lissa would take the classifieds. Why the classifieds first? she asked herself. *In case*, her self answered. *Houses Wanted*. Perhaps she would deprive Cheryl of a commission.

The pharmacy's appearance had not changed: it had the same marble soda fountain, the same inlay of small octagon-shaped tiles for a floor, the same square, mirrored pillar in the very center of the store, with the newspapers stacked up all the way around it. She chose the *Globe* and the *Telegram*. Tales of two cities, she told herself. She was about to say those words out loud to the young woman behind the prescription counter, to gauge the clerk's sense of humor—or her own, she was not sure which—when suddenly and shockingly she saw the man she had conjured up in the distance of her hospital half-dream the morning after the murder. But this time she knew who he was. Striking white-blond hair and—when he turned, something she now remembered, although until this moment she had forgotten that part of the dream—his eyes: a pale, pure blue, like the ice she had seen in films of the Arctic. The man was ahead of her; he paid for a newspaper and brushed past her on his way to the door.

"Goodwin," she said. She had not formed the name in all these years; it sounded like a foreign language.

The man glanced at her over his shoulder and half stopped.

"Goodwin," she repeated, making it familiar by the repetition. "Goodwin Kimball."

And at this he came to a full stop. He turned and looked hard at her. His strange, melting eyes searched her face. "Do we know each other?" he said.

"It's been a very long time," she said. There was more, much more, she wanted to say, but the words would have been unintelligible if they had come out of her mouth in anything like the way a welter of buried images was presently making a chaos in her mind. *This man*, said a voice inside her head; it was both her own voice and her mother's, heard across years and years: *This man*. "Let me pay for my papers; we can talk outside." She hesitated, was all at once self-conscious. "If you're not in a hurry."

"No, no," he said. "My curiosity is piqued."

.   .   .

When she got outside, Kimball was sitting on the front seat of a silver-metallic Jaguar sedan parked beside the pharmacy. The driver's door was open; he was waiting for Lissa with his feet on the curb and the magazine section of the paper open across his lap. He watched her come toward him, one eyebrow slightly raised as if he were trying hard to place her, matching her face against whatever pictures his memory was offering him.

She stood before him, the papers hugged against her. "Melissa," she said.

He shook his head slowly. "I'm sorry," he said. "I really . . ."

"I used to call you Goodie."

He smiled. "Everybody used to call me Goodie," he said. "That's no help at all."

Oh, God, she thought, what on earth am I doing, and why am I doing it? She tried to rearrange her newspapers, almost lost them, and ended up laying them flat on the roof of Goodwin Kimball's car. There she let them stay, for the moment, while she brushed small bits of newsprint off the front of her jeans. She wished she were better dressed for this occasion, and realized that her mother's humorless voice was so strong a part of her turmoil that she had borrowed the woman's sensibility.

"Seventeen years ago," she said, "you paid for my abortion."

She could not have named his reaction, and she thought then that if she could have retracted the words—found some other, less abrupt way of presenting herself—she would have done so, out of kindness, out of caring. His face was a sequence of expressions, of changes that altered the shape of his mouth, the intensity of color in his eyes, the set of his jaw.

"This isn't a joke," he said.

"I didn't mean it to be. You were a friend of Bruce and Vicki Remington's."

His eyes were trying to look through her, as if the glass front of the pharmacy might somehow reflect a knowledge she herself had failed to convey to him.

"Melissa Allen," she said. "Melissa Cooper in those days. I even remember how much money you gave me to have the abortion. It was four hundred and ten dollars, and you gave me twelve dollars extra so Mrs. Leach could buy gas when she drove me up to Boston."

Kimball swung his legs into the car. "Get in," he said. "Don't forget your funny papers."

Lissa gathered up the newspapers and got in on the passenger side.

"The Bakery's just a couple of blocks away," Kimball said. He did not look at her. "It's a coffee shop. We can talk there."

"All right," she said. She sat facing forward, hugging the papers, pretending to be totally absorbed in where the car was taking her, but she managed from time to time to glance at him, his profile, matching the young man she had never forgotten against this older man she could not have dared consciously to imagine, but a man her unconscious had already created for her like a hologram.

When the car was parked in front of the Bakery, he paused before getting out, seemed to take a deep breath. "Maybe you should tell me what it is you want, before we get inside."

"I don't want anything at all," she said. "I just recognized you. I'm sorry; I guess I spoke without thinking. Of the effect."

Now he studied her, as if he were memorizing her.

"I didn't even remember your name," he said.

· · ·

At a booth inside, Kimball ordered coffee for them both.

"I've completely lost touch with Bruce and Victoria," he said. "Bruce was a big wheel with a discount chain in California, last I heard."

"What about you?"

"I was still in med school when I . . . I knew you. Coming home from Tufts on weekends. I got married that fall, to Marian Spenser. I don't think you knew her."

"I knew who she was. Her father was in the savings and loan."

"A vice-president. He retired last year." He stirred his coffee for the third or fourth time and set the spoon down on the table. "Marian and I had a couple of kids. Mary Ellen is sixteen; she's going to be a senior at the high school. Josh is thirteen, in junior high."

"And now you have a practice in town?"

"Actually I'm at Maine Medical most of the time. I still live here—big yellow house out on South Spruce that used to be my dad's. We've lived there five years—the kids and I. Dad sold it to me when he officially moved to Scottsdale."

"Marian isn't with you?"

"She died in 1982. Cancer."

"God," Lissa said.

"Yes, it's rotten. She'd just turned forty."

Lissa groped for something to say. "I'm sorry you thought I wanted something from you."

"I don't know what I thought. Blackmail? Do I watch too much television or see too many movies?"

"I wouldn't have the slightest idea how to go about it."

"And in any event, I don't feel guilty. I'm afraid I never have, that I pretty much—obviously—pushed it out of my mind. Wild oats. I'm not sure if you can hold somebody responsible for things they do when they're young and foolish."

"You were older than I was," she said.

"How old were you?"

"Fifteen."

He bowed his head. "I never realized you were that young."

"It would have made a difference?"

"Probably not." He looked sheepish. "You were very sexy, as I recall."

"I wanted to please."

"You did."

"I meant, I wanted to please Vicki and Bruce. I didn't want to seem inhospitable to a friend of theirs."

"How did you happen to know them? Vicki was much older than you."

"It was her brother, Frank, I knew first. He was my age, and he used to do odd jobs for my father. Vicki sort of adopted me, treated me like a sister. That flattered me, me being an only child; it made me feel less alone, less lonely."

"I see."

"She asked me to be one of her bridesmaids when she married Bruce. And we stayed friends; she talked to me like an equal, and I think she wanted me to *be* equal. I've always thought that's why she introduced me to you—so she and Bruce had another couple to double-date with."

"Ah."

"So I felt I was traveling in adult circles," Lissa said. "And I thought that since I was a sophisticated woman, I had to act like it." She glanced around the room. There were glass cases filled with pastries, a window that opened into the kitchen, a U-shaped counter. The men at the counter had faces that seemed familiar. Scoggin faces, she thought. Generations of Scoggin faces. "I don't mean I didn't like you," she said. "I did."

"Have you been living in town all this time? I don't think I've seen you."

"I live in Chicago. I've lived in the Midwest for quite a few years."

"Married?"

"Widowed."

"Kids?"

She looked into his pale eyes. Were these the eyes of the child she never gave the chance to be born? "Finally, yes. A daughter."

"What brings you back home?"

"My class reunion."

"Which one?"

"Fifteenth."

"Marvelous, aren't they? I went to my twentieth a while back."

"It hasn't been a very marvelous trip. My father was killed last week.

It sort of undercut the festivities—and in fact I haven't done any of the socializing."

"Your father . . ."

"Raymond Cooper. It was in the papers."

He sat back in his chair and shook his head—the way people do, Lissa thought, when something they've only heard about is presented to them in a real way.

"So that was your father," he said. "What a terrible thing for you."

"I expect I'll get over it," she said.

"I expect you will." Kimball looked at his watch, shifted forward in the chair, leaned his elbows on the table. He wore a ring—she wondered if it was his wedding ring—on his right hand. It looked expensive: gold inlaid with a single diamond that caught every light. "I'm sorry," he said. "About what happened between us, back then. I don't have any defense."

"It's past," she said. "And it takes two."

"I liked you too," he said. "If I'd been younger—if you'd been out of school—I don't know. Now I appreciate how much family—children— means to me; if I'd known better, if I'd been wiser, I might have wanted you to have the baby, maybe put it up for adoption so someone else could at least have had the pleasure of the child."

"I wanted it. I would have kept it, if they'd let me have it."

"Who's 'they'?"

"My parents. The family doctor. Everybody." She looked out the window; the sunlight was deep green on lawns across the street, and yellow in the leaves above. "You."

"I couldn't. I had ambitions—or my father had them for me. In his footsteps."

"So what kind of doctor did you become? I hope you didn't end up in obstetrics."

"No. But not far off. Pediatrics."

"It's curious, seeing you," Lissa said. "The day after I found my father dead, I was in the hospital, floating on some sort of drug they'd given me, and I had this hallucination you appeared in."

"Me?"

"I didn't realize at first what I was seeing, but I think it was your house—or your father's—and then I saw you. It was from a great distance, that whole distance between being asleep and being awake, so I couldn't see your face. But a man came out of the house, and he had your almost-white blond hair."

"Interesting."

"Persistence of memory," Lissa said. "When I knew I was pregnant, I used to ride my bike past your house—your dad's house—and I'd say to myself: 'That's where I'll live.' "

She looked straight into Kimball's eyes, swam there, shrugged and turned her face away.

"I have to get home," he said. "Hindsight doesn't manage to *do* anything, does it?"

"Gives us a different perspective," she said. "For whatever that's worth."

She stood up when he did. He put out his hand, the diamond of his ring brilliant for an instant in the light through the windows, but she chose not to take the hand, not to touch the man he had become. He dropped his arm at his side and turned toward the street.

"Nice to see how you grew up," he said. "You're a lovely woman."

"Thank you."

"Need a ride somewhere?"

"It's all right," she said. "I'll walk. I'm staying close by."

Lissa stood in the shop window and watched him unlock the Jaguar, slide behind the wheel, drive away without looking back. *And you're a handsome man,* she thought. Then she bought a half-dozen jelly doughnuts for a treat and walked home to Nana's house along streets that used to be hers.

.   .   .

Donnie stopped by in the middle of the afternoon. Lissa saw him coming, a brown paper bag cradled in his left arm, and she went to the front door to open it for him before he could ring the doorbell. She held a forefinger to her lips.

"Nana's taking a nap," she said. "What's in the bag?"

"Something to celebrate with," he said.

"Well, we'll have to be quiet about it." She led him into the kitchen. "What are we celebrating?"

"Good news." He set the bag on the table and drew out a fifth of gin and a paper carton of orange juice. "I hope you like orange blossoms. It seemed like a good drink for the season."

She found glasses and got ice from the refrigerator. Was it possible he didn't see the irony in the name of the drink? Wedding business, all her rambling about Edwin, her driven memories. Bitter orange blossoms. Donnie mixed them—hers was a bit strong, she thought—and they sat at the table in the kitchen, across from each other.

"You'll get me drunk," she said.

"Maybe that's the idea."

She shook her head. "If you think what happened last night was because of the Scotch at your house, you're very mistaken."

"I hoped you'd say that."

"I can't explain it."

She sipped, waited for what else he had to say. The house was close and hot; the day had again warmed into the eighties, and she kept having to push little damp tendrils of hair away from her temples. She already felt as if she hadn't bathed in a week. There was a fan in the window over the sink, and it hummed along at its slowest speed, a tiny rattle once in a while reminding her that she should tell Nana to have someone fix the bearing. Suze was on the porch; she had finished with the comics, and now she was sprawled on the coarse carpeting with a box of crayons and a huge pad of drawing paper. "Fish," she'd said in answer to Donnie's question when he paused on his way to the kitchen to look down at her handiwork. "I'm making a school of fish."

"Zebra fish," Lissa said. "She saw them once at a pet store on Michigan Avenue."

"I saw them twice," Suzanne had reminded her. Now she came into the kitchen with an empty plastic tumbler, dull red, in her hand. That morning, when she came home with the papers, Lissa had laid out corduroy slacks and a white T-shirt, but Suzanne had put on dark green shorts and a green tank top.

"Is there orange juice for me?" the girl wanted to know.

"Yes, sweetie. On the top shelf in the fridge."

"How about a little splash of gin?" Donnie said. "Good for what ails you."

"Nothing ails me," Suzanne said. She took the carton to the counter and poured juice into her glass. "I don't drink that stuff."

"How are the fish?"

"The fish are done. I'm doing the ocean." She replaced the juice and closed the refrigerator door with elaborate care. "It's a lot of boring blue."

"That's blue for you," Donnie said.

Suzanne rolled her eyes at Lissa and went back to the porch.

"It isn't that she doesn't like you," Lissa said, "but she gets preoccupied with her projects. Don't think you're being dismissed."

"She's a doll, isn't she?" He added gin to his drink and shook the tumbler. The ice cubes, mostly melted, made a light wind-chime sound against the glass. "She's like a miniature woman. Perfect features, perfect legs. Everything done to scale."

"Except above the waist." Lissa studied her drink. She remembered how, even in the hospital, Donnie's eyes stayed on Suze when the child was nearby—not in a scary way, but idly, persistently, as if somewhere in the back of his mind he was defining her, perhaps projecting her into the future. Lissa did that herself sometimes, trying to see herself in Suzanne, imagining the girl as a teen, a young woman, a married lady. You couldn't look at boys that way: they were anything but "miniatures"; their heads were too big for their bodies, they were unmuscled, they were utterly without poise. Maybe Donnie wanted children. Maybe Cheryl didn't. She thought about Goodwin Kimball, how he hadn't wanted her child but had allowed Marian two.

"Guess what we're celebrating," Donnie said.

"What are we?"

"We've made an arrest."

She felt a chill. "Who?"

"An ex-prizefighter, a guy with a record of beating people up."

"You've really got the person who killed him?" How ought she to react? "You're sure?"

"It looks good," he said.

Good. She thought of her own words in the hospital: *And that will bring him back, won't it?* when the doer of the deed was finally caught.

"I think I'm ready for another orange blossom," she told Donnie. She drained her glass and chewed the remaining ice cubes. She found their crunch satisfying. *I don't know how you can do that,* Daddy had always said to her. *It sets my teeth on edge.*

"Aren't you glad?"

"No," she said. She wished Donnie could read her mind. "Not till they prove he's guilty. Sentence him. Execute him, if I had my way. You hear all the time about murderers who get off scot-free. He'll get a smart lawyer. He'll laugh in my face. Then what?"

"I thought you'd be pleased. Relieved."

She pushed her empty glass toward him. "I'll try to be," she said. "Maybe it has to sink in."

Donnie stood at the refrigerator and dug a handful of ice out of the tray on the freezer door. "I'm off tomorrow afternoon," he said. "What do you think? We could all go to the beach—you and little Susie and me."

"Tomorrow they're burying Daddy."

"I forgot."

"You want to hear *my* news?"

"Sure. What?" He set the glass of ice on the table and poured in the gin and orange juice. He swirled the ice and slid the glass toward her.

"I went to the pharmacy for the Sunday papers. I bumped into a man I hadn't seen in years. Goodwin Kimball."

He waited.

"You know him?" she said.

"By name. I didn't know you traveled in those snobby circles."

"I used to. In a manner of speaking." She took a drink; the citrus bit at the glands in her throat. "He's the man who got me pregnant—back in school."

Donnie stared at her. "My God," he said.

"So now my celebrity has a sequel," she said. "Small world."

"I'll be damned," Donnie said. "He's not the one I would have picked. He's older than us."

"He seems like a nice person. A family man. Maybe I should have fought harder to have his baby."

"That would have been an awful life for you."

"Maybe. Who would you have picked?"

"For what?"

"You said he wasn't the one you would have picked to get me pregnant."

He shook his head. "Doesn't matter. Did Kimball remember you?"

"Not at first. Then we went over to the local coffee shop and talked."

She saw herself accosting Goodie, finding it still difficult to believe she'd had the nerve. "I don't know what made me introduce myself to him in the first place. I just saw him—saw who he was—and I spoke right up. It must be my year for reunions after all."

"Old times. All that."

"God, Donnie, it was amazing what I remembered. I remembered exactly how much money he gave me to have the abortion. I remembered what day of the week it was. I even remembered what the weather was like."

"Is that what this is?" Donnie said. "Old times? Just filling in a gap, and a week from now I'm history?"

The words startled her. She studied Donnie's face, feeling a small shiver of surprise run through her. "No," she said. Jealousy, she thought; it was a reflex in men. "Why do you say a thing like that?"

"Sorry," he said. He avoided looking at her. "I guess I'm not happy about you going back to Chicago."

"You're married."

"That didn't bother you last night."

"Jesus," she said. "Is that what you think of me?" And then she had no idea what to say next. She could not imagine the roots of the jealousy—if that was really what she was hearing—or of his apparent notion that by sharing her bed he had somehow *captured* her. Could not imagine any of it, that is, until it occurred to her that somehow he had already begun to build a future for himself that included her—that she was perhaps perceived as rescuing him from Cheryl. Or perhaps this was a perverse trade-off: he had brought her the man who killed her father, in exchange for her continued love. *Aren't you going to thank me for my good news?*

"I'm sorry," Donnie said. "I shouldn't have said it that way."

"Last night was last night," she said. "Don't make it into something it wasn't intended to be."

"I said I'm sorry."

She drank. Now what? she wondered.

"Look," he said, "why don't we all go to the beach right now—you, me, and Suzanne. Make a day of it, have dinner at the shore. It'll be fun."

"The beach is too crowded, too touristy."

"We could go to Ogunquit. It's crowded, but the beach is so big you hardly notice."

"I don't think so. Not today. Certainly not tomorrow." Lissa pushed herself back from the table. "I'm sweltering," she said. "I'm going to take a shower." She drank the last of the second orange blossom and swallowed some of the ice. "That's my idea of fun," she said. "As many showers as you want, any time you want them."

"How about Tuesday then? I'll get Putnam to take my shift."

"We'll see."

"We'd look like a family," Donnie said.

"Family is the last thing I want to think about," she said. She didn't tell him she wanted to think about Goodwin Kimball.

.   .   .

Upstairs, she undressed slowly, standing out of sight behind the curtains to watch Donnie drive away. It was the first time she had seen his own car—a pickup truck, actually, small and gray and Japanese—and it made him look like a stranger. It was his police uniform she would remember whenever she thought of him; it was a police car she would associate him with; it was her father's murder that would always be the context of her seeing Donnie again. Nothing could come of all that. Now he had made her begin to regret last night, her intemperance, her loss of control, the sheer recklessness of giving herself to a man she liked but did not love. It had been Edwin she was under, Edwin whose weight burdened her, Edwin's hot breath on her face, and Edwin, rampant and slick with the last traces of her monthly blood, putting his seed into her from the grave. She shuddered, turned away from the window, dropped to the floor the last of her clothes. Blood inside, blood out; death outside, death in—would she ever be cleansed?

She let the spray of the shower bathe her face, so that she could not tell the difference between her tears and the warm jets of water on her cheeks. So they had the murderer. *I thought you'd be happy.* Well, she would try—really she would. Though it was true that nothing would bring Daddy back, at least she would have revenge, and that was better than nothing. She had seen the artist's rendering of the "suspect"; she had seen it in the papers, she had caught a glimpse of it when Nana was watching TV, Donnie had shown her a Xerox of the original sketch. It was a broad, ugly face, with blank eyes and a hard jaw; it didn't even look like a real person's, and that made the face all the more menacing.

Trying to recall it, she saw now that it could have been anyone's, that the man in the picture was every-killer, every-threat. No doubt the police had arrested a man who resembled that drawing—that in itself was horrifying to her. Captured, indeed. He should have been killed on the spot; he should have been clubbed to pulp, like a dangerous snake, like a wild animal. She could feel rage blossom inside her, starting from her heart and growing like flame through her whole body. She thought she would burst with it, and at its most intense, when it was about to crack her bones with its amazing force, she screamed—or would have, except that the water half-filled her mouth and choked her, and she had to turn her head down and away, coughing, to recover herself. But now she *was* calm, relaxed; the violence of her rage—or her hatred, if it was that, if there was a difference—had purged her, cleansed her. *God, dear God.* She felt how weak she was.

She leaned, panting, against the tiled wall to wait for her breathing to return to normal, and then she bathed—soaped and rinsed, soaped and rinsed again; shampooed her hair and rinsed, conditioned and rinsed again. Easy rituals that put her life in a different perspective. Now: Goodwin Kimball. It was as if the telescope of the years had been turned around, its lenses arranged to remind her of what she had forgotten, how much she had been infatuated with him—nine years her senior? ten?— how ironic it was that he had married a different, a contemporary love, and that *that* love was dying even as Lissa, who had carried his very first child, was burying the contemporary *she* had married. Destiny loses track of its times, she thought. Then it tries to atone for its carelessness, and here she was, once more in the same place and time with Goodwin Kimball. And the chemistry of the meeting: it was a palpable bond she felt at once, a bond that she was sure disarmed him, made him trust her. What if something came of the two of them, now and after all?

And Donnie was jealous. She turned off the shower, stepped out, dried herself. And Donnie was a lot of things. Toweling her hair, she thought that once she was back in Chicago she would find the barber scissors in the kitchen drawer and cut Suzanne's long blond hair. She would give her daughter a pageboy sort of cut, something that would fall just below the jawline and tip under, some style whose modest length would not draw the attention of men who saw young girls as "miniature" women, and who pursued these miniatures in order to dream on them, and who sometimes, sometimes—it is that kind of world, Lissa knew now—acted on the dreams in ways that were perverse and violent and final. Poor Donnie; she was making this man who had been her nearest help into a pervert and a maniac. It was shamefully weak of her to have shown him the mix in her of grief and lust. But he'd read it all wrong, and now how was she to explain to him—to make him understand—what she had really meant?

Perhaps simply by leaving Scoggin for good. Now that the murderer was caught, she could call ExecuFind, talk to Jeremy Chapman, tell him she'd be back in the office on—when? If she stopped to see Mother . . . She could book a flight to Burlington on Tuesday or Wednesday—say Wednesday, so that if there were things the police needed her to do, to sign, she could oblige them. Chicago on Thursday. She could go in to the office on Friday morning, catch up on messages, plan for the following week, get back into the flow of her real life.

Real life, she thought. It seemed a startling notion.

10

AT TEN O'CLOCK Monday morning, Michaud gathered the press people in the Edison basement, seated them on folding chairs, and himself sat on the edge of a makeshift stage usually used, Strand imagined, for school assemblies. Len Haverkamp, in his short-sleeved summer uniform, lounged casually in one chair with his arms spread across the backs of two others in the front row. One of Michaud's men—the inscrutable Putnam—stood nearby; Eleanor sat against the back wall under a double row of coat hooks. Strand dragged one of the metal chairs aside and straddled it, backward, in such a fashion that he could watch, alternately, both Michaud and Eleanor without its seeming obvious. This was an event arranged without his consent and against his better judgment, but Michaud had been adamant and—as Strand reminded himself with relentless and growing dissatisfaction—it was the chief's show.

In fact, he had raised the "show" question with Haverkamp over breakfast at the bakery-cum-coffee shop uptown. "I'm not crazy about the way things are being manipulated, Len," was what he had said, and all Haverkamp had seen fit to answer was, "Let's keep an open mind. I've got great faith in Al; don't be put off by his grainy exterior." And then, almost as if it were an afterthought, he had passed on to Strand a large brown envelope. "From the lab. Al has his copy of this. I think every print was identified—even several young people, thanks to the hysteria of the local PTA a couple of years back. Bart Anson—you know him?—even threw in the photos, suitable for displaying on milk cartons." "What happens," Strand asked, "if something here contradicts Michaud's case?" Haverkamp had licked powdered sugar off the tip of one finger and wiped the hand with his napkin. "I'd want to know about it," he said. "But you've got to remember to keep things in perspective."

By now a half-dozen men and women had assembled to listen and ask. Here was plump Mrs. Adler, whose face had "good bone structure"— and who already knows more than the others will ever find out, Strand thought—and a fortyish, bald man with a vintage Speed Graphic to take pictures for her; here was the young woman who claimed to be from a television station, still without a "cameraperson"; here were the stringer from the Associated Press, a young man from the local weekly, and a red-faced older fellow from the *Globe*. The *Globe* man probably wished he was back in Boston, keeping a rendezvous with a glass of Irish neat.

Strand took a last drag on his cigarette and looked around for someplace to dispose of it. Finding nothing, not even a metal wastebasket, he stubbed it out on the sole of his shoe and placed it on the windowsill behind him. His watch told him that it was now ten minutes after ten; he wondered what the chief was waiting for. He looked over at Eleanor, who raised an eyebrow and pointed to her own wrist. Strand shrugged. The press fidgeted. Putnam rocked on his heels, with his cap tucked under his left arm, his hands joined behind his back.

Finally the door at the rear of the hall creaked open and Cooper's daughter appeared, shepherded by Officer Savage. Michaud stood, waved for her to come to the front of the room, but she stopped about halfway and took an outside seat; Savage sat directly in back of her. It was only then that Michaud was ready to start the proceedings, standing, waiting a few moments for the attention of the group seated before him.

"I believe the inspector—Inspector William Strand—from the Attorney General's department in Augusta, has some words," the chief said.

Strand was taken by surprise—sufficiently so that he did not react to having his name misspoken—but he stood and moved to the front of the room. He did not climb the two steps to the stage, but spoke from the floor, conscious of Michaud behind and above him.

"I told you on Thursday," Strand said, "that we would hold press briefings whenever we had genuine news for you. Now it's only four days later, and we have tried to be true to our word. The local police, as well as the county sheriff's people and troopers from the Scarborough barracks of the State Police, have worked very hard, very efficiently, and the A.G.'s office feels it's only fitting and proper that Al Michaud, who is chief of the Scoggin police—and whose expertise I have learned to admire in a very short time—should make a statement and answer whatever questions you may have."

He walked back to his chair. Eleanor put two fingers to her lips and wafted a kiss in his direction. Sweet praise for rank horseshit, Strand thought.

"Since the Cooper homicide," Michaud began, reading from a sheet of paper in his hand, "the following has occurred: The burglary of three summer cottages at Long Lake and Sand Pond, belonging to Whittiers and Andersons and Langleys, which transpired in February of this year, has been solved, and the burglars—five juveniles—are in custody. A 1985 Pontiac station wagon stolen from Reid Motors in late April has been recovered after incurring only minor damage, and the thief, also a juvenile, incarcerated. Investigation is continuing, with new leads, into the New Year's Eve hit-and-run killing of Norman Morton, shop foreman at the Scoggin shoe factory. A number of smaller crimes—I'll pass out a list mimeographed by the Scoggin Municipal Police Department— have also been cleared off the books."

The man from the *Globe* interrupted. "Is all this stuff the result of 'rounding up the usual suspects'?" The edge of sarcasm in his voice Michaud either missed or ignored.

"That's right," Michaud said. "The Cooper murder stirred the little fish off of the bottom of the pond." He looked toward Strand, and then at Haverkamp; he seemed pleased by the image.

"But nothing on the Cooper case itself?" the *Globe* man said.

"I'm coming to that next." Michaud referred to a blue notebook, turned a page, began to read. "Early this morning, acting on a tip from a Department informant who is nameless and under police protection, officers of this Department arrested Mr. Roland Thibodeau, forty-one years old, on suspicion of murdering the late Raymond Cooper."

Strand bowed his head. He wanted at that moment to stand and tell everyone that suspicion was one thing, but it was not everything. He took a long look at Melissa Allen, who appeared—or so he thought— to be either uninterested or absorbed in something else. He glanced quickly at Eleanor, who sat calmly, contemplating her hands folded in her lap.

"Did he do it?" the *Globe* man wanted to know. "Has he confessed?"

"He is a suspect," Michaud said.

"But how does it happen that he's a suspect? Are there witnesses? Is there hard evidence?"

"An item belonging to the victim was found in the suspect's possession. We believe we have located a witness who places the suspect in the vicinity of the crime scene."

"What's the item?"

Michaud looked at Strand; Strand shrugged and opened his hands.

"A small handgun, registered to the victim's former wife."

Mrs. Adler put up her hand. "Is this the same Thibodeau who was once a well-known boxer?"

"Mr. Thibodeau was—" Michaud consulted the notebook—"from 1967 to 1973 he was the light-heavyweight champion of New England, and from 1966 to 1974 he was the heavyweight champion of the state of Maine."

" 'Flash' Thibodeau," the *Globe* man said aloud. He looked at Strand and leaned toward him, tapping meaningfully at his own right temple.

"Is this his first arrest?" The television child.

"Mr. Thibodeau has an arrest record," Michaud said. "A long arrest record. Assault, robbery, assault with intent, public intoxication."

"Any convictions?"

Michaud referred to the book. "Three," he said. "Both assault charges, and the public intoxication. All inside of the last five years."

"What's the motive for the murder?"

"If Mr. Thibodeau did the murder," the chief said, "we speculate the motive may have been robbery."

At least he's *trying* to be careful, Strand noted.

"Robbery of a gun?" The *Globe* man seemed bemused by the whole exercise.

"There's other items not accounted for. The investigation is continuing."

"What other items?"

"I'm not free to say."

Because you don't know, Strand said to himself.

"Has Thibodeau actually been charged? And if so, with what?"

"He has been charged. B and E, theft, suspicion of murder."

"What's his bail?"

"Bail hearing was held this morning; he is incarcerated without bail. His case will go to the August grand jury."

The reporters were making notes. EX-CHAMP HELD WITHOUT BOND IN COOPER MURDER; OTHER CRIMES CRACKED; SCOGGIN CHIEF SMUG. Strand got up, letting the chair scrape noisily against the cement floor.

"I simply want to add," he said, "to underscore what Chief Michaud has said: that the investigation is ongoing. That while we are all encouraged by these developments, the Cooper case is not closed. Mr. Thibodeau is not yet convicted, and the charges against him are, presently at least—even though they are serious charges—only allegations."

"Where was Thibodeau picked up?"

Strand turned away and strolled to the rear of the room. While the questions to Michaud continued, he held out his hand in Eleanor's direction, and was pleased when she followed him up the stairs to the classrooms.

"He did all right," she said. "Didn't you think? All things considered?"

"Better than Thibodeau's going to do," Strand said.

"Are you going to try again with Haverkamp?"

"No. Len's coasting. He's not ready to interfere with an old school chum."

"Did you watch the daughter?"

"I didn't notice any joyful reactions. I get the impression she didn't show up here because she wanted to. Isn't her father being buried today? That's tough, but maybe the Bear is smarter than I thought; he understands a little bit about symmetry, and quite a lot about public relations and pacifying the press."

·   ·   ·

In the third-grade classroom, Strand cleared the top of the teacher's desk and Eleanor spread out the contents of the envelope Haverkamp had delivered.

"Snapshots," Strand said.

"Fingerprint cards." There were a dozen or so; she lined them up at the edge of the desk, then arranged the photographs—Polaroids, black-and-white, the same size as driver's license pictures—in a double row below them. "God bless the PTA."

"God bless panic. I never approved of this program, all this dumb hysteria about kidnapped children, just so the parents could pretend their kids weren't really running away from home. If you carry it far enough, it's a psychology that makes every kindly grandfather look like a pervert."

"Leave it to you to look at that side of it," she said.

"I know. My 'age thing.' " He straightened the rows. "Or did you mean my perversion thing?"

"I'd have to see more of that," Eleanor said.

"So what's the report say about this stuff?"

She turned the page of a printout. "Oh," she said, "here's the handgun report. No prints."

"None? Wiped clean?"

"Apparently."

"That's strange. It must have carried Thibodeau's prints, and Michaud must have wanted it to." He sat behind the desk and turned a perplexed look toward Eleanor. What in the hell? he thought.

"Someone else's fingerprints were on it too," Eleanor said. "No?"

"The youngster who sold it. Yes. One of these in the rogues' gallery spread before us." Strand shook his head in dismay. "Shit," he said.

"But the prints on Cooper's office wall? They belong to a Joshua Todd Kimball." She came around beside him and began turning the Polaroids over to read the names on the back. "Here," she said. "Joshua Kimball."

Strand put on his glasses to see. A blond boy, longish hair, very young-looking. "When were these taken?"

" 'Eighty-one." She found the matching fingerprint card. "Born in 1972."

"Thirteen years old now." He put the photo in its place, found a cigarette and match. "My first since Al-Bear's show," he told Eleanor.

"I'm impressed."

"Did I listen to this boy's interview before the mysterious vanishing act?"

"I don't know. I don't think we had names then."

"What else is on that sheet?"

"Names of adults—three—whose prints turned up in the house."

"Anybody else named Kimball?"

"Of course not." She folded the printout down the middle and laid it on the desk in front of him. "There you go again," she said, "wanting the case to solve itself."

Strand stubbed out the cigarette. "Let's have lunch," he said. "Let's think about something less frustrating."

Eleanor collected everything off the desk and replaced it in the brown envelope. "I won't ask what," she said.

.   .   .

Walking out to his car, Strand was overtaken by Officer Savage and Cooper's daughter. A light rain had begun to fall, and the woman held one hand to her face to shield her eyes.

"I wanted to say thank you," she said.

"For what?" The daughter looked tired, but not as disconnected from things as she had seemed to be during the press conference. He glanced at Eleanor, who had already opened the door on the passenger side. Don't say anything unkind, warned Eleanor's eyes.

"For whatever you and your partner had to do with arresting that man. I'm sorry if I wasn't ever much help to you."

"I'm not sure we did anything useful," Strand said. And then he said, "Remember: 'that man' isn't convicted yet."

Melissa compressed her lips. She seemed to want to say something more, but couldn't find the words.

"I just mean we have to be careful about conclusions," Strand said.

"Come on," Savage said. He held the woman's arm and steered her toward a nearby police cruiser.

She let herself be moved. "Thank you anyway," she said. "I'm sorry, but I have to go bury my father."

Strand followed for a few steps. "Savage," he said, "I need to talk with you. Is late this afternoon possible?"

Savage paused, his hand still on Melissa Allen's sleeve. "I guess."

"Four o'clock?"

"All right. Where?"

"How about that bowling alley by the river? They have a bar; I might buy you a beer."

Savage nodded. "I'll be there."

Strand got into the car beside Eleanor. "Now what?" he said.

"I thought you were going to say too much to her."

"Not yet."

"You're always right on the edge of hurting her."

"I know that's what you think."

"You don't expect Haverkamp to interfere," Eleanor said, "but what are *you* going to do?" They sat, the gentle summer drizzle blurring the windshield, droplets gathering and breaking into rivulets across the glass, and watched as Melissa Allen drove away with Savage.

"What would you suggest?"

"Eventually you have to file your report with Henderson in Augusta. So does Haverkamp."

"True."

"Both of you should tell him what's happening."

"No, that won't work. Michaud's going to pile up as much circumstantial evidence against Thibodeau as he can. Henderson would call me up, say, 'What the hell's wrong with you, Strand?', chew me out, make me rewrite the report."

"You're going to endorse the charges against Thibodeau?"

"We've got the stuff Haverkamp just gave us," he said. "We'll see what we can put together, see if we can get the locals to do more work. If we don't end up with a case stronger than the Bear's, then we'll have to back off—say the local investigation speaks for itself."

"That's not like the real you. That's surrender."

Strand took out the cigarette pack, found it empty, crumpled it and dropped it onto the floor of the backseat. "How do you know what's like 'the real me'? You've known me how long?"

"You can't say we haven't been close."

"Let's change the subject, shall we?"

"What about the daughter? Are you going to have to tell her what you think about all this?"

"That's a change of subject?"

"All right. What's going to happen to *us*?"

"What do you want to happen?"

"What *I* want is probably beside the point. You're a man. I'm fallible about men."

"I've known two women in my life—my wife for thirty-one years, you for less than a week. I'm a babe in the woods about women."

"A match made in heaven," Eleanor said.

Strand shook his head. "Jesus," he said.

"So what *is* going to happen to us?"

Good question. He leaned back against the headrest and silently cursed himself for forgetting, over and over, to buy Luckies. Maybe it was Freudian; maybe he secretly wanted to quit smoking. Maybe he would already have consciously quit, except for the way these small-town types were running him around. Or running around him.

"What if I retire?" he said. "Go home and tell Henderson I want to be pensioned off."

"Is that the plan?"

"I didn't say it was a plan. I said 'What if?' I'm eligible."

"All right. You retire, I keep on working—because I'll want to—and maybe we live happily ever after." She nudged him. "Violins. Syrupy saxophones. End of scenario."

"My scenario," he said, "is you and I, evenings in the summertime, walking around the block. Me a little slower every night. You holding on to my elbow so I don't tip over. Younger couples saying something respectful to us both. Little kids avoiding us." He put his hands across the steering wheel and cocked his head toward her. "Is that what you want?"

"It isn't exactly that I look forward to it," Eleanor said. "And it isn't the way I envision it. But I could live with it."

"I've seen those people. Those couples. That's all they do: walk around the block every evening, slower and slower, the old man smelling like shit and talcum powder."

"That's not us."

"I've got more than twenty years on you."

"You're a whiz at arithmetic."

"I'm a dead end," Strand said. "You're too smart to love me."

Eleanor faced front. "I see," she said. "Ram, bam, thank you, ma'am."

"Oh, for Christ's sake," he said, "it's nothing like that. You know it's nothing like that."

"What is it like?"

She looked out the window into the wet. When he tried to read her expression by the gray light of the rain, he believed he saw that she was genuinely unhappy with what he was saying—that it was important to her to pursue the question of their future. But what could anybody tell in this emotional weather?

He took her hand and kissed it. "Can't we leave it the way it is, for now?"

She drew her hand back and sat stiffly.

Strand faced her. "Look, I was married to the same woman for thirty-one years, and meeting you has turned me into a kid in a sexual sweet-shop. I love to be in bed with you, I love to be with you outside of bed, I'm proud to have—to have attracted your interest."

"You were a pushover," she said.

"But I'm going to be dead while you're still young. This machine that's me has got sixty years on it. . . ."

"Jesus, you're obsessed with that."

"You will be too—"

She put her hands to his mouth and half-covered it. "Listen. You're an attractive man, in spite of yourself. At least you attract me, even when I want to slap you and go running back to my own solitary life. You're older, yes. You're old-fashioned and silly about the past and terrified about the future—I can see all that. You make fun of my computer because it's newfangled—

"It is, damn it."

"I know. It's beyond you. I've watched you work the computer keyboard at the office like it was a manual typewriter you had to pound into submission. I've wanted to stop you, to say that a feather's touch would do as well, and that if you're not careful, you're going to break something. I want to say the same thing about the way you work the Allen girl, Michaud, me: a feather's touch will do as well. I don't want you to back off from this case, or from me, but I don't want you to bruise us, either. Find a middle ground. Jesus God, Will, don't you know how to care?"

He held her wrists and leaned to kiss her. "I do," he said. "Dear God, you know I do."

"Just because I threw myself at you, don't throw me back," she said.

He buried his face in the perfumy softness of her hair. He felt her hand stroke the back of his head, and then her voice changed into something lighter.

"I have to tell you," she said. "Mrs. Adler stopped me before the press conference. She said she hoped you and I were enjoying our honeymoon in Scoggin."

.   .   .

At a few minutes after four, Strand watched Savage come through the door of the Riverside Lanes and stand uncertainly in the smoky light between the bowling alley to the left and the lounge to the right. At this time of the afternoon the place was relatively quiet: a retired couple on lanes three and four, a trio of older men who might have been truckers, or workers just off the shoe factory's day shift, drinking beer and razzing one another's splits and gutter balls. The lounge was busier, but not by any means filled, and Strand was pleased he'd picked this as a meeting place. Three or four men were at the bar; two couples were playing cards at a table next to a window overlooking the river; the barmaid—she had explained that a regular table waitress wouldn't come on until later— was taking orders from two old men in the corner. On the table next to his was a discarded copy of today's *Evening Express*. Large headline: SUSPECT HELD IN COOPER MURDER. Fast work by Eloise Adler.

Strand waved, and Savage strolled over. He was wearing his uniform, but without hat or tie.

"Sit," Strand said. "Tell the girl what you want."

Savage sat.

"I'm deep in thought," Strand said. He gestured toward the drink— rye, neat—and drew a cigarette from the new Luckies pack. "And I need your input, as the feller says."

"Where's your sidekick?" Savage said.

Strand smiled, lifted the shot. "To taking care of business." He downed the whiskey. "Which Miss Watkins is presently concerned with." Love and duty, he thought. They seemed at last to have come down to the same thing.

Savage caught the barmaid's eye and she came over to him. "Narragansett," he said. "I left Cooper's funeral about an hour ago," he told Strand. "What sort of input are you after?"

"How did the daughter handle it?"

"Okay. She's glad it's over with."

"She have anything to say? About this morning's events?"

Savage shook his head. "You sort of took the wind out of her sails."

"I didn't mean to upset her. Just trying to be prudent." Strand took a deep breath. "Now," he said, "help me understand this town of yours."

"I'll do my best."

"What if the rest of the town manages to find out Cooper was gay? And not only gay, but a corrupter of young boys?"

"All hell," Savage said. "A lot of people would be flaming mad and embarrassed. But they won't find out."

"And if the murderer is tried by a jury of Scoggin County yeomen—and yeowomen—good and true? A jury that knows Cooper was gay, that he buggered children?"

Savage hesitated. "You mean would they convict?"

Strand nodded, sipped his whiskey.

"It would depend."

"I wondered if it would," Strand said. "Thibodeau?"

"Probably they'd convict."

"But if the killer were an upstanding citizen, a God-fearing type, a pillar of the community."

"But he isn't."

"Stretch your imagining," Strand said. "Suppose it isn't Thibodeau."

A long, tense silence. Strand studied his whiskey.

"This is all what-if bullshit," Savage said.

"You're right." Strand sipped. "Thibodeau is the ideal suspect. I don't doubt Thibodeau could kill anybody with his bare hands."

"He damn near killed that storekeeper in Shapleigh."

"And the only witness he has that locates him away from the scene of the crime is the woman he lives with. I know all of that," Strand said. "I know exactly how it appears, and I also think I know exactly what Michaud and the town fathers have in mind." He finished his whiskey. "What I'm saying is: I don't care much for the way things are happening."

"Thibodeau isn't being framed, if that's what you think."

"Do you *know* that?"

"I believe I do."

"Seriously— Who's Michaud protecting?"

"I didn't say I knew that."

Strand put his elbows on the table and looked at his hands. He could make out the blue outlines of his veins, but without his glasses he didn't see the crepe-paper texture of the skin, and the liver spots on the back of his left hand were diffused and pale. Beauty marks, he thought. He lowered the hands.

"Listen," he said to Savage, "this is a bizarre case for me. Almost from the start of it, what I felt about it had a lot more to do with me than it did with poor old Cooper. I admit that. I admit I didn't want to be here. I even admit that I've let myself get sidetracked by Miss Eleanor Watkins—the same way it looks to me as if you've gotten sidetracked by Mrs. Melissa Whozis. But it hasn't made me totally deaf and blind. I know in my bones that Thibodeau isn't the man, and you ought to know he isn't the man, and I can't escape the idea that somebody in your department knows who *is* the man."

"I doubt that."

"Listen: when I go to look for something simple and obvious like interview tapes, all at once I'm not finding them. You and Putnam and Michaud and whoever else—you guys have talked to scores of people: neighbors, friends, acquaintances, clients, fellow Legionnaires. Christ, you must have a couple of hundred hours of tape—I've seen them, once, and I've heard some of them, once; now I find squat. I can't even find the tapes Eleanor and I made on our own, because when the department moved our things out of Cooper's house, this, that, and the other got selectively mislaid. When I go into your file room to find transcripts and photographs and preliminary reports, it's like the mice have got there before me and eaten up all the good stuff. You hear what I'm saying? If it weren't for the fact that the Scoggin police department is too small to have its own lab, I wouldn't have anything at all to show for my troubles."

"I hear what you're saying. And I don't know anything about all that. All I'm saying is that this is an honest police force and nobody's going to railroad Thibodeau."

"You're damned right they're not. Because the state of Maine doesn't go to the grand jury unless I tell it to, and I think I'm not going to tell it to do anything until I'm sure we've got a viable suspect." Strand signaled the waitress. "I'm not really a heavy drinker," he said. "My stomach's too old to put up with the regular abuse of alcohol. But I'm a little bit frustrated right now, and a lot pissed off, and I figure a good solid hangover will make me more docile tomorrow. I wouldn't want to offend the town fathers."

Savage looked down at his glass. The lounge was beginning to fill; the floor waitress had arrived for work and now sat at the bar, chatting with the barmaid. They would be talking about ordinary things, normal things. The subject wouldn't be sodomy, you could put money on that. Maybe in Boston or New York, but certainly not in Scoggin, Maine. God, Strand thought. God, God, what happens in this world.

"Your girlfriend knows what I think—I mean she knows I've got misgivings," Strand said, "and I'm sorry if it made her unhappy. And she doesn't know yet about her father—his 'preferences.' "

"She isn't my girlfriend, by the way."

"All right."

"And it's true: she doesn't know about her dad," Savage said.

"I think she ought to."

"What for?"

Strand spilled a cylinder of ash onto the table before he could reach the ashtray. "I think what happens next isn't going to make much sense to her unless she knows."

"I don't think so. What is going to happen next?"

"I don't believe Michaud is going to be able to hold Thibodeau—at least not on the murder charge. There's no real evidence that he was ever inside that house."

"The gun."

"That's crap," Strand said. "Thibodeau's telling the truth. He bought it from one of those kids Michaud's got on tape."

"Maybe."

"Which brings me to you."

"My input," Savage said. He poured beer into his tilted glass, letting it fill slowly.

"I need you to find the tapes, the transcripts, the lab reports. Anything you can ferret out."

"They've got to be at the station. Everything's kept there."

Strand shook his head. "Eleanor says not. She was told they couldn't be found."

"So somebody mislaid them," Savage said. "They'll turn up."

"Then turn them up for me."

"Ask Michaud."

"Michaud wouldn't give me spit for a postage stamp, and you know it. I need you to find them. I need to make copies. I need to see local reports."

Savage shook his head.

"Which do you want?" Strand pursued. "The truth, or some safe way out?"

"We all want the truth. But you're asking me to steal from my own boss. If there's something you want to know, why don't you just ask me straight out?"

"That's such a simple idea," Strand said, "I'd never have thought of it." He slid Haverkamp's oversize printout from between the pages of his green notebook and unfolded it. "Let's see what you know."

"What's that? A list of suspects?"

"Close. It's names of people whose fingerprints were found in the Cooper house. Maybe you can tell me something about them."

"Maybe. Can I order another ale?"

"Be my guest. How about Alden Robinson? Know him?"

"Runs the restaurant on Main Street—Walden Pound."

"I saw that place. Cute name. Why would he be in Cooper's house?"

Savage shrugged. "He's divorcing his wife. Maybe Cooper was his lawyer."

"Plausible. How about a chap named Robichaud?"

"Which one?"

"Paul."

"TV repair."

"Wayne Waterman?"

"Never heard of him."

"Okay." Strand turned up the fingerprint card. "One of the kids who did odd jobs for Cooper; parents named Goodwin and Marian Kimball."

"Mrs. Kimball's dead."

"What do you know about Mr. Kimball?"

"*Doctor* Kimball. Melissa knows him. He was her lover."

"Really?"

"Once anyway. A long time ago—back when she and I were in high school."

"That still going on?"

"No." Savage filled his glass from a new bottle. "Well, I don't think so. She hadn't seen him in years until yesterday. Or so she told me."

Coincidence: the word echoed in Strand's head. "You know those palm prints on Cooper's wall? They belong to Kimball's son, Josh."

Savage drank. "So you're telling me you think it's Kimball who really did it?"

"I'd like to find out."

"I would too," Savage said. "So would the chief."

"Then why not find those missing tapes for me. Find out where all that stuff has gone." Perhaps Savage would be helpful after all. Strand leaned back. You couldn't trust men when they were all tangled up in feelings for women.

Savage was hunched over his beer, scowling into it. "Goodwin Kimball's kid," he said.

"I'm sure Kimball's an upstanding citizen," Strand said, "but for Christ's sake, we need the truth."

"I appreciate that," Savage said. "I won't make any promises."

Strand let his shoulders slump. "You're right," he said. "This is not a promising situation."

11

LISSA MET GOODWIN KIMBALL, the second time, at the cemetery.

When she saw him—she couldn't have explained even to herself why this happened—her knees went watery and for a frightened moment she thought she might fall. It was a side effect of grief, that weakness, or it was simply fatigue or the confusion of the morning—Michaud's and Strand's contradictory messages about the arrest of her father's killer. In any case, here he was, a solitary figure removed from the small knot of graveside mourners by a distance of several yards. The Cooper plot was on a shallow hillside, and above it, farther up the slope between her and Kimball, lay a succession of family monuments centered in their own plots: Bartlett, she could read from here, and Turner and Emery—large stones, granite or marble or reddish sandstone, carved to represent the shapes eternity might assume in its larger dimensions beyond Earth. The gentle rain had stopped, and the air was as oppressive as it had been before the shower. Kimball looked down on them all, bareheaded and shirtsleeved, his pale gray suit coat draped over one arm, standing just within the shade created by a cluster of small pines planted at the crest of the hill. She thought he was looking at her; it was unlikely that he could hear the graveside eulogy from such a distance, with a light breeze drifting toward the mourners out of that pine grove.

Once she had recovered her balance, she felt a physical lightness that seemed to mean she welcomed his presence. After the burden of the brief church service, the Reverend Winslow doing his ministerial best to sound as if he had been a close friend of the deceased, yet mispronouncing Daddy's middle name, "Hussey," as if it were spelled "zz" instead of "ss"; the tasteful but dreary piano music, the sympathies of men and women whose names she could not call to mind—after all of that, the sight of Goodwin Kimball elated her. What had prompted her to look toward him? Lissa shivered. If she was too far away for words to reach, she was not too far from the pressure of his liquid eyes; of course: she had felt him watching her. My God, she thought, what must be the matter with me? It had been all these years since she had even thought of the man, and now, in a matter of twenty-four hours, she was smitten by him all over again—and this time there was no Bruce and no Vicki to please, no sense that she was obligated to prove she could do what the grownups did.

The minister's voice drew her attention back to her father's casket, balanced on a frame of silver rails, the open grave under it an opaque, rectangular darkness, the dirt dug out of it partly covered by a blanket of green artificial grass. "Raymond Cooper, we return you to this earth and the mystery from whence you came." Lissa bowed her head, as much to keep from looking at Goodwin Kimball as to show reverence for the words of commital.

"An honest man lies here at rest,
A solid friend, a voice of truth,
A friend of age, a guide of youth. . . ."

Why did he read the words so woodenly? What was the good of poetry if no one understood its emotion?

". . . If there's another world, he lives in bliss.
If there is none, he made his best of this."

"The lines are from Robert Burns," said Winslow. He took a step back from the grave. "Let us pray."

She lifted her gaze toward Kimball; he was gone. The casket was lowered, the webbed straps played out around the metal frame, the movement of the polished box sluggish and even. She could see that the sides of the hole were not bare earth, that the vault—*cemetery requires outer burial container*—was in place to receive the box. Then the activity was finished, the straps rolled up, the frame taken away.

"May love renew and inspire us . . ."

Afterward: nothing. No close friends appeared to reminisce; no neighbors waxed nostalgic; if any school chums from out of town had stayed to pay their respects to Daddy, they did not come forward. Two of the pallbearers—men from the Legion Post—had stripped the shockingly clean American flag from the casket and folded it deliberately. Mr. Hunter brought it to her, a white-starred bundle shaped into a triangle; he mumbled something about "a nation's gratitude," and that here was a gift not only from the local American Legion, but from the Veterans Administration. What would she do with it? She hadn't known what to do with the one they gave her at Edwin's funeral, and it was still wrapped in butcher paper at the back of a closet.

Reverend Winslow appeared and took her hand in his. "He has peace now," Winslow said gently.

"Yes," she said—as if her father's life until a few days ago had not already been peaceful. She pressed the flag into the minister's arms. "Would you take this? Would you tell the Legion people it's a gift from me?"

Then for a short time she was alone—Donnie had not come with her to the cemetery—and she was about to make her way back to the limousine she had arrived in when Goodwin Kimball was beside her.

"Let me drive you," he said.

He steered her down the hillside to the silver Jaguar by gently holding her elbow, opened and closed the car door for her, got in on the driver's side without seeming to note that she had slid across to unlock the door for him.

"Thank you," she said. "This is more pleasant than riding with Mr. Hunter in that black Cadillac of his."

"I think all of this was pretty tacky," Kimball said.

"It doesn't matter," Lissa said. "What's important is getting it done with."

"I suppose."

"Was your wife's service tacky?"

He looked sideways at her; she thought she must have startled him, and she wondered how she could have said such a thing.

"You think it's an awful question."

"No, it's okay," he said.

"I was only wondering if you thought any of it made a difference."
She leaned her head against the window beside her. "To your wife."

"Point grasped," he said.

Kimball did not start the car. Instead, the two of them sat, silent now,
watching the other cars leave the deep vegetable-green surroundings. A
hundred yards away, in front of a brick building with white-trimmed
windows and a white-railed porch, two men in overalls loitered—one
of them leaning against the fender of a battered pickup truck, the other
seated on the damp grass, smoking—waiting for everyone to be gone,
she imagined, so they could draw aside the artificial grass and push the
concealed earth into the hole which was now her father's home.

"Formalities," Kimball said.

"What made you come to the funeral?"

He pushed a forelock of hair back from his brow. At first she thought
he wasn't going to answer, was only going to look pensive, but then he
managed to find something to say.

"I'm not sure," he said. "It must have had something to do with my
feeling guilty."

"Guilty for what?"

"For yesterday. For jumping to conclusions; for thinking you wanted
something from me when you introduced yourself at the drugstore."

She shifted uneasily. "You certainly shouldn't have felt guilty about
that. You didn't remember me. I might very well have been some kind
of wacko."

"But you weren't. And you made me think, afterward, how much I'd
changed since Marian died—how I rarely give anyone the benefit of the
doubt, how I expect the worst from people."

"Right now," she said, "I'm not feeling any too generous toward the
world."

"And then I felt. . . how serious your loss was. When I thought back
to Marian—that wasn't so long ago, you know—I realized all over again
what a wrenching experience it is to lose someone near, someone related.
And I knew you'd been away from Scoggin for a long time, which meant
probably there weren't any close friends to help you through."

"Don Savage has helped—the man I was with at the church. We were
classmates. And there's a woman named Pris Simpson who used to baby-
sit me when I was small. But you're quite right: I don't have anyone
close."

"I feel—I don't know. As if I owe you something. For what I did to you."

"It wasn't so much what you did to me. It was more what those 'close' friends and relatives did."

She watched the two men climb into the cemetery pickup, heard the engine start. The truck moved away, made a left turn and disappeared over the horizon, the image of it shimmering in the heat from the blacktop of the road. What would the men do? Have a drink in town, come back to fill in the grave when they could do it without witnesses?

"I really did want the baby," she said. "Your baby and mine. You couldn't have known that at the time. I wanted it desperately, with all my heart and all my strength. But when you're not even sixteen, and when you won't tell anybody who the man is, you don't have much negotiating power. I think my father was slightly sympathetic; Mother wasn't at all. Mother was the one who would have had to put up with the talk—the town gossiping, the bad opinion of her women friends."

"It's true that I didn't know you wanted to keep it."

"You didn't have a vote anyway. By the time I even told you I was pregnant, all the right decisions had been made for me."

The car phone rang. Kimball answered and listened.

"It's true, isn't it?" Lissa said. "What they say about not getting involved with doctors because their time isn't their own."

He looked almost sheepish, and she thought then that he had probably been honest about his guiltiness for being uncharitable toward her in the pharmacy. "Where shall I drop you?" he said.

"At Simpson's. It's on the corner of Grove and Main."

"I wonder if I could see you again. Take you to dinner, or a movie." He waited. "Something," he said.

"You can phone," she said. "I'm not going to be here much longer."

Kimball started the car. "This is just as well," he said. "This interruption. If we go on talking, those two men won't ever come back and bury your dad."

"Is it serious, this call?"

He looked at her, the blue eyes startling her, and she remembered they had startled her then, those years ago when she had been a child, frightened of what he would do to her even as she wanted it done. Eyes like a pale sky, like a surreal painting. She had flown upward, into those eyes, that sky, that terrifying heaven where she had first nurtured his seed.

"Probably not serious," he said.

On the seat between them Lissa laid the small cardboard box Hunter's daughter-in-law had given her, wondering what she would do with the white booklet inside, its list of names of those who had attended the service. Sign in, please. Kimball was still in his shirtsleeves, his tie loosened, a faint shape of perspiration showing under his arms. He seemed to her to smell not of sweat, but of something inoffensive, even reassuring, that she could not have described. She supposed it was all part of the old, memorable desire.

.   .   .

Kimball didn't telephone. Instead, early that evening he appeared at Nana's and rang the doorbell. Lissa found him sitting on the porch rail, waiting, arms folded, blue eyes tentative.

"I decided to take a chance you'd be home. I gave Josh money so he could have supper out, and here I am."

"McDonald's?"

"What?"

"You sent your son out to have supper at McDonald's? Or some such fast-food place?"

"I suppose that makes me a bad father."

She studied him. The years—possibly his profession—had drawn lines at the corners of his eyes and mouth, had made him coarser, his body more wiry, rangy rather than tall. Whatever had attracted her all those years ago, never mind Bruce and Vicki, seemed now enhanced. "Possibly," she said.

"I can't undo the deed," he said. "Can I atone?"

"You could take Suzanne and me to McDonald's." She felt playful in Kimball's new presence, almost easy. "I know," she said. "I'm suggesting that two wrongs make a right."

So the three of them ended up sitting inside the Jaguar and ate Quarter-Pounders and Big Macs and fries and unhealthy, milkless shakes. To Lissa's amazement, Goodwin Kimball seemed unperturbed by the prospect—no, the fact—of mustard and special sauce and grease on the car's leather upholstery. "A car is just a thing," he told her, a dismissal she thought only a person of means could have made sincerely.

Afterward he drove them to a Friendly ice-cream place. He allowed Suzanne to drip strawberry swirl all over herself and the backseat, and he took the liberty—Lissa permitted it—of moistening a paper napkin with his own saliva and using the napkin to clean traces of chocolate-marshmallow whip from the corners of Lissa's mouth.

Finally he drove them back to Nana's. Suzanne was sent inside to get ready for bed. Lissa and Kimball sat in front of the house in the car and talked—she would remember later—what Suze called "deep stuff." This was the ritual of reacquaintance, Lissa imagined; it was the way two movie characters who were fated for each other made up for lost years after the impediment separating them was finally removed. It was, in short, pure sentiment and cheap romance.

At dusk she went inside the house to put Suzanne to bed, while Kimball waited. To her daughter's question, "Are you going to drive away with that man?" all she could say was, "Not without you."

When she reported this exchange to Kimball, he seemed more than amused.

"Perhaps someday you'll mean that," he said.

"I mean it now."

"In a different way, is what I'm saying."

She looked away. No, she thought; this was too quick, this was as presumptuous as Donnie tried to be. "You think you can charm me now the way you charmed me when I was fifteen."

"I wouldn't mind trying. Should I not?"

"I'm not the same person. I'm wiser. Or I think I am."

"What's made you wise?"

She leaned against the door opposite him. His face wore a serious look she could just see by the dim light of a streetlamp across the way.

"You have. You didn't intend to, but you did."

"Explain."

"I shouldn't have to. Think about it. Sex, pregnancy, abortion—they put women in a peculiar niche, or did back in those days, no matter how enlightened people think the Sixties were. You changed my whole life."

He had twisted in the seat so that he faced her, and now his whole expression was shadowed so she could not read his wonderful eyes.

"Once I'd done the things my mother imagined had to be done—going to Boston with Mrs. Leach, having the fetus destroyed in the old illegal way—I was an odd sort of damaged goods. Not because I wasn't any longer a virgin—though I'm still amazed at the importance of virginity in this world—but because I wasn't any longer a 'nice' girl. A boy who'd had hardly any interest in me before—I just found this out—suddenly wanted to date me; wanted to screw me. You know.

"And then I wasn't good enough to be sent to a four-year college—I'd spent my whole adolescence counting on Wellesley, even though I've still never met a Wellesley grad I liked—and so I ended up at business college, getting an A.A. degree instead of a B.A. And an M.R.S. before that, of course; it made perfect sense for me to marry Eddie, and to find work as a secretary, and get legally pregnant with a child I would actually get to keep and bring up."

Kimball never turned away from her as she talked; it was an attentiveness she found mildly unnerving. As if he cared. Or perhaps he did.

"Tell me about virginity," he said.

She laughed. "It didn't bother *you*," she said. "Or it didn't seem to; you didn't have the scruples the others had about being first. All through junior high and high school I'd dated boys I really liked, really *wanted*. I marvel at that now: there I was, thirteen, fourteen, fifteen, and I really wanted them, whatever 'want' meant to me then. I think I just plain wanted to get laid. It wasn't that I'd begun to experience the—what can I call it, now that I'm grown up?—the wonderful, unexpected arousal that makes things happen to your body. Things that are a little scary—no, a lot scary. Physical sensations, odors, temperatures, juices; my God, I was giddy with it all. But the boys—excuse me, but they were stupid and impossible. They'd get me so crazy—the boys I liked, the boys I wanted—crazy with their kissing and feeling and putting their hands and fingers where I *certainly* wanted them, and then they'd back off. Like their mothers were calling them. No, *they* weren't going to be first."

"Because it's a responsibility."

"It's terror and ignorance," Lissa said. "Responsibility be damned. They were afraid they'd do it wrong, and they'd look foolish in front of a mere female. My best friend at school—her name was Sara Thurlow; I wonder whatever became of her—was a freshman at Northeastern, and one night she was raped. She didn't get pregnant, thank the Lord, but she dropped out; she was a mess for a long while. She got over the experience, or came to terms with it—however you want to say that she resumed a more or less 'normal' life—but one of the worst things about the rape, she told me once, was that she was a virgin when it happened, and that she'd never have the joy of giving up her innocence to a man she truly desired. She'd been going steady with some guy at Harvard for almost three years, and they'd done 'everything but,' but he'd never gone all the way. Why, she asked him afterward, after the whole question was academic; if he honestly loved her, why wouldn't he ever make love to her? Because she was a virgin. That's what he told her. She was intact, and he wasn't going to be the one to—to what? I wonder."

"Maybe he was waiting for their wedding night."

"No, she asked him that. It wasn't ritual; it was that strange social scruple."

"Awful," Kimball said.

"Yes, awful," she agreed.

"But it's odd, your saying all this. Because that's why I wanted you, back then, not knowing how young you were."

"I don't understand." She shifted her position to make her gaze more direct. "What was the reason you wanted me?"

"That I didn't want to go to bed with Marian before the wedding. I didn't want to be her ruination . . . "

"Oh, please," Lissa said.

"No, I thought like that. You're quite right. I didn't want to 'ruin' her until our wedding night, at which time it wouldn't be 'ruin.' It would be a consummation. It would be sacred."

"But it was all right to be profane with me."

"I didn't say I was proud of that."

"No, you shouldn't be." Nana's porch light came unexpectedly on, and Lissa stole a direct look at him. "Although after that first night, the other times we did it were wonderful."

She watched him smile. He said nothing.

"I was awfully afraid I wasn't doing it right," she said. "I desperately didn't want you to think badly of me. To tell on me to Vicki and Bruce."

Now he looked at her. "It was in the front seat of the old Ford I was driving in those days."

"It was. The first time."

"I didn't know exactly how I was going to do it to you. I must have bruised you. Door handles. The dashboard."

"The steering wheel and the shift lever," Lissa said. "Especially the shift lever; it was a killer. But we'd been to the football game, and you had that stadium cushion we'd sat on in the grandstand. That was what saved me from being killed for love."

She opened the door of the Jaguar, and the interior lights came on. "So this is nostalgia," she said.

"This is it." He took her left hand and kissed it.

"I'm amazed at how nice the evening has been," Lissa said. "Considering our complicated beginnings."

"Likewise."

"I hope you'll call me," she said. "Even if I'll only be around for another couple of days, while the police sort things out."

"Is the case solved?"

"They seem to think so."

"That's great news," he said. "I'll give you a call tomorrow."

"You won't appear at the door without warning?"

"No," he said. "Not again."

She got out of the car and walked up the steps to the Simpson porch. At the front door she paused, but she didn't hear the Jag pull away; she didn't even hear its engine started. When she turned, she saw that Kimball was still looking out at her, one elbow resting against the top of the driver's seat. He beckoned and pushed open the passenger door. She went back down the steps to the curb.

"What is it?" she said.

"What are you going to do right now?"

"I'm going to go up and see if Susie's asleep. Then I'm going to brush my teeth and go to bed and read."

"Why don't you check on your daughter, and then come back? You can bring your toothbrush and your book with you if you'd like."

She stared at him, trying by the car's courtesy lights to read his face, to see if he meant what he was saying. It seemed he did—his eyes intent on her, his mouth serious, the knuckles of his left hand white above the dark rim of the steering wheel, his right hand laid loosely against the leather of the seat back.

"Give me a couple of minutes," she said.

· · ·

When he returned her to Nana's—it was just dawn, the birds nattering as if they were all the life of the summer world, the sun casting elongated shadows of the maples across the gray breadth of Grove Street—she did not even kiss him good-bye. She simply let him squeeze her hand and tell her to "sleep well," and then she was into the front hall and up to Susie's room, guilty and exhilarated at the same time, wondering what kind of woman she was turning into. Saturday night she had practically raped Donald Savage in her dead father's house, on her dead father's bed, and now, forty-eight hours later, she had given herself, freely and thoughtlessly, to a man—a calm, gentle man—whose child she had carried to Boston to kill.

But it had all been adult, sophisticated, had it not? They had sat in the living room of the big house on the edge of town, a house the car had literally climbed to, up a curving graveled driveway and under a portico, and she had sipped brandy from a crystal snifter and carried on a polite conversation with Goodwin Kimball.

In an odd way, the experience had made her again into the girl on the bicycle. The room was rich, high-ceilinged, not like any place she had ever lived. The furnishings were expensive but subdued—earth colors, pale beiges and off-whites, accents of dark, polished wood, of brass glowing dully from the fireplace—and in one corner a black-lac-quered baby grand piano shone as dazzlingly as a Chinese treasure chest. She felt very small, responding to this room as she responded to memories of childhood—seeing in her mind's eye how enormous the world was and how insignificant her place in it. If she had seen the inside of this house when she was fifteen, what might she not have done?

"Most of the really fascinating stuff is in Arizona with Mom and Dad. There's plenty of it. They traveled a lot, and I imagine the Customs people must have started rubbing their hands the minute my folks appeared at the gate."

"Didn't you travel with them?" Lissa had asked.

"Not usually," he said. "By the time they were really into being tourists, I was already in med school."

"Coming here from Chicago was the first time I'd been on a plane in ten years."

She'd said it irrelevantly; only later had she seen how she must have been reshaping herself into the naïve high school kid he'd made pregnant. When he led her upstairs, to a white bedroom with white lace at the windows and a white spread on the enormous bed, she was apprehensive but eager for what they would do together. "Won't your children hear us?" she had asked. "Mary Ellen is at music camp in Gorham; Josh sleeps in the cellar apartment." He had kissed her as he began unbuttoning her. "You're safe here," he said.

Afterward, after the kindest of times she remembered having with a man—though perhaps her judgments were colored by the recollected roughness of Saturday night with Donnie—she lay sleepily in Goodie's arms and listened to him talk about the years since she had been with him. Much of what he said was about his wife, about Marian, and what she had meant to him—how he had always wanted her, how he had feared offending her and thus losing her, how it was honestly the truth that he slept with other women, he couldn't say how many, because he couldn't dream of sullying Marian. "Sully" was his word. He talked about her slow dying, the therapies chemical and radiological that had weakened her without helping her, how impossible it was to have been trained as a doctor and to be all but certain of the futility of such therapies. No, he had not himself been involved in the treatments; she was not his "case," not his "specialty," it would have been a thousand times worse for them both if she imagined the failure of the cures was somehow his fault.

And when she died? Lissa had asked, not turning in his arms to face him, not even opening her eyes, but thinking how her Grandmother Cooper had gone the same way—why was cancer so irresistibly drawn to women?—and feeling the strangeness of so solemn a bond with Goodwin Kimball.

Oh, he had said, it was awful. It happened between Christmas and New Year's, and for months after the death he had moved like a man likewise dead, a zombie, someone in a trance he could not wake from. The children had had to fend for themselves; he remembered them now as pale shadows at the corners of his vision, peripheral beings, keeping out of his way so as not to be sucked into the vortices of his grief that appeared and disappeared as unpredictably as weathers. They were good about it, the children: Mary Ellen nudged him to write checks for the necessary items of food and heat and utilities and cash for the taxis she hired to take her and Josh to school and sports; Josh shoveled the driveway, did odd jobs around the house he knew his father would never get to. Spring came, Kimball said, and it seemed as if everything in the world was renewed and reborn except his own spirit. How he did his work, how he hung on to patients, to parents who must have fretted over the distracted way he treated their own children, how he managed simply to get out of bed each morning—*that* he couldn't tell Lissa—not yet.

When school ended in June—not last month, but a year ago last month—he had sent the kids to Arizona to visit the grandparents. They deserved to escape him, he said; they had earned the R&R and the desert sun and the freedom from a responsibility that was adult and properly his. But then the weight of his grief bore down all the harder, compounded by his sudden solitary condition. The children were gone for a month and a half, and in that time he was, he told Lissa, almost catatonic. Each night when he went to bed, drawing back the covers and propping up the pillows so he could sit staring into the dark and smoking—he did not smoke cigarettes now, he knew the risk, but he smoked constantly then—he would tell himself to change the sheets in the morning, but when morning came he could not find the energy to do it, and so the linens were on the bed week after week. It didn't seem so awful, he said; there was a sense of custom and use that consoled him, and it wasn't until Mary Ellen changed the bed in the middle of August, in weather just like the weather of the present time, that he felt guilt for his sloth and realized how the grief over Marian had turned into selfish remorse over his own life as the survivor. During the whole summer he had never washed a dish, had simply used up the china and glassware in the cupboards, the flatware in the kitchen drawers, and when they were dirtied and he needed a plate or a glass, he would either rinse something under the hot-water tap and wipe it dry with a towel or he would go into the dining room and use the lead crystal or the sterling and add that to the stacks beside the sink. Sometimes he would run hot water into one of the sinks and squirt in detergent and fill the sink with dishes, but after they had soaked until the water was cold he forgot about them. Laundry? He had never done it. When he ran out of underwear, he either pawed through the hamper for one pair of shorts that seemed less filthy than all the others or he wore none. He knew—and deplored—that now sometimes Josh deliberately went without underwear; he told himself that perhaps he had set the fashion for his son, but of course he knew better. He knew he was being lazy; he knew he was indulging himself, pretending grief was an excuse for every failure of self-respect.

How he'd broken the perverse habit of grief, he couldn't now say, except that there came a day—or an event, or a mood—when it dawned on him that he could not continue to function by refusing to function. Perhaps it was the children; perhaps he saw with a father's eyes, or a doctor's, rather than a husband's, that he was ignoring lives, treating them as if they were inferior to the memory of the dead; perhaps he began to be concerned for the whereabouts of his children when the hall clock—it was electric, thank God; otherwise it wouldn't have gotten wound and he would slowly but certainly have lost all notions of the meaning of time—struck late hours. What were they doing? One night would the phone ring, and would it be the police to announce one or another tragedy that meant he had sacrificed them? "Who can say what calls us back to reality?" he said to Lissa.

"I don't know either," she said, "but I know what you mean."

He'd kissed her forehead, both her eyes. "Speaking of reality," he said, "we'd better get you home."

But they had had to wait until Kimball's son left on his morning paper route, his silver-fendered bicycle leaving the driveway, its tires in the dawn quiet making a sound like walking on spilled sugar. Lissa stood back from the bedroom window to watch Josh's vivid blond hair into the distance.

"He's an ambitious child," she said.

"Takes after his mother."

"And he has your hair."

"A little too long for my likes," Kimball said. He turned away from the window and kissed her. "It's okay for us to leave now."

And now in Nana Simpson's house she was crossing the hall into the guest room. In the soft morning light she could see that Suze had tangled herself in the sheet and was sprawled ungracefully, one leg and one arm hanging off the edge of the mattress. Lissa gently freed the bedclothes and nudged her daughter into the bed's comfortable center. As she smoothed the sheet over the child's shoulders, Suzanne sighed and put the knuckle of her thumb into her mouth. Lissa brushed a lock of hair away from the child's face and carefully, very carefully, guided the thumb away from her mouth. Love, and the fear of orthodontia, she thought. It's the ordinary that always calls us back.

12

Strand had not confessed this to Eleanor—he was persisting in the image of his marriage to Harriet as a dream broken and still lamented— but when he was in his middle thirties, he had been the one who wanted to leave his marriage, had considered it seriously, had almost done it. It was not that he had stopped loving his wife or that he was drawn to someone else, but simply that he had begun to feel guilty for not living up to the promises he had made when he courted her. The war that had so energized him was fifteen years behind him, and he had, so far, failed to realize the dreams he shared with her: security, comfort, happiness.

He had come back to civilian life to graduate from Springfield, he had taught and coached in a pair of undistinguished high school programs, he had finally chosen to capitalize on the training of his army MP days because it made him feel that he was once more "his own man" and it brought him a control—or the illusion of it—over the near world. None of this had freed Harriet from the necessity of working to help support the family; it had not brought her a nice home in a neighborhood worthy of her; it had not provided time and wherewithal for travel. At the time, Jackie was eleven years old, and Strand saw not even the remote prospect of money to send her to a decent college.

He never explained his misery to Harriet. When he worked the Turnpike between Kittery and Wells, or Wells and Portland—hours divided between patrolling the pavements that were heat-blistered in summer and ice-sheeted in winter, joining radar teams to monitor the speed of traffic flow, sometimes driving mercy missions from Boston or Portland, delivering drugs or plasma to isolated small towns—his mind worried his situation, fretted over marriage, dreaded the future even as it played with ways to alter it. His radio was always on, tuned to a Boston pop station with the volume low, listening during that most depressed of summers to Roy Orbison's "Only the Lonely." That was his unconscious image of himself as well: the solitary man—never mind the love of wife and daughter—who even in his dreams appeared over and over again stepping from the shoulders of endless highways into the traffic lanes, hand raised to stop a car already marked from the air as traveling over the limit, never certain the driver would stop. Or he turned up the volume on Percy Faith's "A Summer Place," which sent him daydreaming of escape from all failures and responsibilities—a secluded lake, a deserted beach, a green woods too dense for the world to penetrate. What a romantic he had been.

Then duty would break in; the police radio would instruct him out of his reveries or a drunken speeder would provoke him into chase. If he could be always hounder and punisher, he might be always saved from introspection and its regrets, but even the most active shifts came to an end, and he was obliged to go home to Harriet, to Jackie. "You look exhausted," Harriet would say, and night after night she excused him when he had no interest in making love. "It's all right," she whispered in their tense bed. "They're running you ragged." Only once had she said, "Will? There isn't anyone else, is there?" And there never had been. It was only his worse self, his dark self, that came between husband and wife like a smoke that choked him and made him speechless.

Finally he saw he was wrestling not with love but with an order he could not have the management of, and he promised himself to work at the marriage, to substitute attentiveness for control. Circumstances helped him. He was promoted, he made more money, got better benefits, worked shorter hours. He climbed to higher responsibility; he joined the A.G.'s office, moved to Augusta, bought a nicer house. When it was time for Jacqueline to go to college, she won a scholarship, and there was money enough for Strand to make up the difference in her expenses. "How things turn out for the best," he said. But then came the most unexpected of ironies: Harriet's slow but steady retreat from him at a time when he had begun to be so absorbed in his work that it became a true pleasure. He had told her so, bringing home, at the end of days no less long than his days as a trooper, fresh tales of human quirkiness, human perversity, human imagination in the exercise of revenge or passion or jealousy on fellow humans—the behaviors that were the crux and essence of his job as an inspector. Blood he told her about, from stabbings and shootings and sheer animal brutishness; death he told her about, mayhem, tragedy and black comedy in the factory towns and ignorant rural shacks of the sovereign state of Maine. "Willard, how can you stomach it?" she would say. "How can you tell me such things?" "It's the way the world is," he told her, "and I marvel at it." She began turning away from the stories he brought home—first closing her eyes, then covering her ears, then backing away and leaving whatever room they were in. Once she left the bedroom, carried blankets and a pillow down to the living room and slept all night on the sofa in front of the television set. For his part, he began spending even more time at work, looked forward with more and more zest to the next assignment, swapped stories with Frank Carey about the worst—the best—of cases whose responsibility they had shared in times past. He had been blind to the "normal" world; he had immersed himself in the other. One day Harriet had emptied her closets, packed her car, left the note that asked him to "remember the good times," and after the judge signed the dissolution papers three months later, she was vanished from his life forever. If he had paid more attention, if he had held himself back from the attraction of bad behavior, would Harriet, who had recoiled from that behavior, still be with him? If there had been another woman, would his neglect of his wife at least have been more comprehensible? Assuming there was a God, a Fate, a Destiny, would Harriet have grown old with him if he had not loved his work too much? Well, he told himself, no danger of that now.

"Penny," Eleanor said. "For your thoughts."

Her voice startled him. He was standing at the window of the class-room where he had first seen Thibodeau. The window looked out on a clear sky; the landfill resembled nothing so much as a dump. It was clear that the filling in—with broken concrete and rocks and earth laced with the roots of a thousand torn trees—had been going on for years, and now Strand wondered what would happen once this great hole was filled in and earthed over and leveled. Another mall, another parking lot, one more nursing home so the old folks could watch children play?

"What a lousy view," he said.

"That's what you were thinking?"

He shrugged. "So I lie. Ask me later."

"The daughter just parked out front. Shall I meet her, or will you?"

"I will."

"I don't approve of this," she said.

He went down the stairs and met Melissa Allen outside the boys' entrance. She came up the walk briskly, clearly ready to get this meeting, whatever it concerned, put behind her. She wore a dress of summer white with yellow trim, and white open-toed shoes.

"What's it about now?" she said. Annoyed. Angry. Dear God, he thought, you'll know soon enough.

"I've got a dilemma," he said. "I'm not sure I should do this, but if I should, this is as good a time as any."

"Do what?"

"Let's go down to room three." Strand stripped his cigarette onto the schoolyard and led the way up the stairs and into the first-floor corridor. The corridor smelled of a peculiar mix of stale tobacco and custodial lime and pungent floor wax. Strand led the way, conscious that he was slouching, his hands half-tucked into his trouser pockets—hard to know if forcing this woman to know the truth about her old man was going to do anybody any good; harder still to guess how much she would simply be hurt, and he would have gained nothing. Kill or cure, he thought, I need you on my side.

"Why couldn't we have done this yesterday morning?" she said.

"I didn't have the evidence yesterday." Just like Jackie, this young woman—all for efficiency, getting things done briskly and expediently. "This won't take long."

"I hope not. I have an appointment."

He glanced at her over his shoulder. "Officer Savage?"

"Not only."

Mind your own business, Strand thought. Why be wrong about the same thing twice?

"Godawful smells in this building," he said. "I suppose we've corrupted the air the schoolkids will have to breathe next month."

He opened the door into the third-grade classroom. Eleanor had set up a small table under the windows, with a straight chair beside it. Strand gestured toward the chair. On the table was a small portable tape player that belonged to the school—bright green, stereo, its two speakers round and bulging. The player was like a frog with enormous eyes.

"Miss Watkins asked to be here, and I thought it was a good idea," he said.

"To protect me?"

"Something like that," Eleanor said. "We might need to outnumber him."

"It sounds serious," Melissa said; she tried to smile at Eleanor. She sat, not beside the tape machine, but at one of the children's desks, turning to face the window, her hands folded before her. "But then, I remember this school seriously. That basement where you brought me for the press thing— When we were in sixth grade, Harold Wormwood and I sang a duet—'Juanita'—in an assembly program. I was the soprano; he did the alto part."

Strand sat beside the tape player. "It *is* serious," he said.

"This was Miss Littlefield's room when I was here. Third grade." Melissa looked around; she talked without much expression, as if by talking she could evade Strand's kind of seriousness. "The reading circle was on this side, against the blackboard. At the back of the room we had a display table—it was a kind of sophisticated sandbox where you could create landscapes. The Sahara desert. The Rockies. It wasn't papier-mâché; it was actually sand, and you got it to hold its shape by wetting it. Like at the beach. Nostalgia," she said.

"I wondered," Strand said, "if you were satisfied by what Chief Michaud had to say at the press conference. I gather you were brought in as the guest of honor, to be observed by the media."

"I don't know what I felt or how I was perceived. Satisfaction— What you said to me as I was leaving the school made me uneasy, made me think it's too soon for me to feel satisfied."

Strand shifted in his chair. "Would you like some coffee?"

Melissa shook her head. "Aren't *you* satisfied?"

Strand saw—saw what? That this was his last chance to walk away from all of it? Spare the child? He held his ground by temporizing. "A straight answer?" he said.

She stiffened slightly. "Yes."

Eleanor looked out the classroom window. He wondered how much this day would damage the fabric that, like bed linens, presently bound the two of them together.

"I wasn't much in favor of charging Thibodeau," Strand said. "I'm not persuaded he's our man. I wanted you here so I could explain why."

"Why would all of you go to the trouble of that grand announcement about the arrest if Thibodeau isn't the right man?"

"It wasn't my idea," Strand said. "I suppose the police ran close to a hundred people through here—through your father's house—in the first couple of days after he was killed. Neighbors. Friends. People he'd done legal work for."

"And I suppose you asked all of them 'Where were you on the night of July twenty-fourth?' "

"A little of that," Strand said. "But these two tapes in my hand— they're the only ones left from all that were made. Or they're apparently the only two. In any event, they're all we can find."

He put one of the tapes into the player, closed a door over it, pushed a button. Eleanor startled him by shutting the player off, her hand moving so quickly that she almost caught his before he had drawn it back from the machine.

"You don't have to listen to any of this," she told the daughter. "What you're going to hear may be awfully hard on you."

Melissa looked at her. It was as if she were trying to read in the tone of Eleanor's words, in her expression, in the very depth of her eyes, what was coming. "Hard," she said.

"Upsetting."

"Harder than Daddy's death?"

"No. Of course not."

Melissa looked at her hands. "I'm listening," she said.

Eleanor restarted the tape. She raised her gaze to Strand's, just for an instant, as if to deplore this scene. What was she asking him for? he wondered. One more reprieve?

The tape player spoke:

"Interview with Miss Alice Briggs, July the 25th. . . . " Al-the-Bear telling who, giving the interview a number, asking Alice Briggs to identify herself, give her address.

Melissa paid polite, if distracted, attention. Probably knew the woman as one whose occupation in her seventies consisted of sitting at her front window behind a scrim of curtain, watching the progress of life along Ridgeway Avenue. Nothing—no one—escaped her. Maybe she used to spy on Melissa Cooper.

This time Strand was struck by the thinness of the voice—not that it was feeble, exactly, but soft, high, its tremor as much from age as from nervousness at being recorded. Age, years, distance, death. The summer's preoccupations. Of course Melissa wouldn't be terribly interested in Miss Briggs's recollections of her father. A man of regular habits. Liked to wash his car. Otherwise not much for manual work—hired youngsters to do other things for him: mow the lawn, put on and take off the storm windows, trim the hedges in front of the porch. Nice boys. They all seemed such nice boys. Sometimes they came back just to sit and talk with Mr. Cooper. You'd see them sitting on the sunporch. Then they'd go inside for a while—sometimes quite a long while. They'd come back out with cold drinks—orange tonic, cola, you know.

Strand watched Lissa. She looked back at him just as directly, her eyes seeming to ask him: Is this important?

"She's a weird old lady," Melissa said. "She was a weird old lady when she was born, I think. Twenty years ago she was sitting across the street from us in the same chair, watching the same things, thinking the same thoughts. We were her career. She even followed us when we moved."

Strand stopped the tape, rewound it, put it aside on the desk. He loaded the other.

"I want you to hear this one," he said.

"Who is it?" she said.

"One of the boys who did chores for your father," he said.

This time there was nothing cool about her attention. As the interview went on, Strand felt like a man inflicting a public whipping, and more than once a voice, small at the back of his mind, whispered, Stop the tape. Let the woman go. He kept looking at Eleanor, then looking away because her mouth seemed just ready to say that this was too much, too cruel—that no truth was worth such cruelty. As the Kimball boy talked, the soft, sullen voice answering terrible questions, confessing terrible actions, each new revelation brought a freshening of the bright wetness of Melissa Allen's eyes. Finally she put her hands to her face and shook her head slowly.

"It's enough," she said, the words muffled. "Please."

Eleanor moved to put her arm around Melissa's shoulders. Strand shut off the player, ejected the tape. "Sooner or later—"

"Sooner or later I'd have found out."

"You had to."

"So this is why you don't think it's the Thibodeau person."

"This is why."

"And why doesn't the chief of police agree with you?"

"It's a question of how much sympathy this town would have for your father—or for the person who murdered him—if they knew the truth about him. About his sexual . . . choices."

"The chief of police said that?"

"No. That's how I'm reading the man." He started to light a cigarette, then didn't.

Melissa bowed her head. "Shit," she said. She rocked from side to side. "Shit, shit, shit."

"Do you want me to leave?" Strand said. "Do you want to talk with Miss Watkins?" Putting the tape back into its case, he dropped the unlit cigarette on the floor and stooped to pick it up.

"God," Lissa said sharply, "smoke the damned thing before you have a fit."

Eleanor took her hand, tried to hold it.

Melissa pushed the hand away. "I'm not listening to any more tape recordings. I'm not going to let you people brutalize me again in the name of I-don't-know-what—full disclosure, or something like that."

"No, no," Strand said. "No more tapes."

"Who is it?"

"What difference does it make?"

"Who?"

Strand held out the Polaroid. "This is the boy you heard."

She took the print, looked at it. Her hand trembled; she closed her eyes. "It's Josh, isn't it?" she said. "My God, yes it is. It's Josh Kimball."

"You know him?"

"I know his father."

Strand took back the photo. "Don't jump to conclusions," he said. "But we may need your help, to talk to Chief Michaud, to tell him—well, I don't know what you'll tell him."

"That I don't mind if the world knows about Daddy?"

"Something like that."

"That he has my permission to arrest Goodwin Kimball?"

"That he shouldn't try to convict the wrong man."

She took a tissue from her purse, wiped at her cheeks, stood up. "I guess I need to be alone with my new knowledge," she said.

"Perhaps you should talk to Officer Savage."

"Donnie's a friend," she said, "but he's very jealous of Goodwin—

Josh's father—who is also a friend. I don't think Donnie would give me very good advice." She stood abruptly. "That's enough, isn't it? You won't stop me if I want to leave?"

"No, it's all right," Eleanor said.

"You're free to go," Strand said.

"My worst memory of third grade," Melissa said from the doorway, "is of one morning when I came to school with the flu. We were in reading circle, right here in this room, and when it was my turn to read I opened my mouth and threw up all over everything." She smiled grimly at Eleanor. "My stomach feels the way it did then—speaking of nostalgia."

Strand watched the door close. "Go with her," he said.

"Yes."

Finally he smoked his cigarette.

When she came back, Eleanor sat on the edge of the teacher's desk and sighed. "Happy?" she said.

"What did she have to say?"

"Not a word. I didn't try to prompt her."

"Good that you didn't."

"I wish—"

"Think of it this way," Strand interrupted. "If Eloise Adler knows, eventually everybody will find out."

"All right," she said. "And was the Kimball tape the only one Savage could find, or the only one he wanted to find?"

"That *is* a problem," Strand said. "Isn't it?"

.   .   .

"Let me make you a list," Michaud said. "Don't you tell me what the state of Maine is going to do to me until I make the list."

Strand sat back and waited. Michaud was behind the desk, leaning over a sheaf of papers and photos; Savage—an unexpected presence—stood under the windows.

"One," Michaud said, "we got a man beat to death, a homicide. Here is photographs of the scene, here is Doc Pike's report, here is Xeroxes of the State Police log that shows when the crime was reported, who was on the scene first, and et cetera." He pushed the items toward Strand, who took them and put on his glasses to look at them. He supposed that when he went to the A.G. and put in for retirement, it would be because if he wanted to see anything within ten feet he had to find his glasses. At least this stuff was familiar: photos he had been shown on his first day in Scoggin, the log, the coroner's textbook description of how to destroy the human skull and brain, Melissa Allen's statement from the hospital.

"And there's TV tapes of the scene—the room, the rest of the house, the grounds, all that. You can get that stuff from Len Haverkamp."

"I did," Strand said. He slid the papers and photos back onto the desk. "You're doing something to me, Al-Bear, but I'm not sure what. I've seen all this."

Michaud resumed, producing more paper from his desk drawers. "So here's the insurance appraisal of the coin collection."

"Horseshit," Strand said. "You know what I think of that."

The chief put up a warning hand. "And here's an affidavit from the guy in Biddeford who drove over to do the appraising."

"You pull the collection out of your desk, then I'll be impressed."

"I wish," Michaud said. "The Boston police and the Portland are talking to collectors, pawnshop people, hobby stores."

"The coins could be anywhere," Savage said. "Sold one by one."

"What about Josh Kimball's statement? Have you even talked to the kid's father?"

"The kid made it all up. He said so. He was scared. Why should I bother the father again, who's busy doctoring his patients?"

"He could learn a thing or two about 'doctoring' from you," Strand said.

"Watch your mouth," Michaud said. He pointed a finger, the aim between Strand's eyes. "You push me, I got a different list—call it irregularities in conduct of an inspector from the Attorney General's office. Call it extracurricular activities."

"What I do after hours is no business of yours." Strand felt the futility of this conversation. Probably it was the last day in Scoggin; his mind was already in the car with Eleanor, moving north to say whatever needed to be said to the State, and even as he thought of tomorrow's obligations and evasions, images of Eleanor interfered with his reasons for being in Michaud's office.

"I see I got your attention," the chief said. "What else is on your mind? Here: the interrogation of Thibodeau—there's nobody we found who can back up his alleged alibi."

"His girlfriend."

Michaud smiled. "Cock loyalty," he said.

"That doesn't make her a liar, Al-Bear."

"Maybe we should've put her on her back before we took her deposition." Michaud pushed himself away from the desk and began ticking a list on his fingers. "We got Thibodeau, his police record, the gun we found on him, the fact he bears likeness to who Blake saw—" he leaned forward and pushed a drawing toward Strand—"you remember the artist sketch. We got his prints in the house, we got—"

"Wait." Strand put Eleanor out of his thoughts. "You've got what?"

"Fingerprints."

"Thibodeau's?"

"You deaf? Thibodeau's prints, inside Cooper's house."

"How long since? This is the first I've heard of that."

"Day before yesterday," Savage said. "It was dumb luck. I hired Marjorie Vachon to clean up the house for Lissa. She found a water glass that hadn't been washed, and she was smart enough to think it might be important."

"Where'd did she find it?"

Savage looked at Michaud.

"In the kitchen," Michaud said. "On the windowsill, sort of half out of sight behind a curtain."

"Give me a break," Strand said.

"Hey," Michaud said, "don't call me a liar. You come down to my police station to work out what we don't agree about, and I'm telling you what we got, to go to the grand jury with. Period. You hearing me?"

"Dimly," Strand said. "I'm wondering if Thibodeau said 'Excuse me a minute, I need a drink of water before I club you to death' or if he clubbed Cooper first and all that exercise made him thirsty."

"Get the fuck out," Michaud said. "Out of my office. Out of my town."

"And speaking of which: What about all the sweet children Cooper sodomized? That has no bearing on all this?"

"You think bringing it out in the open about these children is going to help anybody? Think about it. I don't say I like Cooper's habits. I said we got a case against Thibodeau. He's bound over to the grand jury. Period." Michaud stood to face him; he leaned across his desk, offering to shake Strand's hand, but Strand turned away. The hand dropped. "Nice working with you," Michaud said.

Leaving the office, Strand had visions: of police investigating police, agencies indicting one another, honest men uncovering lies, abstractions of justice conquering apparent facts, the public taking the wrong side, the town's honor intact. Eleanor giving up on him. Descending the steps of the Town Hall, he realized Savage was alongside him.

"You should've told me how you felt about Goodwin Kimball," Strand said.

"What's that got to do with anything?"

"Your careful choice of the tapes you brought me."

"The Kimball tape was the only one I could find. I told you that."

"I just want you to know," Strand said. "We made a copy of it."

"I thought you would. But now the boy says he got panicky when we questioned him. He says he made stuff up, or used things other boys had told him. He says he answered the questions the way he thought we wanted them answered."

"I'll still use the tape if this business starts to stink in public. I'll use it if it looks like the real killer is going to get off scot-free." Out of the corner of his eye he could see Savage shrug. "I mean it."

"You'd wreck the kid's life?"

"If I had to." No, you wouldn't, said a small voice that might have been Eleanor's.

"Anyway, I didn't think they admitted tape recordings into evidence," Savage said. "And I was thinking what Captain Michaud said about irregularities in the investigation."

"Fuck you," Strand said. He slid behind the wheel of the state car and turned the key in the ignition. Savage waved. I've got to get out of this work for sure, Strand told himself; I used to be a lot more articulate.

·   ·   ·

Later, Strand lay back against the pillows, listening to the shower run, floating—in a haze of bourbon on the rocks, in Eleanor's tangible sympathy. It had been an awful day, shot through with cruelty and irony—the first out of a neutral progression of days to have taken its structure from a desire for justice, for the right thing, until that idealistic structure collapsed under its own weight. The bathroom door was not quite shut; the syllables of dropping water and images of steam swirled and danced through the narrow strip of light. When the water stopped Eleanor emerged, beaded and beautiful, toweling her wet hair.

"I thought you might go to sleep." She leaned over him and kissed him; the air around her smelled like yesterday's warm rain.

"You taste clean," he said.

"A nice afternoon run," she said, "to purge the imperfections of the last day in Scoggin."

"Five miles?"

"More like three."

"Slacker."

"You can't make up for lost days all at once," she said. "It isn't healthy."

"I wouldn't know."

"No, you wouldn't. You're going to be like the wonderful one-hoss shay. You're going to go all at once, in a grand cloud of soot."

"I love it when you talk dirty," he said.

She sat on the bed beside him. Now he would have to report what had happened in Michaud's office. Not that he didn't want to, but that he was oppressed by the sense of futility, of having been outmaneuvered by the locals. To do the right thing—not the "correct" thing—had seemed important, but matters here had gotten so complicated, it was hard to sort out the priorities. And if I were the father of an abused thirteen-year-old, he thought, would there be a limit to my outrage? Should anyone be punished for love?

"Do I dare ask?" Eleanor said. "About the news from downtown?"

He turned a thumb down. "I had no luck."

"So that's that," she said. He thought she straightened, leaned away from him.

"That *is* that. Home tomorrow."

"You sound relieved."

"No," Strand said. "Fed up"

She was quiet for a long moment. We could stop time right here, Strand thought. We could make a pact.

"What about Kimball?" Eleanor said.

"What about him? I couldn't make a real case—and neither can you."

"Did you tell them I copied his son's tape?"

"That didn't faze anybody. The tape likely isn't admissible, and now the Kimball boy is denying he was one of Cooper's toys—says he was scared and gave the police what he thought they wanted to hear, says he knew what the other boys claimed was happening to them, but he has no firsthand knowledge."

"And anyway, I don't suppose anyone explained his rights to him," she said.

Strand grinned. "You're quick," he said. "The rest of it reads just as neatly: his father's a respected citizen, popular doctor—pediatrics, I think, which makes it a perfect symmetry—upstanding, all that, and I'm given to understand that he was out of town when the murder was committed. It's hard enough to arrest the ruling class when you've got the goods on them. You can't touch them if you don't have hard evidence—not even if you were an eyewitness.

"So Thibodeau wins the lottery. He's charged. I think Michaud's actually faking evidence, but I couldn't prove it. Even the police sketch of the man Skippy Blake saw is looking more and more like Thibodeau. The grand jury convenes next month; the State presents Michaud's evidence. Thibodeau'll be bound over."

"For the fall term?"

"Depends. I don't know about your state of Minnesota, but here in Maine we've got a trailing docket system. New cases to the end of the line to wait their turn."

"And he'll be found guilty?"

Strand rattled the ice in his glass. "I'm not even sure the grand jury will indict," he said. "If it does—if the case comes to trial—even with the doctored drawing, unless the Blake kid also perjures himself, I wouldn't be surprised by a hung jury. Maybe a retrial—but more likely not. How much money will the Pine Tree State want to spend on an ex-prizefighter? I'd guess not much. I predict we'll end up with an unsolved crime."

"It's a shame," she said.

"I try to be philosophical. Justice is supposed to be blind; Al-the-Bear takes that to mean that what you don't see won't hurt you." He put the glass aside and held Eleanor's hand. It was a connection he hated to think of breaking. "If there's a killer loose in the town, at least he isn't a mad dog. He isn't going to kill again . . . "

"You hope."

"No, he isn't. Here was an angry father—let's decide it once and for all—who took revenge on Cooper. Let's even admit he went a little berserk. But now, the desire for revenge, the rage—whatever you want to call it—"

"The broken commandment."

"There you are," Strand said. "And Who punishes the commandment-breakers?"

She smiled resignedly. "Different jurisdiction," she said. "I didn't know you recognized it."

"It usually doesn't come up."

"But we're all vulnerable now," she said. "Call it a distraction from the proper assignment."

"You know how I felt—feel—about Cooper," he said. He drew her against him—not to make love; he half feared that they were touching for the last time, that for one reason or another—her shrewdness, his own clumsiness—she would say a final goodbye when they arrived in Augusta the next day. But she had not said it yet. She put out one hand, idly stroking his hair the way a child might.

"You tried to make him your alter ego," she said quietly. "Almost."

"I don't know," Strand said. "I wish I had a cigarette."

"You'll live longer without it."

"Who wants to?"

The words were out before he could stop them, and they seemed to sting the woman. She sat up, turned her back on him. She looked up at the ceiling and for a moment let a shiver take her.

"Stop it," she said. She pronounced the words without turning to look at him. "Just stop it."

"Sorry," he said. "It slipped out. It was only a wisecrack, after all your picking at me."

She said nothing, only bowed her head and hugged herself, sitting in this small room on the bed beside him.

"Really, I take it back," he said. "I didn't mean anything by it."

"But sometimes you do."

"Not this time."

"But sometimes."

"All right," he admitted. "Sometimes. Sometimes I even want to say that Cooper's being dead is a fortunate thing for him. I almost said it to his daughter. Not that he was a villain, a perverted man inflicting himself on others, but that he was an aging and lonely man who was inflicting himself on himself. I know something about that loneliness; it just so happens that pederasty isn't one of the pastimes I use to take my mind off it. I smoke, I drink, I blunder around my job, I fall in love with Eleanor Watkins. Some of those things are a way to shorten my life; some of them—one of them—is a way to make me regret the shortening."

Eleanor shook her head, still facing away from him.

"I've been alone for a couple of years," Strand said. "When you're alone, you talk to yourself. When you talk to yourself, you talk about how you despise being alone." He reached for her, intending to draw her back into his arms, but she refused to respond. "It's no way to live," he said.

"And is that your idea of a proposal?"

"Maybe it is," he said. "Maybe it's the only honest way to get at it. I love you—that's true enough. I admire you—that's also true. We fit nicely in bed—that's spectacularly the truth. But I failed you, and I failed me, and I dread losing you. I dread the whole damned future, because it's clear from my job here that I'd better retire before some sensible bureaucrat gives me the sack. And then what?"

"More of being alone," she said.

"Exactly. No occupation, no hobbies."

"No little boys."

"No little girls either?"

"I told you I never wanted them," she said. "I said no to them. That was the end of husband number one."

"No regrets?"

She faced him. Her eyes glistened and her mouth was compressed into a line that implied she was barely succeeding in holding back whatever she felt. "Don't," was all she said. Then she did lie against him, did let him hold her.

"But you," Strand said. "You're something. And I don't know much about what other people see in sex, but I know I said to you once that entering you was 'magical,' and now I begin to understand that the magic has very little to do with physical sensation and has a great deal to do with what I *think*. What it does to my imagination, what it lets me perceive to be the shape of our future—I think these are the deep solaces of the sex you and I share. Is that sensible? I mean, does it make sense?"

"I don't always ask for sense." She kissed him; he felt her face wet against his. "Whatever happens to dead Cooper, at least you should come back to life," she said.

"Oh, dear El," he said. He hugged her, burying his face in her wet hair. "I'd rather you killed me with kindness forever."

He felt her sigh, her breath warm on his neck. "No promises," she said. "Let's see what happens when all of this is over."

13

"WHAT'S THIS SUDDEN INTEREST in Dr. Goodwin Kimball?"

Donnie tried to make the question sound casual, offhand, but Lissa felt the stress of it.

She had let herself be coaxed to Long Pond partly by Suze's insistence that mother and daughter had done nothing at all together since their arrival in Maine, and now they had only two more days away from the city, and partly by the feeling that she needed to close out this thing—whatever it was—with Donnie. Strand had given her trouble enough; she hardly needed the insinuations of a man who didn't any longer attract her.

They had stopped at the IGA for cold tonic and an extra bag of potato chips, and now they were on the road leading to the pond. Donnie was driving; Suzanne sat in the backseat and read a book she had brought from Nana's.

"I didn't invite him to the funeral," she said. "He came of his own free will. Anyway, is that your business?"

"Maybe," he said. "Maybe I'd like it to be."

"I told you not to make so much of Saturday night." She closed her eyes momentarily; she saw herself in the darkness, shameless under this man. "Please."

He glanced back at Suzanne. "If you say so."

"I do say so."

They drove in silence for a while. Uneven walls of fieldstone bordered the narrow blacktop; pines and birches cast cool shadows across the road, forming them into a tunnel whose lights were deep green. Off to the right, the silver of one of the streams that fed the river past Scoggin's mills showed brokenly among the tree trunks.

"I paid Marjorie Vachon to come in and clean your dad's house—make the beds and dust and sweep. I gave her a key the Augusta people left on the hall table."

"Do I know Vachon?"

"She's a friend of Nana's," Suzanne said from the back. "She comes over for coffee in the mornings."

"This is grownups talking," Lissa said. "Please don't butt in."

Suzanne sighed and turned a noisy page. "You *asked*," she said.

"It's good you arranged for the house to be spiffed up. That will make it easier for Cheryl to sell it."

Donnie looked straight ahead, his grip tightening on the steering wheel. "Is that the plan?" he said.

"Probably. You said yourself, Cheryl's good at real estate." She watched him; his lips were pale.

She leaned her head against the back of her seat and watched the tree branches passing overhead, the high sun flickering between them, the sky an almost-white background. Then there were no more branches; only clear sky and the aching sunlight.

Donnie parked in front of a green oil drum and shut off the engine.

"It has a beach." Suzanne put her book aside and leaned over the seat between them. "And a lot of little houses."

"The water's like glass," Lissa said. "And it doesn't look crowded."

"I'm going to go practice my butterfly kick."

Donnie lifted the picnic basket and the tote bag out of the trunk. The bag he handed to Lissa, who took out a swimsuit and towel and gave them to Suzanne.

"Suze, those little houses are where you can change,"she told the girl. "Bring your clothes back to me."

"Nobody's going to steal *clothes*," Suzanne said scornfully. "I don't see anybody around here who's my size."

"Susie, I just don't want anything to get lost."

"Including me."

"Yes, including you."

She watched her daughter trot toward the shake-shingled cabanas. So much like Edwin; so quick to be contemptuous of advice, and so rational when she needed to be. Eddie would have loved her at this age; surely he could have learned how to express it. I should have worked harder to teach him, she thought. I let him down by going along with him.

Donnie had set out ahead of her, so that she had to catch up and fall into step beside him.

"I was thinking how Edwin would have been pleased by Suze." She stumbled when she felt the yielding sand under her feet and leaned for an instant against Donnie's shoulder. "I hardly ever think of him," she said.

"Except when you're around me."

"Except when I notice Suzanne growing and changing."

"Is that it?"

"Things cluster," Lissa said. She stopped at the edge of the sand. "Here," she said, "take an end," and with Donnie's help she spread the blanket and set the tote bag at one corner of it.

"What things?"

"Chicago things. Next-week things. Job things." She sat and indicated that he should sit beside her. "I have a real life, and it isn't here—so I guess I'm thinking about going back home, and feeling like an odd fish because my father is dead; everybody at work will be curious, and trying so hard to be sympathetic—and Saturday night at your house I got started on thinking about couples, about what my life was like after Edwin died. I don't dwell on Edwin very much, truly I don't, and I'm sorry to keep bringing him up to you."

"I shouldn't make a big deal out of it," he said. He leaned on one elbow on the blanket, facing her; Suzanne had emerged from the cabana and was already in the water, practicing her butterfly stroke amid an extraordinary show of splashing.

"Death attracts death," she said. "Is that it? Another cluster? They must overlap." She took a deep breath. "You knew about Daddy," she said.

"Knew what?"

"About—" How did one say it? "Damn it, Donnie, you know what I'm saying. You knew about my father's being . . . interested in young boys. And you knew Strand was going to tell me."

"Yes. I knew."

"And you knew about Josh Kimball . . . Goodwin's boy."

"Yes."

"You bastard." She squeezed her nails into the palms of her hands.

"Are you so damned jealous you'd lie? You'd accuse a man of murder just to keep him away from me?"

"Hey," he said. "I didn't do that."

"What do you call it?"

"You don't know what's going on. I was caught between a rock and a hard place. Michaud doesn't want the town all ripped apart over your old man; Strand wants everything brought out in the open."

"I'll say." She wondered if her mother knew, if that was why her parents divorced. *I wouldn't put anything past your father.* Hadn't her mother told her that?

"What in hell did you want me to do?" Donnie said. "I took an oath. Strand and Michaud, both of them are my bosses."

She thought about it. "You could have warned me. You could have given me a chance to prepare myself."

"Then I'd have been the one to tell you."

"I guess I'd rather have bad news from somebody I know than from a stranger." She squinted against the sun's brightness. Suzanne was splashing toward shore, and now she ran up to the blanket. Lissa held out the bath towel, but Suzanne spurned it.

"Now I'm going to do bobs," she said. "Keep count."

"Okay. Don't wear yourself out."

Suzanne ran off. Lissa refolded the towel and laid it on top of the tote bag.

"What are 'bobs'?"

"She likes to stand in the water and duck under, and then jump straight up before she goes under again. It's an exercise. You have to see it to believe it."

Suzanne was a few yards out, waist-deep in water. "Ready?" she called.

"Ready."

The child began jumping, holding her nose as she ducked underwater, emerging like a porpoise into the sunlight, her long hair plastered tight against head and shoulders. Over and over she jumped, while Lissa kept count and Donnie looked on, smiling and shaking his head.

"How many's that?" he said after a while.

"Eighty-nine, ninety, ninety-one . . ."

"Jesus. She's amazing."

"I told you. Ninety-four, ninety-five . . ."

Suzanne stopped. "How many is that?" she wanted to know.

"Ninety-nine," Lissa told her.

The girl pushed the wet hair off her brow and took a deep breath. "I'm going to do three hundred," she said.

And did.

.   .   .

"Do you think Goodie killed Daddy?"

The three hundred bobs were accomplished; Suzanne had gone off to look for tadpoles, at Donnie's urging.

"I don't know."

Her breath caught. "But he might have?"

"He says he was in Boston, that he didn't get back until after midnight."

"But you don't believe him?"

"He says his boy was with him." Donnie pulled a thread at the corner of the blanket. "We haven't found anybody who saw him in Boston."

"Have you looked?"

Donnie shook his head. "Yes," he said. "But it doesn't make any difference. Michaud really believes it's Thibodeau."

"He really does? Really and truly?"

"Really."

"And you?"

Donnie shrugged. "It doesn't matter what I think."

She thought she read in the tone of his voice that he honestly wanted it to be Goodie, that he honestly wanted her all to himself. It was a crazy notion.

"What about us?" Donnie said. As if he had read her mind.

"Nothing about us," Lissa said.

"I'm serious. Can't we be what you called a 'cluster'? Only a cluster of good things, just for a change?"

"Including Cheryl?"

"Not including Cheryl."

"And not including Goodie."

He had no answer. He was looking away from her, his gaze fixed, apparently, on Suzanne, watching her without expression. It was as if all his responses were private and hidden away for the time being—as if his blank eyes were a screen keeping out the impersonal world. Lissa had the sudden notion that Suzanne was with him, behind that screen, and it was as though the sun had slid behind clouds and a cold wind had swept over her.

She stood and shielded her eyes against the glare from the water to follow his gaze. Suzanne was at the end of the dock, lying on her stomach to look down into the water. The dock floated on oil drums painted shiny black, rising and falling with the motions of the green water. "Suzanne?" she called. "We have to go."

"We haven't even been here a half hour," Donnie said.

"I don't want her to get too much sun," Lissa said. "She doesn't get outdoors much in the city." She walked toward the water's edge. "Come on, Suze. We have to go now."

"I'm watching minnows," Suzanne said. "They're so skinny you can see almost right through them."

"We've got a lot to talk about," Donnie said. He had followed Lissa, was standing just in back of her.

"You can write me a letter." She took another step toward Susie. "Suze, please."

"I'm floating," the girl said. "I'm pretending I'm a minnow too."

In the end, Suzanne walked to the car barefoot, a towel around her shoulders, her hair damp down her back. Lissa walked beside her, one hand light on her daughter's shoulders. Donnie brought up the rear.

"After you've changed," he said, "we could drive down to the beach for dinner."

"I have a date," she said.

"With Kimball?"

"If you must know—yes." She glanced back at him. "Don't sulk," she said.

"I'm just disappointed."

"Did you tell Strand you thought Goodwin Kimball was the man who killed Daddy?"

"That's what he told *me*."

She looked at him. "Truly?"

"Truly."

"Then I'm sorry," she said. "I thought it was your idea."

·   ·   ·

That night, when they came back to his house after dinner in Portland, Lissa lay in the enormous bed with Goodwin Kimball and talked about her own despair, thinking she owed him that much in exchange for the secrets he had shared with her the night before, arguing with herself that whatever Strand might think about the man who killed Daddy, and whatever the boy Josh had admitted or denied, she could not bring herself to believe it was Kimball. And even if she believed him capable of murder, how was she to confront him with it now, in his bed, in his arms?

"What was the worst of it?" Goodwin said into the back of her neck.

"I guess it was after Edwin's suicide. After he was ashes. After they gave me the flag. I went completely to pieces. I stopped doing housework, washing dishes, cooking—I did nothing. Absolutely nothing. I'd lie in bed until I had to go to the bathroom, I'd watch the soaps all afternoon, I'd take Suze out to McDonald's or Burger King and then let her stay up until midnight while I drank beer and stared at the television some more. If she didn't want to go to daycare, I'd say okay, do what you want. If she did go to daycare and came home with a note saying what a good girl she'd been or how well she'd worked with the other children on some dopy project, I'd say okay, that's nice, do you want to have a cheeseburger or shall we go to Taco Bell for Mexican or what? Once in a while some guy would call me—some guy I'd met at the lake with Edwin, or somebody from a place where I used to work—and maybe I'd go out with one of them, to a movie, or a decent dinner. Sometimes I'd invite him in, and we'd sit on the sofa and I'd let him sit close, maybe even put his arm around me, maybe actually kiss me.

"And then this absolute terror would come over me. I mean, I'd break into a cold sweat and my stomach would start to go crazy, and I'd think: Jesus, if he touches me again, even innocently, even gently, even lovingly, I'll go over the edge. Scream. Hit. Something really paranoid. All at once I'd think of Susie, and all at once here'd be this poor fish watching Mother playing Mother with a passion. One minute he's getting to first base, putting his tongue in my mouth, resting his hand on my knee, thinking whether now's the time to brush my nipples accidentally and let out that moan men make when they want you to know they've reached the helpless stage, the God-forgive-me-I-can't-stop-myself stage, and the next minute he's stroking thin air and this batty mother is fretting about whether she did or didn't hear her darling daughter whimper in the back bedroom. Or was it me that was whimpering? Oh, God; spare me that experience again."

"That flatters me," Kimball said. "Your letting me be with you like this."

"No, it flatters me—that I came through that craziness far enough to let you. And don't ask me how I did it. I just did it. You're right: A day comes when you open your eyes and see how bad you've made things around you." She let him kiss her, kissed him back. "Besides," she said, "you're some kind of an exception to the rule of men."

Keep talking, she told herself. Tell him everything you can think of to avoid asking the one question you need to have the answer to.

"What had you done that seemed like 'craziness' to you?"

She closed her eyes. "What hadn't I? I came home one afternoon from the library—I'd been antsy all day; I decided I needed a walk in the fresh air, and here was this overdue book—and first I took a good look at the place where I was living. It was like a trash heap. The lawn hadn't been cut in weeks. There was stuff on the front walk—broken toys, dog crap, candy-bar wrappers—and in the tall grass, wastepaper growing like flowering weeds all around the house. On the front steps there was a pile of newspapers, five or six days' worth, all wet and gray and stuck together. I thought: I wonder if there's any mail; and when I opened the box to look inside, there was a pile of letters, also wet, also stuck together. My God, I thought, how long has it been since I even looked into the mailbox? It was like I'd lost track of everything—time, place connections, myself, my reasons. I picked up all the soggy papers and as much of the junk on the walk and the lawn as I could manage, and I carried it around to the back to put it into a trash can. And the trash cans!" She laughed. "One of them was tipped over and the lid had come off, and there was garbage strewn all over the driveway in front of the garage. Rotten bananas—you know how black they get—and eggshells and milk cartons and brown foliage that might have been carrot tops. Oh, God, and the stench of it all. I thought: What am I doing? What is this? Am I human, or what?"

"You're human," he said. "A lovely warm body."

She turned away from him and hugged her knees. "Jesus, what a phrase to use on me of all people." Now they were not touching; should she ask him?

"I'm sorry. That was thoughtless."

"No, no," she said. "It's all right. I've got myself all wired again; it'll pass."

Just as the depression in Chicago had passed. And if she had survived that, she would survive murder as well. I'll even survive truth and the sins of my father, she told herself. For an instant she thought she might have trusted this man—this original lover—enough to tell him the whole story of her flaking out after Eddie's death, how really bad it had been—but she was glad she had held it back. If something does come of us, she thought, I have to have something private, I have to hide at least one skeleton. She smiled—noticeably, for Kimball caught it.

"What?" he said.

"I was thinking what a fake I am," she said. "How I beat despair not by standing up to it, but by moving away from it."

"Literally?"

"Literally. I moved out of the house—it had got so awful that there wasn't even toilet paper in the bathroom. I used facial tissues until they ran out, then brought a roll of paper towels in from the kitchen, then found a stack of newspapers— Dear God, I kept forgetting what I needed when I went to the store. One day I just stood at the checkout, nothing in my hands, blank as a cloud." She stopped. "I wasn't going to tell you that," she said.

"What happened?"

She shrugged and lay flat, feeling the coolness of the pillow on the back of her neck. Why shouldn't I? she thought. Here the two of us are, tied up in a world of life and death, of murder and suspicion, and all I'm trying to hold back is a little touch of madness. "They carted me off. Just like that. Off to the hospital, a locked ward, the whole trip."

"It was bad?"

"You can't imagine, if you haven't been there." She sat up and clutched at his hands. "You know physical hurt; you understand that because they taught you in school and you can verify it with your patients. But you're not a psychiatrist, and I bet you only have the barest notion of what mental pain is like—how you feel, knowing that the world sees how crazy you are, knowing that the world doesn't realize that you see it too, because it's as if there was a sane person at the back of your mind watching the antics of the crazy person at the front of your mind. The sane person tries to say 'Stop that nonsense!' but the crazy person doesn't listen, doesn't hear. All the crazy person hears is threats. They wanted to give me electroshock therapy; they told me I'd always be crazy if I didn't have it. I said no, and thank God, my mother said no."

She folded her hands to keep them still. "That balanced the books for her, I think. She'd made me kill your baby, but she kept the doctors from killing me. I think it balanced me too; it made me believe there was some justice in the world, some possibility of order. So I persevered. I got sane. I reclaimed my kid from the neighbor across the street. Then I moved away from the squalor and the black bananas—to a nice upstairs apartment in Rogers Park, with a sunporch that looked out on a 7-Eleven and a liquor store and a corner grocery and a gay bar—God, if I'd known—and a street lined with mulberry trees. Two blocks from the lake."

And reclaimed her life, she might have gone on to say. Got up with the sun all summer long, left Susie asleep and walked to the heaved-up breakwater at the end of Jarvis, where she sat on the shattered concrete and looked out onto Lake Michigan, where Edwin's ashes had sunk—watched sailboats gliding not far from the shore, and steamships farther out, perhaps bringing ore down from Superior, from Duluth and the Upper Peninsula, and overhead the great silver planes settling into the wide patterns that would land them at O'Hare—then strolled back to the apartment and its efficiency kitchen to make coffee and toast.

Sitting at the sunporch table, sipping from the mug decorated with the spindly giraffe picture that Susie loved, she watched the neighborhood come to life—the shopkeepers unlocking their doors, the drunks loitering around the front of the liquor store, the traffic rousing itself for the morning rush to work, the first elevated trains clattering past. When the mulberries bore fruit, mothers paused with their children in the deep shade and reached to pull down the berries; all the rest of the summer the sidewalks were stained purple. From this vantage, she remembered the apartment as perpetually alight from the sun, the wood floors an orange glow, the walls pure white. Now there was always toilet tissue, the mail brought up daily. Now she bought the Sunday paper at the 7-Eleven, and orange juice at the grocery store. Lissa and her daughter healed together.

"Suze stopped asking about her dad," she said. "That was the greatest improvement in the world. And then—"

Kimball reached out and laid his arm across her naked back, slid his hand down to her buttocks. "Then?" he said.

"Then I realized I'd spent most of Edwin's GI insurance, and then, finally, I went back to work."

"To make a long story short," he said.

She faced him and gently pushed his arm away. "I have to ask you something. I've been putting it off, but I can't do that forever."

"All right." He sat up, folded his arms across his bare stomach. "Ask."

Here goes, she thought. "Strand—the man, the investigator, who came down from Augusta to help solve my father's murder—had me in today for a talk. He told me some things about my father, horrible things, things I didn't know. About—" God, how was she to say this? It felt like killing Daddy all over again, murdering him with gossip, with slander. "About his sexual tastes. Preferences. About his fondness for young men. Boys."

She stopped. The room was deadly quiet; she thought Kimball was not even breathing.

"Is it true?" he said.

"Strand played me a tape the police made, of one of the boys my father—did things with," she said.

"What kinds of things?"

"You know—sexual things. Sick sexual things men shouldn't do to men. Things they usually don't do even to women."

"That seems unkind and unnecessary," Kimball said.

"The things some men do?"

"To force you to listen to such a tape."

"I wasn't exactly forced." She took a long breath. "But it's worse than you think."

"How could it be?"

"The boy on the tape. It was Josh."

She looked at Kimball. His jaw was set; he did not seem surprised; he did not meet her gaze.

"You already knew that," she said. She did not make it a question.

"I knew."

"He showed me Josh's picture; he said Josh's fingerprints were in the room where they killed Daddy."

"So I was told."

"Strand thinks—"

"I know what he thinks. I also know what he knows. I know what

Josh said to the police. We talk, Josh and I; we share, we are not like the fathers and sons you hear about who don't communicate."

"Still—" She wasn't able to ask the direct question, to find the strength to make the words. She waited, could feel herself trembling for fear of an answer she hadn't asked for, thought how glad she was not to have said anything more, that even if Goodwin Kimball were a murderer, why would he confess it to her?

And then he asked the question himself.

"You think I'm the one?" was what he said. "You think I'm the man who beat your father to death?"

He looked at her, calmly, as if he were daring her to answer, as if he were almost sure she couldn't find the words.

.   .   .

"I knew who your father was, of course. Everybody knew him, the way you know people who've lived in the town all their life and yours. I knew he liked kids, liked schoolboys. I keep my office hours in Scoggin two days a week, so nobody thinks I'm too good for the town, or that I think Portland is where the action is with its gentrified ambitions and its new money and its snobbery in general. Mothers would tell me about their sons hanging around the Cooper house on Ridgeway—but they were always positive about it, always saying how kind Raymond Cooper was, how generous, how he was teaching their sons the virtue of hard work, how the boys were learning that you got value back only for value given.

"It all seemed perfectly straight to me. I watched these kids grow up to be young men, took them through their vaccinations and bandaged their lacerations and splinted their broken bones, told them what I thought about football and hockey and indiscriminate tree-climbing, gave them advice about sex. If I live long enough, by God I'll be beloved in Scoggin—'old Doc Kimball.' I'll have a football stadium named after me. And during the Vietnam thing—I know you'll despise this—I did whatever I could to keep all these mothers' grownup sons out of the army. Once in a while I even loaned the families money so the sons could go to Canada and live."

"Edwin could have avoided it," she said. "He chose not to."

"Yes, choice. He chose. And I didn't do a soapbox number on the mothers of Scoggin. But when they asked, I gave them my opinion. And I offered them my help if they needed it.

"But as for Josh—"

"You don't have to," she said. "I'm not accusing; I wouldn't know how."

"No, it's all right. Josh— Well, I told you about Marian's illness, her long dying, my not too mature response. And I think that was about the time Josh started running with these kids that helped out at your dad's—lawn mowing, car washing, the kind of 'character-building' stuff"—the phrase carried sarcasm—"the mothers glowed over. I wasn't paying too close attention. He had an allowance; if he wanted to earn extra money on his own, that was fine with me. He wasn't underfoot. I could devote myself to watching Marian waste away."

He was still sitting up beside her. Lissa leaned her cheek against his back, so that his words resonated in her ear.

"Then this odd thing happened. It was a few months ago, and I got a phone call from Ted Melanson—you remember him? Runs the hardware store on the square?—who said that Josh had stopped in the store that afternoon and wanted to buy some ammunition. He'd had a small handgun with him, which he showed Ted, and said the ammunition was to fit it. Ted said it was a small caliber—I don't remember if it was a twenty-two or what—and he was sure he had bullets to fit it, but he'd put Josh off by pretending that particular item was out of stock, and could Josh come back in a week when the new order arrived. Then he phoned me.

"Well, I didn't know what to think. Had he bought a gun? Had he stolen it? Hell, what had been going on while I was in my self-pitying funk over a dead wife? So I confronted Josh. Gently. You know. I know kids, I see fifty a week, from cradle to high school. I think I've got a certain amount of insight."

"Did he say where he got it?"

"Yes and no. He admitted he'd stolen it, but he wouldn't tell me where. I told him he had to return it, and he said he would—no, I take it back. He didn't say he would, but he implied it. All I know is that the gun left this house. I mean, I've searched his room two or three times since, and nothing."

"The police arrested a man who said he'd bought a handgun from a teenage boy," Lissa said. "You knew that?"

"I do now," Kimball said. "All hell broke loose when your father was killed. I found out about that gun when the police talked to me, and that's also when I found out about your father's—" He paused. "Preferences," he said.

"Yes."

"But Josh wasn't one of the victims. I'm quite sure of that."

"Strand played me a tape—"

"No. Josh told me about that interview. He was frightened out of his wits. He knew what other boys had been doing with your father, and he knew he'd been propositioned—he didn't use that word—by your father, but he never did whatever he said on that tape they made of him. He was so scared, he just confessed to whatever he thought would make them let him go home. No, he's not one of those abused kids. I'm sure of it."

"You love him," Lissa said. She hugged him, kissed him behind his left ear. "You're a loving father. I wish Suzanne could have had one like you."

.   .   .

Later he lay alongside her, kissing her, stroking her. She sat up in bed and hugged his face against her bare thigh. "I love your pale hair," she said softly. "It's as fine as a woman's."

He turned his face up to her. "Thanks," he said. "I think."

"And your eyes. They're like blue stones melting away into the wind and the sea around them. It's like a marvelous erosion that goes on and on."

"My God, Melissa—"

"That doesn't take away your virility, does it? That kind of talk?"

"No, but those are odd things to say to a man."

"To a steely-eyed doctor."

"I'm not a steely-eyed anything," Kimball said.

She leaned to kiss him. "That's because you've got such delicate hair."

She watched him nuzzle her thigh, watched him lift his right hand to her stomach and slide the hand down over her pubic hair, his fingers just for an instant brushing the exposed pale edges of her secret membranes. So these were a doctor's hands when your feet weren't in stirrups.

She closed her eyes. Edwin was never this gentle, would never have known how to be so; how could she even think of him?

"Shall I write you?" he said. "Does Chicago have mail service?"

"Please write. We're very up-to-date."

"Will you learn to trust me?"

She put her hand over his. "I hope so," she said.

Kimball pulled himself up on one elbow and kissed her where he had just touched. "When I was in med school," he said, "we made fun of everything: the doctors who taught us, the patients who trusted us, life and death. We played practical jokes with the cadavers we learned to do autopsies on. It was all hilariously funny—in the retrospectoscope."

"The what?" She kept her eyes closed, waiting for his kiss to return.

"An instrument used for hindsight," he said. "The truth was that everything was awful. Grotesque. We made fun of it only after the fact; we pretended we weren't frightened, that we weren't afraid of the ghastly things that happen to people. It was a different kind of bedside manner, the dark side of it."

Then he did kiss her, very lightly.

"This is a confession," he said. "I mustn't keep it from you."

"Why?" Lissa said.

He pulled himself upright and sat alongside her so that they both shared the pillows propped against the wall at the head of the bed. She opened her eyes and laid her cheek against him. She couldn't tell if the pounding she heard was his heart or her own.

"I want you to see," he said, "that I wouldn't hold anything back from you. That if the police—or this Strand, or you yourself—are even implying I would kill another human being, you can trust me if I tell you I wouldn't. But I have to say: I can see why a man might want to kill your father—if what they've told you about him is true, if what the other boys say is the truth. You should put yourself in the place of one of those fathers: What would you do if you found out your boy was being—being abused that way by someone? Laugh it off? Look at your kid and decide it's just a phase he's going through—something he'll outgrow?"

"I'd talk with him."

He cradled her face in his hands and looked squarely into her eyes; she felt herself drowning in the blue irises, saw herself helpless in the black pupils. "No," he said, "it's beyond language; it's beyond anything you know. Think of this: Your daughter is raped. What is she? Eight years old? Nine? Doesn't matter. Your daughter is raped, and you know who did it, but the authorities won't do a goddamned thing about it. What do you think now? What do you feel? What do you do? Do you walk away? Do you hope you'll both heal, and let it go at that?"

The passion in his voice frightened her, and she had to lower her blurred gaze, to look away from the anger that had so swiftly changed his face. Oh God, she thought, I know the answer. Forgive me, Daddy. Please forgive me.

Epilogue

Augusta, Maine
October 7, 1985

DEAR MRS. ALLEN,

The desk at the Scoggin Municipal Police Department was kind enough to supply me with your Chicago address.

By now you are probably aware that when the Grand Jury convened in August, a no-bill was returned, which means simply that the Jury felt the State had offered insufficient evidence in making its case against Roland Thibodeau, and was not persuaded it should return a true bill of indictment. The murder charge against Mr. Thibodeau therefore collapsed. It is my understanding that, while he was cleared of the charge of killing your father, he has nevertheless been detained by the county on a charge of violating parole.

You probably are not aware that the investigation of your father's death remains open, which is to say that the case file is considered current, and the local authorities have no present intention of labeling the case "unsolved." That may be small consolation to you, I know, but it means, among other things, that the search for a weapon, and the follow-up of questions of motive (was it robbery, for example, or was there a connection between your father's unhappy private life and his untimely demise, etc.) continues. Should the murder weapon be discovered and provide further forensic evidence, or should a suspect appear who is recognized by the neighbor who saw a stranger on Ridgeway Avenue on the night of July

24th, you may be assured that the Attorney General's office will be on the scene forthwith.

Chief of Police Michaud informs me that your father's law practice was purchased in late September by a firm in Portland, and the proceeds of that purchase have been added to your father's estate. I'm told that the house on Ridgeway has also been sold, and that the closing is scheduled for later this week. I have no knowledge of where probate of your father's will stands at the moment; you probably know more about that than I do. These latter items are of course no business of the State of Maine's, but inasmuch as my own involvement in the investigation was somewhat unusual, I have, as they say, kept in touch with activities in Scoggin.

I am, personally, sorry that your father's case is not resolved, especially in light of the emotional distress suffered by you during the investigation subsequent to the crime. I hope nevertheless that you have put the worst of this behind you, and that your life in Chicago is a pleasant and full one.

Best regards,
WILLARD STRAND

• • •

The last night in Scoggin, Lissa had given Susie a bath and tucked her under the makeshift bedclothes of the narrow bed in the guest room.

"I was bored silly," Susie said. "I played with Nana's button collection."

"I'm sorry, sweetie. I meant to be home early."

"Sixty-three different kinds of buttons. The biggest ones look like huge earrings, except there's no way to hook them to your ears, and the smallest look just like baby teeth."

"That's fascinating," Lissa said. "I know Nana's pleased you got them all arranged and catalogued."

"They aren't exactly arranged; just divided up. Sixty-three kinds, and three hundred and eighty-seven separate buttons." Susie had put her thumb in her mouth, then thought better of it. "It got to be kind of dumb."

"I can imagine." For an instant, Lissa thought of Edwin and his con-

tainer lids, of asking him if he wanted to quit that boring job, of his answer: And do nothing?

"Are we going to live in Grampa's house?"

"No, of course not. Grampa's house is going to be sold, and we're going back to Chicago."

"Just the two of us?"

"Yes. For now."

"And then with the policeman?"

"No, not with the policeman."

"With the man who has the silver car?"

"I don't know. Maybe. Are you going to stop asking questions and decide to go to sleep?"

Susie wriggled further under the covers and turned her face up to be kissed. Lissa kissed her and noticed what Donnie had once mentioned: the sweetness of the child's breath, the mild smells of the soap and shampoo, the soft warmth of her skin.

"If you get a new husband, what will I call him?" Susie said.

Lissa stood, her hand poised to turn out the lamp beside the bed.

"I don't even know silver car's name, anyway, but will he be Uncle, or will he be a mister, or what?"

"His name is Goodwin Kimball. I guess 'Goodwin' will do for starters."

"Is he really going to be my new father?"

"I hope he will be." She kissed Susie, thinking, I mean it. "I really do."

"Then will I be Suzanne Kimball?"

"Not at first. At first you'll still be Suzanne Allen. Maybe after a long time, we'll talk about changing your name. But only if you want it changed." She switched off the light. "If it happens, you'll also have an older brother and sister. Notice I'm saying a big 'if.'"

"God," Susie said. "That's something to think about."

"Goodnight, sweetie."

"A full-grown brother and sister. I don't even get to see them be babies."

"Goodnight, Suze. Sleep tight."

"Goodnight." Resignation. A long, little-girl sigh. "Don't let the skeeters bite."

Lissa smiled. After she had taken a long, warm shower and crawled into the big bed in the guest room, she lay in the dark with her eyes *wide open and thought of Goodwin Kimball, of love and its actions, light and dark; of stepfathers and adoptions, of the way Goodie talked so passionately about Josh. She thought about how she had gotten up at dawn this morning, before she even started packing, and driven out toward the corner where she knew the paperboys picked up their papers; about meeting Josh a block away, stopping across the street from him. "Can you sell me a paper?" "I'm sorry, ma'am, I don't carry any extras." She thought what a sweet face he had, a full lower lip like a girl's, eyes long-lashed, irises a deeper, darker blue than his father's; she thought about the high, clear brow, the unruly blond hair. No wonder Daddy was in love with him; no wonder he lusted after this pretty boy. She weighed the absurd and horrible chance that the man whose child she had killed so long ago was the man who murdered her father, and what if he had done it not only to avenge the honor of his living child but partly, unconsciously, to punish Lissa for her own act of murder? How did you know where the monsters hid, if nobody ever told all their secrets?*

Then she tried to put herself to sleep with happier thoughts. Or were her "happier thoughts" only false visions? Perhaps happiness was nothing more or less than a matter of not knowing the facts. Even then, she could imagine what her friends in Chicago—Naida Kostas, for instance, who lived across the hall—would say of her trip home. "You heard about Lissa? Flew home for her fifteenth class reunion, met an old flame from her high school days, and by the time the week was over they'd fallen in love all over again. Did you ever hear anything more romantic?" And for her friends, that was sufficiently true, Lissa realized—as if the whole truth were not a threat to anyone but herself.